FIRE GAMES

ARCTURUS ACADEMY, BOOK 3

A.L. KNORR

Edited by
NICOLA AQUINO

INTELLECTUALLY PROMISCUOUS PRESS

Copyright © 2020 by Intellectually Promiscuous Press

All rights reserved.

No part of this book may be reproduced in any form or by any electronic or mechanical means, including information storage and retrieval systems, without written permission from the author, except for the use of brief quotations in a book review.

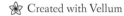 Created with Vellum

PART ONE
THE WAGER

ONE
WHY NAPLES?

Gage thanked the Deliveroo driver and took the two plastics bags containing our order, then stepped back as the scooter took off. It sprayed stones in its attempt to gain enough momentum to tackle the Academy's steep driveway. I took a bag and fell in step with Gage as we passed under the arch and headed around to the stone tables at the back of the villa.

Dr. Price stood a short distance away on the lawn, murmuring into her mobile. She glanced up as we set the food on the table and began to unpack takeout boxes. Her eyes rolled heavenward and she mouthed, "Thank God."

It was only mediocre Chinese food from the nearest restaurant, but given that Palmer and her kitchen staff had left for the summer, it was delivery or opening a few tins of beans, it smelled like heaven.

Dr. Price said goodbye and came to sit across from Gage, watching as I spooned fried rice and chicken balls onto three plates.

"Basil is dealing with the funeral director and lawyers today." Christy swallowed audibly as I doled out three servings of greasy green beans.

Gage set out the cutlery we'd taken from the kitchen. "Isn't there anyone else who can do that? He just lost his father, for crying out loud."

"Unfortunately, making funeral arrangements and dealing with lawyers falls on the shoulders of the grieving. It's not fair, I know." Christy replied.

I slid a plate of food in front of her and sat down beside Gage on the bench. Mouth watering, I speared a chicken ball and dipped it in some neon-pink goo that smelled a lot like cotton candy. I almost took a bite but paused, deep fried poultry-ball held in mid-air, as I noticed Gage showing exactly zero interest in the food. I glanced at Christy, then took the bite.

"Aren't you hungry?" the doctor asked Gage before shoveling in a mouthful of egg-fried rice.

Gage threw a glance at his plate, frowning. "I don't have any appetite, thanks."

Swallowing, I chased it with a bit of water. "Christy got her SUV back and she's not going to press charges. Is that what you're worried about?"

It had been two days since Ryan had vanished with Dr. Price's vehicle. The police had found it the following morning at Luton airport. Inquiries with airport authorities uncovered that Ryan had purchased a one-way ticket on the red-eye to NAP—Naples International airport.

The Arcturus students (except for me, Gage and Cecily) and most of the staff had gone home yesterday. Cecily was visiting a friend in London while her mom helped Basil and would return to the academy by train when Dr. Price was ready to go home to Inverness.

Mrs. Fairchild was currently—with an army of a dozen seasonal staff—giving every corner of the academy a thorough spring cleaning before she left for summer vacation. When they were finished, only Dr. Price, me and Gage, would be here when Basil returned. At least the villa would be gleaming when he came back.

I had called my parents and delayed my flight by five days. I didn't feel right leaving Basil, Christy, and Gage after what had happened, but I couldn't hang around the villa all spring. I felt some level of responsibility for what Ryan did, even though it had nothing to do with me.

"I'm grateful," Gage was saying to Christy. "If you don't press charges then he'll be able to return the UK without problems. I just wish I knew what the hell he was thinking, and what he's going to do next. Why won't he answer my calls? I know he can see my texts."

"Have your parents tried calling him?" Dr. Price asked between mouthfuls.

"Of course, they have. They're ready to get on the next flight out of Halifax. But showing up in Naples without knowing where he's staying would be useless. We could arrive just as he's leaving. I never would have thought my own twin—" He looked away and cleared his throat.

An awkward silence descended over our table. I put my fork down, swallowing food that suddenly tasted like ashes. I hated seeing Gage so fraught, and wanted to throttle Ryan for putting his family through this. Was I surprised? Not in the least. Especially not now that

Ryan was Burned. Surely, his descent into thoughtless egotism had begun, though it was hard to tell if he was any worse. Ryan had been self-serving since the day I'd met him, but it didn't make the current circumstances any easier.

I noticed that Dr. Price had stopped eating as well, and was now gazing off into oblivion with a frozen stare.

"Was it Basil's father the triplets got their fire from?" I asked, as much from curiosity as wanting to break the tension and distract Gage from his misery.

Dr. Price's focus returned. She looked at me, brow pinched in the bright afternoon light of an English spring. "Yes, Viscount Chaplin was the mage. Basil's mother was a natural. She died not long after Bellamy was killed."

The mention of Basil's murdered triplet seemed to suck the remaining oxygen out of the air. So much for distracting from misery.

So Basil was an orphan now, if an adult could be considered an orphan, estranged from the other surviving triplet, and at only fifty years of age. At one time in my life, fifty seemed so old, certainly old enough to be without one's parents. But my perspective had changed. No one was ever ready to lose a beloved parent, no matter how old they were, and Basil had been close to his dad.

Gage rooted his phone out of his pocket and tapped the screen. Probably typing out his hundredth pleading text to Ryan. He muttered, "Why Naples?"

Christy and I shared a look. Gage had murmured the question so softly it was obvious he didn't expect either of us to have an answer. We did have an answer, or at least a pretty strong theory, which neither of us had dared mention to Gage yet.

"Gage, dear," Christy began, her words halting. "Ryan is a newly Burned mage, he'll be looking for a mentor. Saxony was only one factor in his survival. Ryan wasn't taking chances. We think he contacted a ... somewhat infamous Burned mage who resides in Naples, according to the Agency's latest intelligence."

Gage turned a stare toward the doctor. His cheeks were pale under two days' worth of stubble. "What?"

Gage looked at me. When he saw my expression, he could tell that I was also in the know. He pushed his plate of cold Chinese food away and nailed me with another look.

"You knew about this, too?"

I wilted under his gaze, but nodded.

"Why didn't you tell me before? I've been going out of my mind—"

"That's why," I explained. "It's just a theory, and it's not good news."

"Basil alerted Arcturus Agency of Ryan's movements." Dr. Price laid a hand on Gage's forearm. "When they get eyes on Ryan, you and your parents will be the first to know."

Gage dropped his head and laced his fingers behind his neck. After a few deep breaths, he loosened his hands and looked up. "Who is the mage in Naples?"

"His name is Nero Palumbo," Christy replied, letting the name sink in.

Gage's expression shifted. My stomach dropped as dismay filled his blue eyes. He wiped a hand across his pale lips. "I recognize the name. I haven't heard it since

I was little, but—" he paused, thinking. "He's the guy who murdered Basil's brother, isn't he?"

Dr. Price nodded, looking miserable.

Gage was horrified. "Why would Ryan go to *him*?"

My chest ached. Gage was ever the tender heart, a little naive, always kind. How many times had Ryan disappointed him in their lifetime? How many times would Gage forgive? I already knew the answer because I knew Gage. His forgiveness was endless because his love was unconditional. It was something I admired, maybe even aspired to, but thought I would never achieve.

In calm tones, Christy explained to Gage how Basil's report about what had happened back in 1988 between the triplets and Nero had been 'borrowed' by Ryan. The report detailed Nero's claim that he'd found a formula, one that Basil believed was a fabrication, but—as written—might convince a reader it was factual. Ryan had reached out to Nero and made some kind of agreement with him in exchange for the formula.

I added my speculation that Ryan had promised Nero the artifact, and had gone to Naples to make good on his promise.

"He might even be back in a day or two," I suggested, wanting to wipe the misery from Gage's features.

Gage's phone vibrated on the stone table. He fumbled for it with both hands, almost dropping it as he swiveled away from Christy and me.

"It's Ryan," he said, the muscles in his shoulders and back visibly tight.

Christy and I waited, watching Gage as he read the

text. When he turned around, the relief in his face made us look at one another with hope.

"He's okay." Gage turned back to the table, tapping out a response. He hit send, closed his eyes and breathed, holding his phone close to his chest. Opening his eyes, he smiled at me. The blazing white grin almost knocked me backward. My heart surged against my ribs in response.

"What did he say?" I asked, dazed.

"He's still in Naples. He says," Gage lifted the phone and read aloud, "I'm sorry I've been ignoring you. I haven't been sure what to say. I am okay. I'm in Naples. I'm safe. Forgive me for embarrassing you, and tell Dr. Price I'm sorry for stealing her SUV. Tell her the brakes are a little warped and the alignment needs adjusting but it wasn't me that wrecked either." Gage chuckled and I could hear lightness in his laugh.

Christy rolled her eyes and shook her head. She began to eat again.

"I asked him if I could meet him in Naples," Gage continued, "but he said: When my business here is finished, I'll come find you, brother."

Gage gave me a look of unadulterated relief. "I think you're right, Saxony. He's gone to give the relic to Nero. He'll be back. At least now I know he's okay and that I'll see him soon."

Ice-chips formed along the lining of my stomach. Why was it that no one else seemed concerned that Ryan would be delivering an artifact of some unknown power to a murderous Burned mage? Surely Basil had warned the Agency that the artifact had to be intercepted. With all my heart, I wished that Basil were here.

Gage pulled his plate toward himself, grabbed a fork and dug in.

"That's cold by now," said Christy.

Gage took a bite and shrugged. "Still good."

Pushing my plate away, I massaged my temples with my fingers. Now I was the one without an appetite.

TWO

THE IMPOSITION

Gage and I stood on the second floor with our elbows on the banister, overlooking the foyer. The chandelier's lights were out, leaving a few sconces and lamps to light the large, marble-floored expanse. Both fireplaces were dark and the plush furniture were mere silhouettes against the Turkish carpets and I couldn't quite see the old-fashioned phone box. A lazy spring rain drizzled against the diamond-paned windows, sending cascades of water down the glass and a slur of mesmerizing shadows along the floors and walls.

Gage threaded his fingers together. "I always liked this old building. But I have to admit it's downright creepy with no one but us running around and only half the lights on."

Propping a chin in my hand, I partially agreed. "Creepy, sure. But also peaceful. If Basil's father had to die, the end of the semester was the best time to do it. Imagine him trying to run exams while grieving."

"Dr. Price would have taken over, kind of like now,

except there's no classes to oversee." He straightened and cocked his head. "Listen."

My ears perked but all I could hear was the soft patter of rain on the windows and the gravel outside. There wasn't even any wind. I was about to say that I couldn't hear anything when two car doors slammed, one right after the other.

We shared a wondering look.

"Christy said Basil wouldn't be back until Thursday."

"Maybe it's not Basil." I looked toward the big double doors. "Besides, I think he'd come in through the back. Whoever it is parked in the front, like they're not planning to stay long."

Foot falls and the murmur of a man's voice and a woman's voice preceded the double doors being flung open wide. The woman came in first. The man, who was at least a foot shorter than her, stumbled in holding a brolly over her head until she was well out of range of any moisture. The large black umbrella was snapped closed, shaken off outside, then propped in the umbrella holder around the corner from the phone-box.

The woman wore a black wide-brimmed hat, black gloves, and a raspberry colored trenchcoat I was certain was a very expensive Burberry. She swept the hat off in one smooth gesture, looking around with a self-satisfied sigh. Shoulder length auburn curls coiffed in a neat forties-like do lay against her shoulders. Without looking at the man—a rotund, balding, but well-dressed fellow with a close-cropped ring of silver hair—she handed him her hat. He found a home for it on one of the many brass hooks lining the paneling.

I was about to greet them when Gage's hand

closed around my bicep. He put a finger to his lips and jerked his head toward them; a 'just listen' gesture.

Neither of them called out to let whoever might be nearby know of their presence. The woman tugged off her gloves, gazing around the room in obvious pleasure, and handed them to the man as well. Taking those, he set them on a nearby side-table, a table she could have easily reached herself.

Working at the belt of her Burberry, she shrugged gracefully out of her coat. The man appeared at her back to take it, finding a home for that too, on the hooks beside his own coat. It was like watching a doting husband and spoiled wife arrive home after a long vacation.

A glance at Gage revealed that he was as bemused as I was, only he was holding back a laugh. I didn't feel so much humor as annoyance. Unless they made themselves known, and soon, they were trespassing.

The woman smoothed the wrinkles out of her snug-fitting purple dress; a knee-length frock with three-quarter sleeves and a bow at the throat.

"Let's begin." She didn't look at the man as she gave this command. Her voice was so soft it was barely above a whisper. She sounded like a Marilyn Monroe impersonator. It was so fake that the hair on the back of my neck lifted.

The man produced a small notebook from an inner pocket of his sports coat, followed by a pen. "Here, madam? In the foyer?"

"Why not?" Her black patent leather pumps clicked against the marble, then went quiet as she passed onto carpet. Moving with the turnout and posture of a dancer, she walked slowly through the furniture to reach the fireplace.

She gestured to the Arcturus logo set in the mantel, a delicate 'A' in the middle of an ornate crest. "These will have to go. When you send Christopher through, be sure to have him count them and note every location."

"Yes, madam. I won't place an order until we have a complete inventory and measurements." The man drifted along behind a sofa, scribbling furiously.

So far, neither of them had looked up. The compulsion to yell at them was strong, but Gage's hand on my arm kept me silent. Annoyance transitioned smoothly into alarm as she addressed the crests and fixtures.

"This furniture is hideous. Old, moth-eaten, and ugly. We'll replace all of it." She made a sweeping gesture to indicate she meant everything in the entire room.

"Yes madam."

Gage and I exchanged another wide-eyed look. The furniture was old, sure, but it was antique and well cared for. It went perfectly in the lobby. Getting rid of it seemed a crazy idea, and replacing it all would cost a lot of money.

The woman moved toward the exit leading to Victory Hall and paused there, looking into the corridor where the cases of academic memorabilia were on display behind glass.

"Ah, yes." Her feminine voice drifted up to us, turning derisive as she continued. "Victory Hall. What a shame."

She disappeared from view as she passed through the archway, her footfalls echoing once more on marble.

Gage and I moved as one. Leaving the balcony, we ran silently through the corridor toward the stairwell leading down to the ground floor at the other end of Victory Hall, keeping to the carpet runner. At the top of the stairs, we descended like shadows to the landing. The woman's voice drifted through the cavernous Victory Hall, increasing in volume as she closed the gap between us.

"All these years of teaching," she clucked, "wasted on an inferior syllabus. Accomplishments. Top Marks. Achievements." Her tone dripped with sarcasm.

"Madam?" Her minion was a little impatient to get on with it.

"All of this goes in the trash, not the least of which is this hideous thing. Ugh."

I clamped a hand over my mouth. Judging from how far away her voice was, I knew exactly which 'hideous thing' she was assigning to the trash heap. The beautiful onyx sculpture of the male and female magi, the Top Marks trophy. Basil must have spent a fortune on it.

I made to take the rest of the stairs down, steam whistling from my ears, but Gage's arm snaked around my waist. He pulled me back against him and whispered, "Wait."

Anger kindled, my mind began to spin like a top. She came in like she owned the place and clearly had plans. By the time she was through, it sounded like there would be no Arcturus left.

"Might it not be best to keep these things for posterity, madam?" The man asked in a placating tone. "History has always been important to you, and while the way things have worked out might be ah, an unpleasant thorn for madam, erasing the history of the building might be something you'll regret. Down the road."

Silence.

I couldn't see her face and wondered if she were going to blow up on him. She struck me as the volatile type. But her answer was calm.

"Perhaps you are right, Mr. Bunting. Thank you for being the voice of reason during these times of transition."

Her voice was full of emotion, pure pageantry. I cocked my head, wondering if she was crying. She sniffled. My stomach clenched with nausea. She sounded as genuine as a Louis Vuitton bag purchased from a street vendor in Istanbul. Dislike for the woman burned at the back of my throat.

Gage's arm released me at the sound of her lament and I didn't let the opportunity slide. He didn't stop me from taking the rest of the stairs down into Victory Hall.

I rounded the corner and stopped at the end of the trophy cases. "Shame on you."

The woman—who had had her back to my end of the hall—whirled and lifted a hand to her mouth. Her auburn hair bounced against her neck and shoulders. "Goodness!"

Her minion—standing behind her—poked his head from beyond his madam, adjusting his glasses for a better look.

"Headmaster Chaplin isn't here right now." I crossed my arms and sat into a hip. "Don't you know it's rude to come into a private estate unannounced? You're trespassing."

Unabashed at my admonition, the woman lowered

her hand. Her eyes gleamed with fire and curiosity but her tone was sweet. "Who are you, dear?"

The kindness in her voice took me off-guard, this time it sounded genuine.

"I'm Saxony, a student here. Who are you?"

The man provided the answer. "You're speaking to the Viscountess Barbara Chaplin."

My anger deflated like a pricked balloon and I felt like smacking my forehead. I should have known. Basil had told me that her moral values had deteriorated after her Burning—enough for him to be believe that the Burning process really did pose a danger for some mages—but she was still family. Nothing would change that.

A tumult of emotions crashed through me. Maybe she did have the right to come into the villa unannounced. Surely though, the changes these two were discussing weren't at Basil's permission. Of course they could have had a conversation I wasn't aware of. I hadn't spoken directly to Basil, not that I expected that Basil should share private family business with me. Still, it was weird. Gage and I were students here, and Basil and Christy knew we were here. If there were going to be big changes coming up, surely we might have been given some kind of notice? Then again, grief did different things to different people and Basil had been unusually absent-minded lately.

Her voice penetrated my fog.

"I see you've heard of me." She seemed pleased. I noted she had a hand on the forearm of Mr. Bunting, as if to prevent him from speaking.

"You're Basil's twin, one of a set of triplets." The words were just out and I second guessed them, following them up with an awkward, "I'm sorry about your brother."

Her eyes widened, but not unpleasantly so. "Thank you, but I'm surprised to hear my darling brother shared such a personal event with a student."

I didn't know what to say; I wasn't about to blurt out that I was Burned. She could guess that from my voice if she was astute, which I was certain she was. The reason for her put-on Marilyn voice struck me then. Babs was also Burned. She was trying to cover up the sound of it.

She approached, walking casually. Her eyes flicked once to my left as Gage joined me.

"Two of you," she said, still closing the gap between us. "How many students remain here, though school is out for the summer?"

"Just us. We're here to support Basil."

"And you call him by his first name." She was close enough now that another step and she'd be able to offer a handshake, but she stopped there. Mr. Bunting had shadowed her down the hall and stopped just behind her, still looking out from behind her like he was afraid of us.

"Basil is my godfather," said Gage. "I'm Gage."

"Ah, you're one of the twins!" She threw her hands up then pressed her palms together, seemingly delighted. "Of course, you wouldn't know me. But I did meet your handsome father once. Chad Wendig, right?"

Gage nodded.

"And you?" Her eyes—hazel, I saw, now that she was close enough—fell on me. "Why do *you* call him Basil?"

Prickling with discomfort, I clasped my hands

behind me. It was difficult to break the habits of a well-behaved student who had always respected authority figures, or even just adults who acted like they had authority.

"He told me to," I replied.

"Then you must both call me Babs." She reached out a hand for a shake, suddenly and rather aggressively. I fought the urge to cringe away from her.

This was a pivotal moment. Shaking her hand meant skin on skin contact, which meant the question of whether we were bonded or not would be answered. And how might that change things? She was Basil's sister, and I was bonded with Basil. Ryan and Gage were twins. Basil and Babs were two of a set of triplets. The odds were good, weren't they? I reached out, fully expecting a flare of heat to pass between us.

Our eyes glued meaningfully to each other's as we received our answer. No bond.

I worked to hide my surprise. Her expression fell, just a little, as she let go of my hand and shook with Gage. She released him and took a step back. I thought I could guess from her face that she didn't share a bond with Gage, either.

"Sorry about your dad," Gage said.

I also murmured a condolence, embarrassed I'd addressed her long-dead brother and not her recently deceased father.

"Thank you." Babs brushed at her cheek in a delicate motion. "He was a good man. No doubt you're wondering how it is that I've come to be wandering these halls, discussing the changing of the drapes, as it were."

"Perhaps it would be best to wait until after the signing—" Mr. Bunting began.

"Nonsense." She cut him off with a wave. "These are academy students. The fate of Arcturus affects them, I'll not keep them in the dark." She clasped her hands. "My father's will has been released. My dear brother and I are to inherit the estate fifty-fifty. It was our father's wish that we run the school together. So you see, I have every right to be here. For too long my meek and timid brother has hobbled the fates of young mages. I am here to change that. I am here to push you to your maximum, to improve the syllabus, to open the doors to heights Arcturus students could never achieve in their wildest dreams under Basil."

My skin marbled with goosebumps of horror as her tone hardened. This woman seemed as changeable as the wind, and she wasn't finished.

"Arcturus Academy will become Firethorne Collegiate. My students will migrate here in the new school year, doubling the student population and putting these marvelous facilities to real use."

"What about Headmaster Chaplin?" I rasped as I took a step back and bumped against Gage, who took my hand.

"He'll be my second, of course. He has some value in certain subjects. Now, run along home. It's nice that you're here to support my brother in his grief, but you're no longer needed. I'm here now. We'll see you in September."

She turned away and began to discuss the changing of stained-glass windows which lined Victory Hall. Not all of them. Just the ones with the Arcturus crest in the center.

THREE

!

"The trick with this dish," I said as I unpacked the shopping bags and lined up ingredients beside one of the industrial stoves in the academy's kitchen, "is to steam the smoked haddock and poach the eggs for the right time. The fish takes roughly six minutes to steam, but the eggs take half that time to poach. If you overdo either, the dish doesn't work."

Gage pulled a pot down from the row of hanging copper vessels, filled it with water and set it over a burner. "How do these gas burners work? I've only ever worked with electric ones."

"There'll be a lighter around here somewhere." Raking through a stainless-steel drawer full of odd bits, I paused at the snapping sound as Gage triggered a spark. The gas caught from the flame on the end of his finger, lighting the hob.

I straightened. "Wow, I've rarely felt quite so silly."

Gage winked and rubbed his flat stomach. "Now what? I'm starving."

After our interaction with Babs and her minion the

day before, Gage and I had told Dr. Price, who'd alerted Basil. We still hadn't seen the headmaster since the graduation dance, but Christy had been up early and gone today, texting that she was to meet Basil at the funeral home. She said they'd discuss Babs when the opportune moment came.

I wondered what state Basil was in. Gage and I offered to go to the funeral home but Dr. Price said she thought it better if we didn't. There'd be tension between Basil and Babs, and she didn't want Basil to have to worry about students observing the state of his family dynamics.

"First we do the garlic mashed potatoes, since they take the longest." Retrieving a couple of knives, I handed one to Gage and we set to work on the potatoes.

"I can't wait. I'm so sick of takeout." Gage took the potatoes as I peeled them and cut them into the pot of heating water.

"It's only been a couple of days but I know what you mean. Dover doesn't have a lot of options. I still have the taste of old french-fry grease in my mouth." I sent him a sideways glance as we peeled, changing subjects. "So, are you just going to wait for Ryan to show up before you head back to Canada?"

"What else should I do? He's stopped answering texts again. All I know is that he'll find me when his business is concluded."

"That doesn't strike you as inconsiderate?"

Gage rolled his eyes.

"What? Doesn't it?" I spread my hands, accidentally flinging a potato peeling. Picking it up, I dropped it the compost collector. "I mean, it's great that he let you know he's okay and all, but doesn't he care that you've been stressed and worried?"

Gage's brows arched as he transferred a potato wedge to the pot. "I'm fine."

"Yeah, *now* you are. You couldn't eat until Ryan deigned to answer."

"Don't your brothers have quirks that drive you crazy? This is just like Ryan. Maybe he's not polite, but he's my twin. It's just the way he is. Besides," Gage leaned over a planted a kiss just under my ear. Sparkles of heat whooshed from the place his lips pressed, making my stomach flutter. "It's not every day I have a huge abandoned villa and one smoking hot redhead all to myself."

Desire and exasperation spiraled in my gut. "My brothers would never ignore my messages," I muttered. "They love me too much for that."

Gage stiffened but didn't answer, which made me feel bad. Maybe I should apologize for implying that Ryan didn't love Gage, but I meant it. Ryan didn't know what love even was, in my opinion.

We finished the potatoes in a tense silence and stared listlessly at the pot as it began to simmer. I found a little ceramic bowl full of salt crystals and took a pinch. As I stirred it in and reached for a lid, Gage moved to stand behind me. He wrapped his arms around my waist and pressed his face into the side of my neck, which resulted in all kinds of fiery and delicious sensations.

I squeezed his face gently between my cheek and neck, placed the lid on the pot, and lay a hand over his. "I admire how forgiving and unconditional you are with Ryan, I just also think you let him walk all over you."

"I hate that you dislike him so much." His breath tickled my neck.

"He dislikes me even more."

Gage pulled me away from the stove and turned me to face him. "That's not true. He manipulated and used you, yes, but he did it because he admired what you're capable of. And he was right, in the end. You saved him. Now that he's achieved his goal, I'm hoping the two of you can be friends."

I snorted.

"Friendly acquaintances?" His expression was as hopeful as a puppy eyeballing a bag of treats.

I let out a sigh, considering reminding Gage of what had happened to Nero, when the sound of a door slamming jarred us from our conversation.

From outside the manor in the opposite direction of the fire-gym, men were conversing. Though we couldn't make out actual words, they spoke in loud, casual tones. There was laughter. There was a thud, followed by another door slamming.

Gage headed for the cafeteria.

"There's a short cut back here." I crossed to the rear exit, a door that looked like it led to nothing more than a pantry.

Gage followed. "How do you know?"

"I chased the thief through here. It connects to the west wing."

We took the narrow set of stairs to the second level, passed through the door at the top and followed the jagged hallway until it dumped us onto a landing. A rarely used window seat beneath a set of arched windows gave us a view into the back yard.

A white moving van was parked on the grass with

its rear doors open. A ramp connected the deck to the ground. Slashes of mud where the tires had ripped up the lawn revealed just how little the driver cared about academy property. A burly man appeared with a couple of boxes, took the ramp and entered the academy through a back door. Another muscled man in a tight t-shirt came into view, going the opposite way.

As the men passed, one said in a voice that carried up to us, "That desk isn't going to fit through this door."

"She said we could use the front doors for the bigger stuff," replied the other over his shoulder. He kept talking but I couldn't make out what else was said.

Gage and I shared a wide-eyed look.

"Babs," he said.

"She's moving in?" Incredulous, I fumbled for my cell. Opening the camera, I snapped a photo of the van and a mover holding a stack of boxes. I texted it to Christy with the caption: *Babs is moving in. Does Basil know?*

"The biggest suites are accessible from that door. Do you think she just helped herself to one of the nicest ones?" Gage muttered, nose pressed against the glass as a third man joined the moving team. "Unreal."

I didn't bother to point out the irony at Gage's disbelief over Babs rudeness but his lack of the same for his brother.

My phone vibrated with a response from Christy.

I held my screen up so Gage could see the contents of her text, a single character: *!*

Gage peered over my shoulder, resting his hands on my hips as we watched the trail of dots that meant Christy was typing another text. A few seconds later she followed the exclamation point with: *Don't approach them. We'll be there in less than half an hour.*

"Oh boy, oh boy!" I infused my voice with false enthusiasm. "Just when we thought we had a boring afternoon ahead of us."

Gage pressed his body against mine, fingertips sneaking under the hem of my shirt to trace the skin by my belly-button. "I had other ideas about how to keep things interesting."

My stomach did a triple-flip as fire blossomed under my skin. My breath hitched as I turned in his arms like a rotisserie chicken. His lashes cast enchanting shadows along his cheekbone, his lips parted. I ran my fingers through his hair and was about to draw his mouth down to mine when he pulled his head back, eyes flying open.

"Crap, the potatoes!"

IN SPITE of having to clean up gooey potato-foam, which had dribbled down over the stovetop and the front of the stove, the meal was a success. We ate in the kitchen while at the other end of the academy, Babs' furniture continued to be moved in.

Gage looked longingly at his empty plate. "You should have warned me the portions were so small. I would have eaten two servings, even if it is incredibly fattening."

I laughed. First, because Gage was so lean you could count the veins in his arms—and second; he'd had a portion big enough that my brother RJ—who outweighed Gage by a good twenty pounds, wouldn't have been able to finish it.

"Can we make it again tomorrow?"

"We bought that pot-pie dish for tomorrow." I didn't remind him that my flight back to Canada was booked for Friday evening. I'd already delayed it once and had a powerful urge to delay it a second time. When I'd explained to my parents that I wanted to be here to support Basil, even if it was just for a few extra days, I hadn't realized that I'd be spending more time smooching Gage than attending Basil. I wasn't about to set my folks straight.

Voices intruded on our stainless-steel picnic once more, only this time they were coming from the front lobby and they were anything but happy or casual.

Leaving our dirty dishes on the countertop, Gage and I scrambled through the cafeteria and emerged in the hall connecting with the lobby.

"What are you doing?" Basil's voice thundered loud enough to make the crystal chandelier tinkle.

Gage grabbed my hand and yanked me into a lounge. We paused just inside the door, not daring to appear in the foyer.

Babs answered with infuriating calm. "My desk and my piano are too large to fit through the back door so we're bringing them in through the front. Calm yourself. You look pale. Perhaps you should sit down."

"Gentlemen," Basil addressed the movers through clenched teeth. "You are trespassing. If you bring in one more item—I don't care if it's a bloody paperclip—I will press charges."

"Don't listen to him," Babs scoffed. "I'm perfectly within my rights to be here. This building and all its grounds and assets are half mine."

Basil seethed. "The will takes effect only after the

paperwork is agreed and signed."

"A formality. There is no reason to delay."

"Take a smoke break, lads," our formidable headmaster snapped.

There was a short span of silence—during which Babs gave a longsuffering sigh—followed by shuffling footsteps as the movers left the foyer.

"Shall I—?"

I recognized Dr. Price's voice. I hadn't realized she'd been there. I felt bad about eavesdropping but not bad enough to reveal myself or take myself out of earshot. This was too important to miss.

"Stay, please." Basil leveled his voice to address the doctor. "Take a seat, won't you?"

Their footfalls went silent as they passed from the marble onto one of the Turkish rugs. I dared a peek. Christy and Basil took the large sofa, the one with its back to us, while Babs took a wingback kitty-corner to them.

"Let's work this out like adults, shall we?" Basil was making an effort to sound in control.

Babs crossed one long leg over the other, tugging the hem of her navy dress down in a ladylike gesture. She tucked a lock of hair behind her ear, her face turning a quarter to look at her brother.

"Yes, lets. We can start by reminding ourselves that the will stipulates that we only receive our inheritance if we agree to run the Academy together as partners. That was our father's wish."

Worried that I'd catch her attention, I pulled back behind the doorjamb. Gage—who hadn't chanced a look—slid down the wall to sit on the floor, his head tilted to listen.

Basil made a sound of forced patience. "You know that will never happen. We would sooner kneecap one another than agree on the yearly menu, let alone how students should be instructed."

"There's no way around it." Babs sounded as haughty as she was confident. "We steward the school together or we lose the property completely. We can make it work so long as you follow my approach. Face it, your students have been gagging for an opportunity to become real mages. Something you'll never allow them."

I shot Gage a look of incredulity. He put a finger to his lips, expressing much less indignation than me.

"Actually," Dr. Price interjected, "Headmaster Chaplin's methods have introduced powerful but highly ethical mages into supernatural society, not the least of which is the contribution to the Agency's ranks. Thanks to Basil, the Agency itself has become the most trusted and reliable organization of its kind."

Babs made a sound in her throat, a gentile scoff. "Trusted and reliable, yes. Effective? Not by half. When are you going to learn that you cannot serve two masters? If you serve virtue and integrity, you sacrifice competence and potency."

"I disagree," Basil replied, tightly. "And the discussion is pointless, at any rate. I'll buy you out. There's nothing in the will that prevents it."

Babs snorted outright this time, foregoing her ladylike front. "With what fortune? This estate is half mine. The retro-fittings it's undergone make it unique the world over—thank you for that, by the way. Firethorne's facilities pale dreadfully next to this place. The academy is priceless."

"Perhaps," Dr. Price ventured, "an agreement could be made? A house with two heads of equal power divided against one another cannot stand. If you agree to Basil's headship with a fifty-one to forty-nine—"

"Christy—" Basil began reproachfully.

There was the sound of palms hitting flesh, like Babs had whacked herself on the thigh. "Nonsense. I plan to exercise all of the power the will legally gives me and not a drop less, and yes, that includes where Burning is concerned. If students wish to take the risk, who are we to stifle such desires?"

"*Who are we?* We are their caretakers and guardians. We are responsible for their lives while they are under our roof," Basil's voice was beginning to climb again. "We are responsible to see them graduate safe and sound, in possession of a beating heart."

Babs sighed heavily. "When are you going to accept that Burning is natural to our species? It's a shame its risky and painful, I agree, but you know that we can minimize the risk. I have hopes that one day we can eradicate the risk completely."

"No," Basil barked. There was another sound, like he'd hit the arm of the sofa. "No. No. No. I cannot allow such roulette to be played under my roof!"

"Our roof."

Basil sputtered. "Restrain me, Christy, or I shall—"

"Unless—"

The lobby went silent at Babs' soft voice. Gage and I locked eyes, his were as round as mine felt. My heart pattered and scampered like a field mouse dodging the shadow of an owl.

The grandfather clock ticked eight seconds.

"Unless?" Basil sounded breathless.

"Well," Babs paused, probably enjoying the tension and Basil's agony. "You know how much I enjoy a good wager."

Silence.

If a beetle had emerged from under the carpet to trundle past the phone-box, we all would have heard it.

"You're insane," Basil said, matter-of-factly. There was the sound of fabric sliding on fabric, like he'd shifted on the couch to face Christy. Then: "She's insane."

Babs sounded both smug and alluring, neither affected nor deterred by Basil's reaction. "Come, now. You're always going on about how superior your way of teaching is. A simple tournament between our students would decide things for good. If my students win, I take over the school. Fully and completely. If your students prevail, you shall have Arcturus back unchanged, free to continue relegating its alumni to the dusty annals of mediocrity."

"I really don't think—" that was Christy, overtop of Basil, who was making a choking sound.

Babs cut her off. "I'll leave it for you to mull over, though the fear in your eyes speaks loudly enough. You'll not dare take a wager you're sure to lose. If such is the case, then you must accept our partnership from this point on, as you cannot legally stop it. If you need me, I'll be in my suite—the Rose Room, by the way— working on the Firethorne syllabus for the upcoming school year."

Stunned silence was broken only by the sound of Babs rising to her feet, followed by her pumps as they clicked on the marble. She crossed to the double doors where she called to the moving men: "Hop to, lads!"

FOUR
DESPERATE TIMES

Around the corner from Basil's office, Gage turned me to face him, whispering, "Maybe we should let him alone for the day?"

"We've already given him a full hour," I whispered back. "He knows we're here. Won't he wonder why we haven't come to see him?"

Gage studied my face, blue eyes piercing from under a wrinkled brow.

The situation was strange. On top of grieving for his father, which was supposedly why I was still here, Basil now had Babs to contend with. In Babs' irrational view, the partnership envisioned by their father actually meant she was in control. If that came to pass, Arcturus likely wouldn't exist by the end of the summer.

Gage took my hand and we squeezed each other's fingers, fire threading from his hand to mine and back again. He nodded.

Keeping his hand in mine, I led him onto the landing in front of Basil's office.

The door was open.

Approaching the doorway, Gage and I slowed as one, then leaned forward for a peek.

Basil—seated behind his desk with his chin in his palm—saw us immediately. Brows arching, he twitched a finger for us to enter.

Dr. Price was seated on the largest sofa, a steaming mug of tea sat at her knee. Her expression didn't change when she saw us, but she shuffled over and gestured for us to sit down. I sat by Christy and Gage sank onto the sofa beside me. We looked at Basil.

"Thank you for staying." He leaned back against his chair and let his hands fall into his lap. "It wasn't necessary but it was very kind." His gaze drifted to Gage. "Christy tells me Ryan has texted you?"

Gage nodded, shifting on the seat and making the leather squeak. "He says he'll find me when his business is done in Naples. He won't tell me what he's up to, but I'm hoping he'll be back in a matter of days."

Basil and I shared a look. The headmaster's mouth flattened into an unhappy slash.

"You'll be wanting to get off home, I'm sure?" Dr. Price addressed me.

I nodded. "But I won't go so soon if I can be of help. I haven't arranged for a summer job, and my besties aren't even in Saltford right now, so—"

"I'm not sure there's anything you can do." Christy raised her teacup to her lips.

I'd personally lost all interest in hot drinks, except coffee, the moment I became a mage, but to each their own.

The office fell silent.

"What about Arcturus?" I asked.

Basil looked down at his fingernails, as though they

might hold an answer. He didn't look surprised that I'd asked.

Dr. Price set her cup and saucer on the table. "You overheard the conversation in the foyer, I take it?"

Gage looked at the ceiling, the chicken.

I cleared my throat. "I'm sorry we eavesdropped, but we were incapable of tearing ourselves away."

"I can imagine," Basil muttered without looking up.

Dr. Price angled her knees toward us on the sofa. "Then you'll know that the future of the school is quite uncertain. Basil will never agree to share the running of the academy with Babs, and Babs will never relent her share of authority. As you've already seen, Babs is acting as if her take-over is a done deal." She looked at the headmaster.

Basil chewed his cheek, still inspecting his hands.

"But Basil can't just step down," I sputtered, mentally begging the headmaster to look up. "Keeping half the authority is better than handing the whole lot over to Babs, isn't it? From the sounds of it, she'll change everything."

"That's just it." Dr. Price crossed her arms. "Babs' methods and dealings would soon drown the school in a cesspool of mistrust within the supernatural community. She'll ruin its reputation and everything Basil has worked so hard for these last thirty years."

Basil's eyes flicked up, homing in on me with such intensity that I felt goosebumps run up the back of my scalp. But he still didn't say anything.

Christy, meanwhile, seemed to be hitting her stride. Disdain had crept into her features. "Her ultimate goal has always been to take over the Agency. Chaplin senior's death has provided the perfect stepping stone—

using the Academy to begin her infiltration. She'd turn both the school and the agency into the same soulless operations so many of our competitors run. Mark my words, before the year is out she'd have multiple deaths on her hands."

My jaw drifted open. Christy didn't miss my horror.

"Oh yes, she's already allowed three students—that we know of—in her care to expire, chalking it up to collateral damage. Part of her interview strategy involves asking potential registrants how willing they are to attempt a Burning. If she finds them cowardly—according to her own standards, naturally—she doesn't allow them in. Her relentless pursuit of her goal of one day graduating only fifth-degree mages has already left a trail of—"

"That's quite enough, Dr. Price." Headmaster Chaplin lifted his chin. "Thank you."

Dr. Price pressed her lips together and looked down at the carpet. Her mouth was bracketed by white lines.

The headmaster got out of his chair and went to the small table in the corner, where he poured a glass of water from the carafe. He twisted to look at the three of us on the couch, holding up the carafe with a brow raised in a question.

Gage and I shook our heads mutely. We'd downed several glasses before approaching Basil's office. In fact, my bladder was beginning to send signals.

Basil drank before setting the glass down and coming to stand behind the spinning wingback chair. He faced us, leaning his elbows on its back. "There is something to said for Babs' idea."

Christy recoiled. "The wager? You can't be serious, Basil!"

Basil's glasses had slipped down his nose and he pushed them back. He was sweating. "A tournament. Winner takes all."

"It's madness!" the doctor cried. "You said so yourself when she suggested it."

A cold stone had settled low in my gut, growing heavy as I realized that Basil was seriously considering taking the gamble. But wouldn't I if it were my school? Babs had suggested he wouldn't take a wager he was sure to lose. But Basil and his staff were excellent teachers, in my limited opinion. Wasn't there was a chance that Arcturus alumni were in fact superior?

"In some ways, it's the only open door." He straightened, brushing the velvet covering of the chair. "Think of the alumni we have access to, the number of competent students Arcturus has churned out over the years, some of whom by now may even be Burned. My students are incredibly loyal, a few are talented enough to hold agency positions. Surely, when they learn what is at stake, they will gladly champion our school."

Christy made a sound of incredulity.

Gage was silent but he pressed the side of his hand against mine.

"I must object." Dr. Price got to her feet, looking to Gage and me. "Tell him it's foolhardy, please. He won't listen to me."

"If I were Basil, I would consider it," Gage said.

I lifted my chin. "Me too."

Dr. Price frowned, bemused. "I'm the only sane person in the room."

"Think about it, Christy," Basil's voice was soft and

hopeful. "If I can't buy her out and I can't overrule her authority, what else can I do?"

"Where is your faith in the student body?" Gage asked Christy.

Dr. Price crossed her arms, her blue suit jacket straining at the shoulders. "Are *you* going to take on the responsibility of winning or losing millions of pounds in assets, Gage Wendig?"

Gage looked uncomfortable. "No. I'm only a second-year."

The icy pinpricks of her pupils came to me. "How about you, Saxony Cagney?"

I shrank. "Of course not. Basil already said there are plenty of alumni fit for the job."

"My point is not that the alumni wouldn't be fit to compete; Basil is right, there are many competent mages among them. My point is, who would be willing to perform under that kind of pressure? Losing a trophy is one thing, losing Basil his entire fortune and inheritance is quite another."

It was a good point, and the silence in the room meant we all realized it.

Then Gage plowed ahead, having found his hill to die on, apparently. "But if you believe that Arcturus actually does turn out the best students, then isn't the risk manageable? It could all be over in a matter of weeks, maybe even days."

"Never overestimate an opponent," Basil said, lifting a finger. "But equally, and perhaps more importantly, know your own capabilities."

"Basil—" Christy warned.

"What? Losing only means I have to find something else to do." Basil had begun to pace. "So what? It's something I bandy about every summer. But winning —" He swept back to the doctor, face alight. "Winning might even mean giving some of the poor Firethorne students a chance to try their hand the Arcturus way, out from under the threat of death by Burning, and the pressure to try it."

Christy turned her back on all of us and put her forehead in her hands. "God save me from rash individuals."

Basil, Gage and I watched her recover herself.

She turned, plastering on a serene smile and directing it at Basil. "That is quite enough madness for one day. At least sleep on this. You've been under a lot of stress. You're grieving. You're upset. Just—" she interlaced her fingers and put them under her chin, "— please? Sleep on it?"

"Christy, we train young mages for a living, in all kinds of competencies." He pushed his glasses back into place for the second time, then gripped the back of the chair again, knuckles turning white through the skin. "If I'm truly afraid of losing it all to Babs, then don't I have to ask myself what I'm doing running a school for mages in the first place?"

FIVE

THE COMMITTEE

The hardwood floor of the lecture hall creaked underfoot as Gage and I snuck in and took a couple of seats in front of the Audio-Visual booth at the back of the room. Basil looked over from where he was pouring himself a cup of coffee at a side-table. I held my breath, thinking he might kick us out. This meeting was important. The means by which the future headmaster of Arcturus would step into their post would be determined here by committee.

Basil only smiled. Well, his mouth flattened into a line and a dimple indented his right cheek—an attempt at a smile.

The lecture hall creaked with every movement. Everything was made of ages-old oak and smelled of wood-polish and chalk. It was part of what I loved about the villa, a mixing of old-school and cutting-edge technology. But, I resisted the tug on my memory to relive the events in the abandoned mine. For me, the smell of chalk had forever changed.

Semi-circular platforms equipped with desks and

benches looked down upon a low stage and podium. Sliding chalk-boards and an old wooden desk that probably weighed a ton sat upon the dais. In the space between the dais and the front row, chairs had been arranged around a circular table, at which sat the committee.

Babs shifted in her chair, tucking the edges of her snug-fitting teal dress under her hips. I had begun to wonder if she even owned a pair of trousers. A matching fascinator was pinned at a jaunty angle on her head. She looked like she's stepped straight out of a WWII epic love story. I could now see what I hadn't been able to see initially: a likeness to Basil. They shared high cheekbones and square chin, but outside of that, they didn't look much alike.

Mr. Bunting sat beside Babs, and Dr. Price sat across from her. On the other side of Mr. Bunting sat three men I'd never seen before. I leaned toward Gage. "Who are they?"

He shrugged and whispered back, "One of them has to be the executor, right?"

Basil returned to the table with his coffee and took the remaining empty seat, across the table from Babs. He nodded at the gentleman in the pale green tweed suit sitting directly in front of the dais. The table was round, but something about this man suggested that he was the one in charge.

"Right, let's begin. Shall we?" He stretched an arm out and bent it again look at his wristwatch. "It's ten o'clock on the morning of Thursday, May 31, 2018. We are present here at Arcturus Academy—"

"Chaplin Manor and Estate," Babs interjected.

He went on as though she hadn't spoken. "Seated in

Lecture Hall C. I am the host, Mr. Pendleton, the executor and trustee of the late Viscount Chaplin's will and estate. Please state your names and positions for the record." He gestured to a small camera on top of a tripod pointing at the group.

Mr. Pendleton had gestured for Basil to introduce himself, but Babs spoke first.

"Viscountess Barbara Chaplin, Headmaster of Firethorne Collegiate located east of London."

Her minion removed his trusty notebook from inside his jacket pocket and set it on the table before him. He also produced a small wooden pencil as he spoke. "Mr. Bunting, Secretary at Firethorne Collegiate."

"Basil Chaplin." Basil took a sip of his coffee and set it down. "Headmaster of Arcturus Academy."

Beside the trustee sat a sharp-faced man with sparkling eyes. His movements were quick, his body narrow and whipcord lean. He spoke quickly as his gaze darted about the room, missing nothing, including Gage and me. He spoke with a soft accent I couldn't place.

"Mr. Zafer Guzelköy. Hacker, Cryptographer, Cryptanalyst and Code-Breaker for Arcturus Agency. Co-owner of SG."

What is SG? Obviously everyone else knew the initials.

My stomach did a tumble. Wasn't it premature to have such a specialist here? I'd thought the rules of the wager was what they were here to discuss. I looked over at Gage. He sat with one ankle propped on his knee, his fingers tapping his lips. He shrugged when I looked at him with an arched brow.

Beside the last fellow we didn't know yet sat Dr. Price. She introduced herself, looking like she wished she was anywhere else.

The last man was huge, his bulk threatening to break the chair he sat in. He had a short dark beard, and a long ponytail. In contradiction with his beard, his hair was dark blond and threaded with gray at the temples. His pyramid shaped eyebrows sheltered glittering black orbs. He sat back with his arms crossed, looking relaxed. A tattoo peeked out from beneath one rolled up shirtsleeve.

"Demir Davazlar," he said, "Co-owner of SG."

SG again? G for games?

I thought Davazlar looked more like a wrestler or an assassin than a game-designer. There was something attractive and unusual about the contrast he presented; a quiet demeanor with an imposing physical presence.

"Thank you." Mr. Pendleton shifted the legal pad closer and made a note. "The purpose of this meeting is to agree the terms of a recent wager—"

"Do you mind if we call it a tournament or games?" Basil asked. "I hate the word wager."

"They're not uncommon in your world," Mr. Pendleton replied. "I see no reason not to call it what it is." Something about the way the trustee spoke told me he didn't approve of the whole affair but had resigned himself to it. Being executor for the late viscount, he must have known the history of the triplets. Maybe he too thought there was no better way to settle things.

"He's never approved of gambling." Babs cast a familiar, almost loving smile in Basil's direction. It irked me, to see her looking at him that way, like she still had actual affection for him. If she really cared about him, she wouldn't want to railroad the school he'd built.

The trustee glanced from Babs to Basil. "As you wish. Due to irreconcilable differences and your lack of legal freedom to change the terms of the will, now that the aforesaid documents have been signed, we are proceeding with a tournament to determine the future ownership of the Chaplin Estate. The schools will register a specified number of competitors to compete in games Zafer Guzelköy and Demir Davazlar shall design and referee. The winner takes ownership of the present building and grounds as well as the position of headmaster. I understand a consolation prize of £200,000 is to be set aside for the losing party. The parties concerned are Basil and Barbara Chaplin, the rules and outcome will be legally binding. Do I have the matter straight?"

Basil, Babs and Mr. Bunting nodded. Guzelköy tapped his fingers on the tabletop until a look from the trustee had him snatch his hand back. He looked nervous, but I had a feeling he was always high-strung.

"Messrs. Guzelköy and Davazlar will manage the games together." He gestured toward the two men. "I'll have documents drawn up for each of you to sign upon conclusion of this meeting. Have you settled on the nature of this competition?" Mr. Pendleton's pen hovered over the yellow pad expectantly.

Babs and Basil shared a look and Babs gestured at Davazlar. "They're the experts. Can't they outline some options for us to decide on?"

Attention shifted to the two men.

Davazlar spoke without changing his arms-crossed posture. His voice rumbled like low thunder. "The options are endless. Team sport, round-robin, double and triple elimination tourneys. Card games, board games, debates, points based ranking—"

Guzelköy, far too excited, interrupted the big man, speaking so quickly he was hard to follow. "We could do a multi-stage tournament, a best of seven series, or—something that's all the rage and very trendy right now—an apertura and clausura split-season format—"

It was Basil's turn to interrupt. "We can't have this thing drag on all summer, let alone across two seasons. It needs to be decided at a bare minimum of three weeks before the start of the next school year."

Babs chimed in: "Yes, otherwise the new headmaster won't have time to prepare her syllabus."

Guzelköy didn't miss a beat. "In that case, might I suggest a staged, single-elimination series where the loser of each match is knocked out of the tournament straight away?" He snapped his fingers with a loud, dry pop. "Sudden death."

Quiet descended over the lecture hall like the settling of a shroud. Everyone was looking at Guzelköy.

Babs broke the silence, speaking in a rush. "A wonderful idea. But, if anyone dies in these games, the school who has sustained the loss is the immediate winner."

All eyes swung to Babs, the tension in the room thickened to a near unbearable point as expressions took on a look of shock. Dr. Price had actually turned green. Gage put a hand on my thigh and squirmed at the level of tension in the room. I leaned into him. How had things escalated to the possibility of students dying?

Basil looked aghast at what her misunderstanding

had revealed: just how serenely she took the potential of a student fatality. "No one is going to die, Babs."

"Sudden death is a metaphor," Guzelköy supplied gently, rubbing his slender fingers together over the table like he was eager to get to work. I wondered what those code-breaking hands were capable of, and the keen mind behind those bright eyes. He could have laughed at Babs but he'd taken her seriously, which—in my view— displayed a level of kindness Babs didn't deserve.

Babs had the decency to blush but stuck to her guns. "Then you won't mind having the rule in place."

Silence. Again.

I wished I could see her face better, but she sat partially with her back to me. Gage's hand tightened on my thigh until I took it, lacing my fingers through his and taking comfort in the heat swishing between us like liquid in a glass.

Mr. Pendleton looked pointedly at Basil.

The headmaster waved a hand, his expression making it clear how ridiculous he thought it was to add as a rule. But there was no down side to leaving it. "Fine, fine."

The trustee made a note on his pad.

"I'd like to suggest that all alumni are eligible," Basil began.

"Absolutely not," Babs snapped.

Basil looked at his fellow triplet, wide-eyed. "Why ever not?"

"This isn't about the glory days. Arcturus Academy has been graduating students since 1992, Firethorne Collegiate only since 2001. You have a larger pool of mages to invite, giving you an advantage. To keep things fair, only current students or students who graduated this year should be eligible to compete."

"Seems reasonable," added Mr. Bunting.

A look of incredulity passed between Gage and I as this new rule began to sink in.

"I have to admit, I agree," Mr. Pendleton said, looking at the game-makers. "What say you?"

The game-makers nodded.

Basil tapped the end of one blunt finger on the wood, considering, then relented. He gave Mr. Pendleton a nod, who made the notation.

"How many students will each school supply?" Guzelköy asked. His hands had disappeared beneath the table again, but he must have been swinging a leg or something because his body bounced on his chair.

"I was thinking thirty?" Babs suggested.

Basil put up a hand. "No. We can't allow this to get unwieldy. Let's keep it to sixteen students. Eight from Arcturus, eight from Firethorne. Even sixteen students eliminated over four rounds will take time. How much would you need to prepare an inaugural round?" He looked at the game-makers.

They exchanged a pensive look.

Davazlar arched one of those pointed brows as he asked his game-making partner and fellow referee. "Two weeks?"

Guzelköy nodded, the gesture was so rapid it was like he was being electrocuted. "Two weeks should do it."

Basil continued. "Two weeks to prepare and approximately two events per week"—he glanced at the game-makers, who nodded again—"would put us into July. My students need an actual summer break, otherwise they'll begin their studies exhausted come September." He turned to Babs. "So, sixteen competitors?"

She nodded. "Sixteen suits me."

"Excellent." Mr. Pendleton looked satisfied with the progress so far and lifted his legal pad to tap its bottom on the tabletop as he looked around. "I don't need the details of the games, but settling on the broad strokes now would be advantageous. Don't you agree?"

Guzelköy and Davazlar exchanged another look and I wondered if they'd already spent considerable time discussing the games. They looked like they knew what they wanted to do. Davazlar stroked his goatee and some inaudible communication seemed to pass between them.

Guzelköy addressed the trustee. "Basil tends to favor intellectual challenges, while Babs likes action and sport. We thought that since we'll be hosting four rounds, we would design two of each."

Babs straightened. "The last one will be hand-to-hand combat."

"I have a new, state-of-the-art virtual reality system you're welcome to use," Basil said to the game-makers, sending a withering glance at his sister.

"The final simply has to be in the flesh." Babs tapped a palm on the tabletop. "Think of it. It will be very exciting. The best of each school, facing off like the great warriors of old."

Mr. Pendleton's pen hovered over his legal pad as he looked at Basil. "Mr. Chaplin? Do you agree?"

Christy looked at Basil, her face pale. She shook her head but remained mute.

Basil addressed the gathering. "I don't like the idea."

"You get half the input," Babs said. "You want puzzles or quest games, fine. Make three of them like that. All I'm asking is that the final round be real. I'm being more than generous."

Basil looked into his lap and began to rub his temples as though fighting off a headache. His voice drifted out from between his elbows. "Fine."

Babs leaned forward. "Can we discuss ticket sales?"

Basil's head snapped up. "Absolutely not!"

Babs, Guzelköy, Davazlar and Mr. Bunting spoke over one another.

"But think of the revenue—"

"Games can be very lucrative—"

"This will put the winner on the map, will attract the best—"

"No." Basil barked, emphasizing the negative with a slap on the desk. "I'm providing the venue for these games. I'll not have our students paraded in front of the supernatural world to be gaped at like creatures at a circus. This will be a private and confidential event. The stakes are too high to allow the influence of crowds. Family and friends may attend, yes. Beyond that, the doors will be open to no one. Is that clear?"

One by one, the group gave their assent and Mr. Pendleton made notes.

"Right. Then. Shall we agree the starting date is in two weeks?"

The group agreed.

"Then use this coming week to recruit your contestants. I understand Dr. Price and Mr. Bunting will manage the registrations and verify eligibility?"

Mr. Bunting looked raring to go. I wondered if he planned on using his ridiculous little notebook in the registration process. Poor Dr. Price looked like she needed to lie down and put a damp cloth on her forehead, but she nodded her in agreement.

"One thing," Christy said softly, lifting a finger.

It was the first time she'd spoken during the entire meeting so everyone listened.

"We've dismissed our cooking and cleaning staff for the summer, but we'll soon have sixteen students and support staff moving back in. The contestants can keep their own rooms clean and do their own laundry, but Professor Palmer has gone to Malta for the summer and I know for a fact we won't be able to lure her back. So who will prepare their food?"

Mr. Bunting waved a dismissive hand. "No problem. I'll look into hiring temporary kitchen staff. I know a chef-in-training from Utrecht that we can get on the cheap, he's already in London. Perhaps you won't mind arranging for a small medical team to be on call during the tournament? I understand you're an excellent doctor, but in the case of injury, you might want an assistant or two."

Christy nodded her agreement.

Mr. Pendleton made another notation with a flourish. "If there is nothing else, I shall draft the agreements. I'll have paperwork to you by the end of the week, which will need to be signed and notarized."

People stood. Hands were shaken. Babs and Mr. Bunting began a quiet chat as they went to the sidetable for coffee. Already, Davazlar and Guzelköy appeared to be deep in animated conversation, with Zafer doing most of the talking. Dr. Price and Basil exchanged looks as Mr. Pendleton shrugged into his coat.

"It's happening," Gage whispered, squeezing my hand. "I can hardly believe it." He looked at me in the gloom of the outer circle of the lecture desks. "Are you ready?"

"What do you mean?"

He lowered his voice and leaned closer. "Alumni aren't allowed. We thought Basil had decades of graduates to choose from, oodles of highly competent mages. But the number eligible students has just been cut down by a huge margin. You're the only Burned Basil has ever had. You have to compete."

I gazed at him, wondering if a fire had ever gone out from pure dread. Of course, Gage was right. Basil would ask me, and I would be compelled to say yes.

SIX

FIRE INTERVENES

Knocking on Christy's office door, I waited, my heart still thumping from my sprint up the back steps.

"That had better be Saxony," she called from inside.

Letting myself in, I raked my hair back and used the elastic on my wrist to tie it away from my face.

Dr. Price was seated to one side of her enormous desk with her phone's receiver glued to one ear. The usual pile of folders, lab documents, textbooks and white papers had been cleared from her desktop, leaving an enormous expanse of oak upon which sat a notepad, pens, three red apples and a bowl of clementines. The doc was a fan of fruit, apparently.

She stretched a leg and hooked her toe under the seat of a nearby chair, rolling it toward the desk and gesturing that it was for me.

"I'm on hold," she said over the mouthpiece.

"Sorry I'm late. I just got off the phone with my parents." Settling into the chair, I pulled the second office phone toward me and examined it. Surely, it had more buttons than any phone needed.

"What did James and Annette have to say?" Christy drummed her fingers against the arm of her office chair.

I glanced up, surprised. Dr. Price hadn't met my dad when we'd visited the academy, and had definitely never spoken to my mum. "You know my parent's names?"

"I'm a parent. Of course I do. I make it my business to—" she cut herself off to lift the receiver to her lips. "Hello? Yes, is Mr. Felix Kennet available?"

A voice buzzed on the other end.

"Ah, I'm so sorry," her brows creased. "I don't speak Danish. Would you mind leaving a message? Yes, I'll hold."

Felix Kennet was a graduated mage. I'd never spoken to him, but I remembered him because he was so tall. A quiet man (one couldn't call someone with that kind of five o'clock shadow a boy) with a shaved head and intense, hooded eyes. He stood well over six feet tall and had arms like a basketball player, lean and corded with muscle. His skin was perpetually tanned, even through the long cloudy winter while most of us turned pasty. A jog of memory recounted Cecily singing his praises.

Without the list of students to call, I couldn't do more than wait, so I leaned back in the chair and pulled a foot up under myself

"I see," Dr. Price was saying. "Well, all I'd like is for Felix to call the academy when he's back in. Can you do that for m—, pardon?" She paused. "No, nothing is amiss. Wrong. Nothing's wrong, just—"

I hid a smile as Christy closed her eyes in a gesture of seeking patience. "I'll call back. Thank you so much."

She hung up with a sigh. "It's never as easy as one thinks it will be. I've made three calls already and have yet to speak to the student I'm trying to reach. But we shall persevere. Thank you for volunteering to help."

"Not much else to do around here at the moment. I can't even use the fire-gym because Davazlar and Guzelköy have marked it as off limits while they plan the festivities."

"Please don't call it that." Dr. Price sighed again. "I still can't believe he's opted for this route. Where's Gage?"

"He's been on the phone most of the morning himself. Why? do you need him?"

Christy ran her fingers through her disheveled hair. The doctor had a bouncy bob, but right now her do was more bedhead than bedside manner. "We should be enough. It's only eight students we're trying to get in touch with. How hard can it be?"

Basil had delivered his list of preferred contestants to Christy that morning. If any of the students weren't able to commit, Christy was to go down the list in the sequence he'd listed. I'd been hoping for a glimpse at the list, but Dr. Price had secreted it away somewhere.

Instead of asking what I really wanted to ask (where's the list?), I opted for the much more diplomatic, "Who do you want me to call?"

"Yes, let's see." She pulled a folded page out of her pocket.

I leaned over the arm of my chair, if I stretched my neck enough as she unfolded it—

She handed me the page.

Almost falling when the wheels of my chair lifted off the floor, I caught myself and took the paper, heart in my throat. But opening it squelched my excitement. There were only two names, each with a scrawled telephone number complete with country code.

I read aloud: "Tomio Nakano and Tagan Lyall?"

Christy nodded. "You have good rapport with those two. You can leave the rest of the list to me."

"Tomio is a second-year," I pointed out.

"And?"

"Well—" I hesitated to say. Tomio was an MMA expert, granted, but these games weren't a martial arts tournament. If Basil had chosen a mage just entering his second-year, maybe that didn't bode well for quality of the rest of the list, even if Tomio was at the bottom. I decided against voicing my concerns. "No problem. I'll make it my mission to get a hold of them today."

"You'd best get started." Dr. Price nodded at the clock above her office door as she picked up the phone again. "Tagan is in Wales but Tomio is in Japan. Tokyo is eight hours ahead of us."

"Right." I hesitated, dying for more information. "Am I allowed to ask if Cecily will be invited?" Christy's daughter was one of the most skilled mages of the graduating class, in my opinion.

Dr. Price nodded, picking up the receiver. "I've brought her up to speed. She's agreed to take part. She'll return to the academy from London closer to the starting date."

"Great." I grinned.

As Christy dialed whichever mysterious potential contender was next on the list, I decided I didn't want to make these phone-calls right beside her. Getting up, I headed for the door with my super short list.

"Saxony?"

I turned to see Christy pluck an apple from her line up. She tossed it at me. I caught it, gave her a smile of thanks. I turned to leave when she said something else.

"You'll compete for us, yes? Sorry, I should have asked earlier. I have a to-do list a mile long."

I turned to face her, my tongue feeling like a dead thing in my mouth. I gave a kind of wheeze before I formed an articulate response. "Are you sure?"

Her expression changed, as if to say, *that can't be a serious question*.

I nodded and she gave me a thumbs up as she brought the phone in line with her mouth. "Yes? Hello? That's no problem."

I left her office, heading for the librarian's desk on wobbly legs.

IT TOOK all of fifteen minutes to get Tomio on the phone, bring him up to date, and convince him to return to Arcturus for the games. He was livid about Babs' behavior, even though she was within her legal rights. It took even less time to convince Tagan, whose competitive drive was legendary among the graduating class.

After that I lay flat out on top of the librarian's desk, eating the apple Dr. Price had given me. I stared at the scrollwork in the ceiling and contemplated how Tomio and Tagan had agreed with so little hesitation. They'd even sounded eager, like it would be fun. If they were looking forward to it, then I could come at this challenge with a good attitude, too. Plus, it was still weeks away. I had time to get used to the idea, and with Cecily coming, I knew for sure I wouldn't be the only girl in the games.

I wished I could burn off some energy in the fire-gym, but since the game-makers had appropriated the space to plan for the games, I only had access to the dojos in the CTH. Rolling off the desk, I headed for my room to change. On the way, I texted Dr. Price that Tomio and Tagan had both agreed to compete.

The CTH was an echo chamber. With all the lights off and no one there but me, my footsteps sounded loud and obnoxious. The line of skylights next to the ventilation system in the ceiling cast columns of mote-filled daylight across the mats.

I set my water bottle down on the border of the first dojo and kicked off my shoes. Running a few lazy laps to warm up, I stretched, performed some football drills and ran through the katas Tomio had taught me. After the warm up though, I found my eagerness for a workout had sizzled away. It just wasn't much fun without all the gadgets in the fire-gym, the climbing wall, or a fellow mage to spar with.

I was standing in the middle of the dojo, contemplating my shadow and listening to my heartbeat whisper past my eardrums, when the double doors opened and Gage walked in. He stopped, seeing me standing there in the dark hall, as still as death and with my arms resting at my sides. Half his face was lost in shadow.

"I don't know why it's so creepy to come in here and find you standing there like that." He kicked off his shoes and came onto the mat. "For a split-second I thought you were a ghost. You okay?"

"Yes, I'm fine."

As he approached, I studied his face. Shadows cast crescents under his eyes, there was a downward tilt at the edges of his mouth that was rarely ever there.

"Are *you* okay?"

Gage took my hand and let out a breath. "I didn't sleep well last night. Bad dreams."

"About?"

"Ryan, mostly."

I should have guessed. Had Ryan ever been the source of good dreams for anyone?

"You expected him to be back by now?" I suppressed a shiver at the reminder of what Ryan had most likely gone to do. "If he's just delivering the artifact to Nero, it should only take a day or two at most."

Gage nodded. "I texted him this morning, bugging him to let me know when I can expect him back and telling him about the games. Was he on the list as a competitor?"

"I don't know. Dr. Price only gave me two names and Ryan wasn't one of them. But, do you really think that after what Ryan did, the multiple ways he broke their trust, that Basil would want him to compete?"

"No. I just thought that since he's Burned now, maybe—"

I crossed my arms. "Brawn doesn't count for much if there's no goodwill or faith behind it. Maybe one day Ryan will learn that."

Gage's expression fell further and I shriveled internally until I felt about an inch tall. It was always so satisfying to disparage Ryan with these little jabs, remind Gage that his brother was a shark and a rat and everyone knew it. But after it was said, I felt worse than ever. Why couldn't I remember that and keep my mouth shut?

"Sorry," I murmured, dropping my arms to thread my fingers through his.

Gage squeezed my hands but let me go and began to pace. "No, you're right. It's not like I can defend him, it's just that I'll always love him and I'll always worry about him. It must be a twin thing."

"I think it's a sibling thing." I thought of my own beloved brothers, whom I missed more than I ever admitted out loud. I missed them as much as I missed my girlfriends, which was a bit of a shock given how much Jack and RJ could get on my nerves when I spent longer than a week at home. My heart gave an ache. The next time I was home, RJ wouldn't live there anymore. He was scouting for his own apartment in Saltford.

Gage nodded, chewing on his bottom lip and looking at the floor as he wandered.

"Has he texted you back?" I asked.

Gage's tone was bitter. "Yes, he said that he never specified what kind of business he was on or how long it was going to take and if I had expectations that I'd see him within a few days then I should adjust those expectations."

I almost made a comment about how cold that was, but still felt small about what I'd already said, so I pressed my lips together. I hated seeing Gage like this.

Gage met my eyes, looking miserable. "He said I should go back to Canada without him, enjoy my summer." He huffed a humorous laugh. "As if I could enjoy summer while he's off doing who knows what, possibly with a criminal mage."

Chilly fingers caressed the back of my neck as he raised the possibility I had been avoiding to think about in detail. "What do you think they're up to?"

Gage's answer came out sharp and loud enough to echo. "How should I know? Ryan won't tell me anything. I don't know what to think."

His expression shifted right after he said it. Stepping close, he lifted his hands to touch my face. "I'm sorry. I'm not upset with you, I'm just frustrated."

I almost laughed. Gage was quite possibly the sweetest man I'd ever met. "Don't apologize. I know that."

He planted a kiss on my mouth and released my face, beginning to pace again. My lips and face tingled as tracers of fire threaded beneath the surface of my skin. Heat stoked to life low in my belly.

"What are you going to do?" I asked, shoving my desire into a corner for later.

He shot me a look, an expression filled with hope and exasperation. "I just spent an hour on the phone with my parents. We've come up with a plan, but not a very good one. It involves meeting my mom in Naples. They think that if she and I are in the city, Ryan will agree to meet up with us."

Angelica wasn't a fire mage. I thought she seemed an odd choice to go. "Your mom?"

Gage nodded. "Ryan and my dad push each other's buttons. We think he'll be easier to convince if it's just us."

"Convince to—"

"Come home. He says he's finished with Arcturus, that he won't be coming back to England. If we can sit down with him face-to-face, find out what his plans are and if he's in some kind of trouble, then we can help get him out of it. Even if he doesn't want to come home—I wouldn't blame him for that, he's nineteen and sick of Saltford—at least we'll know he's safe."

I nodded, not sure what to contribute. What would I do if it were RJ or Jack who'd gone off to a foreign city on what could only be shady supernatural business? "When do you leave?"

Gage looked up, his eyes dark and bottomless. "Tomorrow."

My lips parted as his words sank in. "Tomorrow?"

He stopped in front of me. "I'm sorry. We both know I won't be asked to compete, so at least I don't have to make a choice. But I hope I can be back in time to watch you show the Firethorne students what a real mage can do. Have they asked you yet?"

I nodded. "Dr. Price did."

Gage nodded. "There you go. I knew they would, otherwise I would ask you to come with me."

Shoving my anxiety about the games to one side, I brought my mind back to the twins and Gage's plan. "I think it's a good plan."

He brightened. "You do?"

"Yes. If you and your mom are there, having traveled all that way, your mom especially—"

"And during the high-season. She wants to turn it into a business trip, as long as Ryan seems okay. We could stay for several weeks. All the best estate sales happen in the summertime," Gage said, seeming to warm to the idea further.

"Exactly. And once you sit down with him, he'll find it a lot more difficult to resist you. Yes, it's a good plan. The best you can do, given the circumstances. I would do the same if he was my brother." I resisted the near overwhelming urge to add that my brothers would never do anything so spiteful and irresponsible.

Gage was nodding, even smiling, a little.

"Did you book your plane ticket already?"

"Not yet." He stepped closer, taking my hand. He began to lead me toward the door. "I thought you might hang out in my room with me while I surfed for the best prices."

"Sure. Oof—"

Gage had put his leg in front of mine and tripped me, catching my weight and taking me down to the ground.

I gave a startled laugh. "Villain!"

He hovered over me, eyes sparkling with mischief, one foot braced on either side of my hips. "I can't let you leave the combat hall without a little actual combat, can I?"

Sliding out from under him, I got to my feet. Fire flared beneath my ribs, awake and ready to go. "En garde!"

Gage flexed his knees and lifted his hands out in a relaxed grappling posture. He turned his palms up and flicked his fingers back in a come and get me motion.

With a grin, I snaked out a hand and grabbed one of his wrists. Spinning to put my hips into his front, I flipped him over my back and onto the floor. He landed looking up at me, startled but laughing. His foot flashed, sweeping across mine. I tried to jump but was a little too late. His toe hooked my ankle and I went down.

Gage loomed, his weight keeping me down on the mat. I bucked, sending him flying over my head and into a summersault. We were on our feet in a flash, taking that same grappling posture. My fire wanted to be tested, see if I could toss Gage across the dojo.

Hooking him behind the neck, I pulled him down then switched my grip to behind his knee, lifting his leg up to take him off balance. Pulling me down with him, we tumbled over.

The atmosphere flipped as he loomed over me. His hands were no longer playfully combative but fierce and possessive. Heat flared in my face as his mouth came down on mine and our fire churned. Wrapping my arms around his neck, wanting him closer, I returned his passion. His hands slipped under the back of my tank top, sending spirals of heat around my spine. Moisture beaded along my upper lip as warmth stoked between us.

Pulling me against him, a hand slipped beneath the waistband of my shorts. Fire flared beneath my skin and my mouth began to tingle. I couldn't tell my lips from his and my body was full of firecrackers, shooting in all directions and leaving a chaos of sparks and embers.

When I reached up a hand to put my fingers through Gage's hair, my fingers slipped along the slick layer of sweat on his scalp. As his hands ran over the skin of my lower back, I broke away briefly to suck in air. My heart was pounding and I felt overheated but I didn't want to stop. I kissed Gage again, breathing through my nose. It felt like an overactive furnace had risen up between us, baking us from front to back.

Gage broke the kiss next, panting.

A look passed between us; desire, but also dismay, bewilderment, worry.

He released me and rolled onto his back, flexing both hands like he couldn't feel his fingers. He sucked in air, his chest rising and falling. His lips were kiss-bruised and his cheeks flushed a bright pink, like he'd been slapped several times. There were even spots of red dotted along his neck and across his forehead.

I lay beside him, gasping. I put a hand over my heart and one to my lips, where I couldn't feel the touch of my own skin. Sweat coated our foreheads. We looked at one another.

"Do you ever get the feeling that our fire doesn't want us to be together?" I asked, my voice hoarse.

"Not until today." He wiped a hand along his forehead then frowned at his palm, perplexed at the amount of sweat that had gathered. He tugged the neck of his t-shirt up over his face to mop up the moisture.

Thinking that was a good idea, I did the same. When I tugged my tank top back into place and looked down, a dark stain of sweat marked a large area between my breasts.

He came up to sitting. Some of the blush in his cheeks had begun to fade. "Your face is so red. Are your lips numb?"

I nodded and sat up, facing him. "I can't feel my tongue either."

"Same here." His voice broke.

All of a sudden I wanted to cry. My breath hitched and I felt my lower lip tremble. I ran a hand over my face to hide my feelings, brushing away at the moisture it my eyes. It was silly, but ... It hit me like a wrecking ball. I was in love with Gage. Truly, madly.

He was one of the kindest, most loving people I'd ever met. The selfless, unconditional love for Ryan which made me want to throttle him, also made me love him even more. I wanted to be loved like that: blindly, unconditionally, completely. I wanted to be closer to Gage than I'd ever been to anyone else. I was ready to give him all of me. The thought of being with him, of feeling his ardor rise to match mine sent a wash of desire through me so powerful it left my hands shaking.

So why had our fires sounded the equivalent of an alarm? It was like our fires had their own consciousness and they didn't want us to be together. Which was crazy, wasn't it? But it was also crazy for a fire mage—who could stand inside of a blast furnace without any discomfort at all—to feel overheated.

We looked at one another as our breathing slowly returned to normal. He didn't smile, and I couldn't either.

What might at first blush seem novel and exciting, was revealing itself to be a serious problem. If we couldn't be together physically, what did that leave?

It left us with a friendship, an unsatisfying one at that.

My fire swept back into its usual place, pulling all the heat tentacles into itself as if it was pleased with a job well done. My fever receded. I felt mutinous about my fire for the first time since before my Burning. *Why are you doing this? I love him.*

There was no answer from within.

Maybe he read the doubt on my face or maybe he needed reassuring, but Gage skootched closer and put his hand on my thigh, answering an unanswered question. "I do want you."

I looked at him, feeling miserable and confused. "I want you, too."

His voice lowered to a near whisper, even though

we were alone. "What happens when we try to go all the way? Will we spontaneously combust?"

It sure felt that way. I lay my hand on top of Gage's, feeling the heat there, already threatening to build.

"I don't know." I wiped at my eyes, embarrassed.

But Gage saw the edge I was on and pulled me into his arms. We sat there on the floor, hip to hip, arms around one another. I let my cheek rest against his shoulder, looking away from him so my lips didn't ignite heat in his neck. I noticed he was careful to keep his hands on top of my clothing.

"We'll try again when I get back from Naples. Okay?"

I nodded and closed my eyes, wondering what the odds were that anything would have changed by then.

SEVEN
TEAM ARCTURUS

I was seated on a sofa in the lobby with a book I was failing to read as I waited for Basil and Christy to return from the Dover train station with the Arcturus competitors. Dr. Price had co-ordinated their travel to ensure they arrived within 30 minutes of each other, including Cecily. Basil and Christy had gone to pick them up with the school's seven-seater van and Basil's Range Rover Epoque.

It had been a long two weeks since the committee decided on the tournament, even with a trip up north to see Georjie, who didn't seem to have any intentions of leaving Blackmouth anytime soon (and with a fellow like Lachlan around, I couldn't blame her). Then I'd returned to Arcturus planning to spend half of every day honing my fire-skills as best I could using only the CTH. Basil had worked with me a few times, but he was also busy with his dad's affairs and seemed to spend a lot of time in private conversation with Dr. Price. Both had been very secretive, so I suspected some agency work was also distracting them.

Dr. Price never had let me in on who the rest of the competitors were. I wasn't sure why the extreme secrecy. Maybe she was thinking that I'd text Arcturus students with the gossip. I had to admit, if I had known, I would have been tempted to get April or Jade on the line to speculate about how things were going to go down. Not having anyone to talk to about what was happening had built up a level of anticipatory anxiety reserved for kids going into kindergarten.

When Basil and Christy pulled up outside, I leapt from the sofa, dumping the book onto the coffee table. I went to the window, my heart skittering around like an excited mouse as I watched the competitors exit the van and the SUV.

Tomio had ridden with Basil. He got out of the Evoque's back seat as Tagan emerged from the other side. Felix Kennet emerged from the Range Rover's passenger side like one of those foldable yardsticks, towering over the vehicle.

Feeling like it wouldn't be cool to be seen fogging up the windows with my breath, I dashed back to the sofa and picked up my book.

Tomio was the first through the door, carrying a duffle bag on his shoulder. The black sack had the silhouette of two men engaged in a fight embroidered along the side.

I put down my book and got off the sofa. "Tomio!"

He set his bag on the carpet to give me a hug as the other students trailed in through the front door. Tagan and Cecily came over to greet me. The foyer buzzed with excited chatter and laughter as the Arcturus competitors trailed in through the front doors, dragging their luggage behind them.

Tagan's eyes were fever-bright. "Should I feel guilty for being so excited? I used to lose my mind on track and field days back in grade school. I hardly know what to do with myself."

"Can I bottle some of that?" I replied, laughing.

Feeling a presence near my elbow, I turned to see a woman with dark curly hair, large brown doe-eyes and tanned skin. I recognized her as a recent graduate but had never spoken with her nor seen her in action. I held out a hand and introduced myself.

Her cheeks dimpled as she took my hand, answering with an accent that hinted she was likely fluent in Spanish. "Everyone knows who you are after that surprise assembly. I'm Brooke Ortega. Nice to meet you, finally."

Her shake was firm and her hand warm and dry, but no fire flared between us.

"You too." I felt my cheeks warm beneath her probing gaze.

The rest of the competitors gathered to introduce themselves since Brooke and I had kicked things off. A slender blonde girl in a camel-colored leather vest and brown wool pencil skirt stood by the fireplace. A silky blouse encased her torso, the sleeves billowing out fetchingly from the form-fitting vest. She lifted a hand, giving me a friendly smile. "I'm Harriet Ashby."

"Nice to meet you."

Harriet looked like she'd make a better librarian than stiff competition, but there was a fierce energy in her eyes which suggested she was not a book to be judged by its cover.

Felix took my hand, towering over me as he introduced himself. No bond revealed itself when we shook, but if he cared he didn't show it. I fought the urge to run around making contact with everyone, just to figure out who I shared a bond with and who I didn't. But I was still relatively new to the supernatural world and fire magi had a subtle culture all their own. Sharing a bond appeared to be no big deal to most magi.

But between Gage and me, it changed everything.

I relegated thoughts of Gage to a rear corner as the last competitor stepped forward. He'd been standing just outside the circle with his hands jammed into his jeans pockets. Hair cut short on the sides and long on top, he had pale gray eyes and a dimple in both cheeks even when he wasn't smiling. In a plain canvas jacket and well-worn sneakers with an oil stain on one toe, he was the kind of guy who might not catch your eye on the street, but once you did notice him you'd have a hard time looking away. He offered a handshake.

Fire whooshed up my arm as we touched and I couldn't keep from grinning at him in surprise. He grinned back, dimples deepening into craters.

"Peter Toft, pleasure to meet you." He looked like a mechanic but he spoke with an accent posh enough to be straight out of Downton Abbey.

Brooke leaned in and gave a stage whisper. "Peter looks like a choirboy but watch him. He can be very ... handsy."

I flushed to my roots and everyone laughed. I relaxed. During the academic year there'd been invisible walls between the students of the different years, the widest gap being between first-years and third-years. But it was summer now and we were here for the same reason. The feeling that we were a team had already begun to take shape.

"Everyone's acquainted, then? Good." Basil gestured that we should find a seat while Dr. Price closed the front doors. He moved to stand in front of the fireplace. Dr. Price joined Basil but stood off to the side, looking ready for business.

Christy—while having taken every opportunity to express how insane she thought the games were—had settled into a grim determination to 'win the bloody thing.'

"You know why you're here." Basil's expression was drawn, as it had continuously been since his father's death. "I'm grateful to you for coming to the academy's aid. I have a few bits of business to address before I release you to settle in. First, the Firethorne students will arrive tomorrow."

He paused here as if wanting to give time for comments, but no one so much as coughed or shifted on the couch. There was an air of restraint from the competitors, as though we weren't entirely sure how to behave. While games were generally viewed as enjoyable, these ones couldn't be approached with as cavalier an attitude as we might like.

The headmaster cleared his throat. "I'd like you to be courteous and professional, but if you find yourself drawn to making friends, I'll ask you to resist until the tournament is over. The outcome should be our focus. Anything that might jeopardize the goal should be treated with caution. That includes trusting our competition. I'll come right out and say that I don't trust my dear sister, therefore you shouldn't trust your opponents."

"You think they might cheat?" Tagan asked from the large sofa, sandwiched between Harriet and Brooke.

"Cheat? No. The consequences would be too dire for them to cheat, but they will try to unsettle you, intimidate you, even manipulate you. So be alert."

"Have you met them?" Brooke leaned forward and rested her elbows on her knees.

"No. But I know Babs." Basil said this like it should be enough reason to be cautious. After having met her myself, I agreed.

Basil glanced at Dr. Price and she stepped closer. "We'll be putting you all in the third-year men's block. The Firethorne students will be given the first-year women's block. We'd like you to be together as a team so you can support one another, but as far from the competition as you can be."

No one complained, but I was disappointed that I'd have to move out of my room. I liked the view from my windows and I felt at home there. I wasn't about to voice any displeasure though, since no one else seemed to mind, and the point of moving us made sense. It was a good thing I hadn't unpacked everything after my return to Saltford was delayed.

"The fire-gym is off limits but you're free to use the CTH and the forge. Internal detonations are now allowed in the dojos for you lot, just to be clear. Babs' assistant, Mr. Bunting, has found us a new chef and temporary kitchen staff given Professor Palmer is not available. His name is Lars Hoedemaker. Dinner will be at seven tonight."

"What can you tell us about the games?" Peter asked from an ottoman, one sneakered foot resting on top of his knee.

Basil adjusted his glasses. "Not much, I'm afraid. Guzelköy and Davazlar have kept the details confidential. What I do understand is that the first challenge will be physical in nature. You're to be timed, and your strengths and weaknesses will be analyzed, which will allow the game-makers to adjust for the second challenge and so on and so forth."

"If we're eliminated, can we stay and watch if we want to?" Harriet asked in the kind of soft, sweet voice usually reserved for reading a bedtime story to a child.

Basil nodded. "Yes, if you like, you're welcome to stay and support your teammates, but please keep in mind that outside of your family and a small circle of our friends and acquaintances, no outside observers are allowed. This is a private affair."

There were murmurs of understanding.

"The day after tomorrow, you'll be addressed by the game-makers together with your opponents, in Lecture Hall A. I know you'll do me proud," Basil said with finality. "That's all I've got for now. Take the afternoon to move yourselves in. We'll see you at dinner."

With that and a nod from Christy, they left us to our own devices.

EIGHT

SLOP & STRATEGY

Walking into the cafeteria for supper that evening, Tomio and I stopped and sniffed before approaching the serving stations with caution.

"What is that smell?" The aroma had my stomach on the edge of queasy.

Tomio wrinkled his nose. "Gym-sock and jock-strap stew?"

We were the last to hit the line. Brooke, Felix and Harriet were already seated at one of the larger tables, staring morosely into their steaming bowls of mystery food. Peter had left the line without a bowl and was making his way over to the fridge.

Behind the serving station was a sweating, red-faced lady wearing a plastic swim-cap instead of a hair-net. Beside her was an also red-faced but more jovial looking fellow adorned with a proper chef's hat and a crisp, white apron. It was nice that we didn't have to worry about him having clean duds to wear, but he also sported a seriously impressive Viking beard.

"Erwtensoep?" He asked as Tomio and I

approached with our trays, eyes bright and beard wagging dangerously close to the industrial sized pot of soup. A peek inside revealed a lumpy concoction with chunks of something that might have been sausage in another life. It was the source of the smell, I'd determined.

"Sorry?" Tomio cocked an ear.

"Snert?" the chef asked, just as pleasantly.

The lady interfered, thankfully. "Dutch pea soup," she said, proudly. "So thick you can stand a spoon in it."

Tomio and I shared a look of dismay but nodded and handed our bowls over. From the looks of it, there wasn't much else prepared.

Lars spooned glops of booger-colored stew into our bowls before sidling a step to the left. Gesturing at a cutting board upon which were stacked slices of bread the color of chocolate, he said with that same hopeful expression: "Roggebrood?"

In spite of the weird smelling food, I bit my cheeks to keep from laughing. "Yes, please."

Using a pair of tongs, Mr. Hoedemaker served us each a thick slice on a side plate. He slid another step to the left and indicated a pile of what looked suspiciously like raw bacon.

"Katenspek?"

My tummy did an unpleasant forward roll and my smile faltered. "I think I'll pass, thank you." I looked at Tomio. "Katenspek?"

He shot me a baleful look before pasting on a smile for the chef and putting up a palm in a policeman's stop gesture. "I'm good."

Looking into our bowls as we wandered over to join

the rest of the team, I made sure to hold it away so the smell didn't go directly up my nose.

Tomio went around the table and sat down beside Felix, who was lifting the slop up with his spoon and watching as it dripped back into the bowl. It had the consistency of over-milked mashed potatoes.

I set my tray down beside Brooke and settled into the chair. I rolled up my sleeves, not certain any of the food besides the bread would make it past my teeth.

"That's Mr. Hoedemaker, I guess," mumbled Felix.

"Did you know that Hoedemaker comes from 'hood maker,' and therefore 'hat maker'?" Brooke added helpfully.

I watched Tomio cringe as he took a tentative bite and returned spoon to the bowl making a smacking sound. "I think a hat would taste better."

Felix snorted, a half-amused, half-distressed sound. He sighed and pushed his bowl away.

"The bread's not bad," Brooke said through a mouthful. She made odd shapes with her mouth in an effort to dislodge the roggebrood from where it stuck to her molars. "A little chewy and sticky, but not bad tasting."

Peter appeared with a Bounty bar and a can of Dr. Pepper. He took the empty seat beside Tomio and tore the chocolate bar's wrapper open with his teeth.

Felix's eyes widened. "The vending machines are stocked?"

I was about to say that as far as I knew, the vending machine supplier hadn't been here since the school year had ended, but Peter nodded, cracking open his can of soda.

The rest of us sighed at the sound.

Felix popped up from the table like a jack-in-the-box. He carried his tray over to the trolley for dirty dishes and deposited it there, a wrinkle in his nose. He left the room as Basil and Christy were coming in. They paused with a moue of distaste as they detected the smell.

I pressed my lips together and looked at Tomio with a jerk of my head in the professors' direction. Brooke caught it too, put down her partially eaten roggebrood and watched as the headmaster and the good doctor approached the serving station with all the caution of alley cats. By the time they reached Lars and his assistant, our whole table was watching.

To their credit, Basil and Dr. Price took what was on offer politely and without complaints. Our temporary chef greeted them as cheerfully and sweetly as he'd greeted us, repeating just the name of the food in the lilt of a question.

"It's probably quite tasty when done well," I heard Cecily say, ever the gentlewoman.

"Where did they find him?" Harriet asked under her breath. She put a hand over her stomach, which issued an audible gurgle. "He's sweet, but if he serves food like this every night we might as well forfeit the games. Sorry to be gross but my innards sound like a clogged drain-pipe.

"Lars is a chef-in-training. Mr. Bunting hired him," I made air-quotes, "on the cheap."

"Who?" three of my teammates asked together.

"Babs' secretary, or partner. I don't know what he is. Her minion."

Looks and murmurs were exchanged as Basil and

Christy took seats at the end of the table. All eyes were on them as they took their first tentative bites.

Dr. Price put her spoon down and held a napkin to her lips.

Basil tore off a piece of bread and dipped it in the soup, pausing as he brought it to his mouth before taking the plunge and popping it inside. He chewed thoroughly, clocking our eyes on him as he swallowed. He sucked his teeth, then took a quick swish of water.

"I'll have a word," he said, getting up and heading for the kitchen. I heard him suppress a burp on his way.

Felix returned with a bag of candy and a can of Coke. Tagan saw it and disappeared a moment later. Peter was finished his vending machine snack, but looked far from satisfied.

Suddenly I missed the days of ordering takeout.

After the evening 'meal' the team, none feeling top notch, gathered in the third-year lounge, eyeing the vending machine as we entered.

"So, what's our strategy when we meet the competition tomorrow?" Peter asked the room at large as he collapsed into one of the plush sofas. He looked less upset about the disappointing dinner than anyone else did.

My stomach gave a growl, but I reminded myself that chocolate would only make me more hungry. I took my phone out of my pocket and opened the delivery app as I took a window seat.

"Takeout, anyone?"

The mood lightened considerably as everyone took a turn scrolling through the options. We eventually settled on pizza and my phone went around the room so everyone could add their order. Pocket money was dumped into a pile on the window seat beside me. By the time I submitted the order, I realized not only had no one had fleeced me, I might have turned a small profit. I didn't know my teammates well, but in that moment, I decided that I liked all of them. Good people, Arcturus grads.

When that was done and everyone had found somewhere comfortable to sit, Peter asked his question for a second time.

"What do you mean, strategy?" Harriet crossed her delicate ankles and tapped a slender index finger against her lips.

Peter shifted forward, putting his elbows on his knees and talking with his hands. "I was thinking, the first thing we do is shake hands with all of them, listen to their voices, see which of them are Burned and which aren't."

"Why shake hands?" Felix stretched his long arms out and interlaced his fingers behind his bald head, in a much better mood now that pizza was on its way. "Shaking hands only reveals bonds, not who is Burned, and Basil said we should keep our distance. I don't *want* to know if I'm bonded with any of them."

"Basil said to be polite," said Brooke from a wingback chair, which was so large she looked like a child sitting in it. "Shaking hands is good manners. I've had bonds with people I despised, so I don't have a problem with it. It's never meant much to me."

"You say listen to their voices." Cecily spoke thoughtfully in her warm Scottish brogue. "But not all Burned get voices like Saxony's. Look at Basil."

I blinked rapidly at this, realizing just how unobservant I'd been. She was right. Basil didn't have a hoarse voice. His voice was a little throaty, but not nearly as husky as mine.

"I always thought the voice was the first clue," I blurted. "You're saying you can be Burned without having scarred your voice box? It happened to me and it changed Ryan's voice, too. Basil's voice is on the line, so I just accepted it as a symptom."

Harriet was nodding. "I've read that it has to do with whether the fire goes up high enough to affect the throat before the lungs and heart have been roasted. The major organs are the most important part to burn, you give water after that. If the throat hasn't been reached—and maybe the way the mage is positioned has something to do with it—then the voice isn't affected."

"I don't know if the position makes a difference," I said. "When I found Ryan, he was slouched against a wall. His organs were low and his voice box was high."

"Yeah but this is fire, not water," Tomio said. "Heat rises."

I felt my cheeks heat. "Good point."

At the mention of the incident with Ryan, all eyes were on me.

Peter turned his head to look at me. He was so far into the couch I wondered if he might have trouble getting up again. "Is there a way a Burned mage can tell another Burned mage on sight?"

The room went quiet as I thought about this. "I might be able to if I use evanescent vision, but it throws off so much heat that it would be obvious I was up to something."

"Dang." He raked a hand through his dirty-blond hair, rubbing the top of his head. "We have to know who's Burned so we'll know who to pitch Saxony against."

Harriet disagreed. "We might not have the option. We don't know how the game-makers will determine who goes against whom, all we know is that it's a one-strike system."

"I heard Babs offers opportunities for her students to go through a Burning, but that can't be right," Brooke murmured, pinching her bottom lip between two fingers.

"That's exactly right," I said.

The room went quiet as unspoken questions hung in the air.

I cleared my throat. "I overheard the headmaster and Dr. Price talking about it."

Cecily looked horrified, her cheeks lost some of their color. "How could he have agreed to pitch us against Burned mages?"

"We don't know how many, if any, of them are Burned."

"He should have made sure none of our competition was Burned. Shouldn't he?"

"Maybe he tried," Tomio said, sitting back in his chair and crossing tanned arms. He'd been able to enjoy some sun before coming back here. "Maybe there are no Unburned at Babs' school. None at all."

"That's a sobering thought," Felix muttered. His pale eyes swung back to me. "You pretty confident you got this, then?"

"What?" I shrank into the drapes behind me. A cool breath brushed the back of my neck, lifting my arm hairs and making me shiver.

"That's our strategy." Harriet brightened. "Our goal

is to help Saxony to be the one who survives to the final round."

"What? No—" My throat closed up and my sinuses followed. I felt a stress headache begin to form in my temples, just above my eyes.

"It's the only thing that makes sense," Cecily said gently. The level of compassion in her voice did nothing to assuage the feeling that she was throwing me to wolves.

I found my voice. A version of it anyhow. "You can't put that expectation on me. Just because I'm Burned doesn't mean I'm automatically the best bet to win this thing. The game-makers are opening with something physical, but even if I do well in that one, there's going to be two intellectual challenges. Ones that won't focus on brawn or flashy fire-skills. That levels the playing field. Everyone will have a chance."

My teammates thought about this, I could see them mulling things over. My headache eased and I thought maybe I'd weaseled my way out of these unrealistic expectations of theirs.

But then Tomio said, "What if the final challenge is all physical? It's still a good strategy, Saxony. It still makes sense."

Peter made a fake expression of empathy, shooting out his lower lip in a quasi-pout which nettled me. "Be realistic, Red. It's likely going to be all down to you."

"I don't know." Tagan spoke for the first time since ordering food. "Shouldn't we all do everything we can to win, regardless of anyone's status? In single-elimination, there isn't much teamwork involved unless we have to face them in pairs or triplets."

"Of course we have to all do our best," Brooke said.

"But our objective isn't personal glory, but to keep Arcturus and all its assets in Basil's hands. Whatever gives us the best chance of making that happen, that's what we have to do."

Tagan murmured: "I wouldn't mind a little personal glory."

"So, we agree?" Harriet looked around, straight blond strands of hair swinging. People were nodding. "We do whatever it takes to keep Saxony in the running. Whatever its possible to do without breaking the rules."

"Unless our enemy starts breaking rules," Peter chimed in. "Then it's a free for all."

Everyone laughed, except me.

NINE
TEAM FIRETHORNE

I'd forgotten all about our temporary chef until I arrived in the cafeteria in the morning with a grumbling stomach and saw a lot of moping faces gathered at the same table as the prior evening. Approaching the serving station with caution, I returned the smile of Mr. Hoedemaker, who manned the station alone this morning.

Breakfast appeared to be an assortment of sliced breads, cheeses, cold cuts. That wasn't so bad. I wasn't sure what to think of the collection of brightly colored toppings at the end of the station, though.

Mr. Hoedemaker watched with genuine interest and earnest hope as I shuffled along with my tray, adding slices of bread, cheese and meats to my plate. I paused at the array of small pots containing spreads, jellies, syrups, and what appeared to be the edible decorations you'd put on a child's birthday cake.

Lars scooped up a spoonful of rainbow sprinkles. "Hagelslag?"

I murmured a polite decline but considered the jams.

Mr. Hoedemaker lifted a spoonful of a thick, dark syrup. "Stroop?"

He looked so hopeful that I hadn't the heart to decline again. "Oh, go on."

I thought his grin would split his face and decided that even if it was pureed liver, it was worth it for that smile. I held out my plate and watched as he put a dollop beside my cheese. "Thanks, Lars."

He winked and went to assist Harriet, who was coming up behind me with a concerned look. Ever the lady, her expression transformed into pure sunshine as she said hello and good morning to Lars.

Carrying my tray of interesting food to the table, I set it down beside Cecily. I exchanged more than one dubious look with the girls, but Felix, Tagan, and Peter were almost finished. So Lars had a better handle on breakfast foods than dinner, if that was any sign.

"What's stroop?" I sat down and bellied up to my tray, catching a whiff of parfum de old-nacho from the cheese slices.

"It tastes a lot like brown sugar," Felix said with bulging cheeks. "It's not half bad with a bit of Edam and a coffee chaser."

"I thought Basil had words with Mr. Hoedemaker about the food," Brooke whispered, her left cheek full of bread, again, which she endeavored to unstick from her molars, again.

"He's a student. I guess we'll have to deal." I took a bite of bread and cheese. It was no Florentine omelet but it would do. Brooke was right though. It was sticky. If I got it all down I wouldn't be hungry until dinner.

A series of popping noises followed by a loud bang coming from outside had us staring at one another. It had come from the front of the villa.

Tagan looked at his watch with the quick movements of someone very late for something, then looked up, grinning. "Firethorne!"

It was like someone had yelled that there were backpacks full of money falling from the sky. Breakfast abandoned, we scrambled from the cafeteria, startling poor Mr. Hoedemaker. I stepped on the back of Cecily's shoe and she almost went down. Tagan and Peter were cackling madly as we took the hall to the lobby at high speed.

Recovering our sanity as we reached the front foyer, we slowed to a walk, putting untidy hair and clothing back into place like civilized young people. It could also have been the fact that Basil yelled at us from the second-floor balcony, reminding us that this wasn't a haunted mansion and we weren't a cauldron of bats.

"I don't know what you're expecting," he said as he descended to the marble floor, tugging his cuffs out from under the sleeves of his tweed jacket.

Dr. Price followed him down the stairs. "They're not movie stars, or even accomplished athletes. They're just students or recent grads, like you lot."

"Yes," Basil added. "And if Babs has rubbed off on them at all, you'll remember my warning."

"Have you met them, Headmaster?" Peter asked as we spread across the foyer.

"I already asked him that," Brooke huffed as she headed to the window.

"No. Of course not," Basil replied, as if the very idea was preposterous. "Why would I have?"

"You ought to see this," breathed Brooke to the lobby in general.

Everyone rushed to the window at her words. The crush of bodies all seemed to inhale together at the sight outside.

In the driveway, on the far side of the fountain, sat a short, orange school bus belching black clouds from its tailpipe. Quite an accomplishment considering the engine was off.

The doors opened and Team Firethorne stepped onto the gravel, partially concealed by the hazy, gray fug. Hands waved, people coughed and moved away from the vehicle's nether-end to gather in a cluster.

I counted eight, all dressed in uniforms of an undetermined color. We'd have to wait for them to stand clear of the pollution for that. I expected numbers nine and ten to step off the bus as well, perhaps more, as I figured Babs might have an entourage, but the bus doors closed. The engine coughed to life, quite literally, spewing more effluent into the air, then rumbled up the driveway at an impressive clip for so sick a conveyance.

Someone gave a soft belch—probably Felix because it sounded high up—and the smell of Edam wafted past my nose. No one turned away from the window or even commented, proof of how spellbound we were.

"Where's Babs?" Cecily asked.

"And Mr. Bunting," I added, feeling sorry for the still-coughing Firethorne team. Somehow, this short episode had banished all my nerves. Basil was right. They were just young mages, some of them looked barely out of their teens.

"*This* is our competition?" Peter's voice drifted from the back of our huddle, sounding unimpressed.

Basil answered in a raised voice from the other side of the furniture, unwilling to appear as undignified as the rest of us. "If they don't have adequate transport, it only means Babs has funneled every last penny she has into their training facilities."

And her wardrobe, I thought.

The Firethorne kids—I had trouble thinking of them as anything else in those uniforms—began to spread out and come into focus as the cloud drifted away to poison the birds instead. Their matching outfits were revealed to be a dingy pastel shade a paint manufacturer might dub 'mint gray', and mostly ill-fitted. They spoke to one another but it was inaudible. Their gestures made it clear the topic of conversation was the building, features, and grounds of Chaplin Manor itself.

I caught a flash of bobbed hair so blond it was almost white and squinted for a better look, but she was lost from sight as the group drifted toward the arch leading to the fire-gym.

"Should we go outside to greet them?" I heard Harriet ask Basil. "Babs wasn't on the bus and they look lost."

Basil didn't respond until the entire cluster of us looked back at him expectantly. The Firethorne team was out of view now anyway. I realized then how close Tomio was standing behind me, bumping chests with him as I turned.

"Sorry," he murmured, stepping back, bumping into Cecily and giving another apology.

Basil gave a sigh of defeat under the pressure of our collective stares. "Fine." Then he added something under his breath that sounded suspiciously like, "Bloody Babs."

Tagan went to the front door and opened both sides. Stepping out onto the front step, we heard him yell. "Oi! This way!" There was a pause and he added, "That's it. These are the front doors, init? Welcome, welcome."

We moved away from the window to stand among the furniture. No one was sure whether we should stand in a line or organize ourselves for introductions and Basil wasn't helping. So we just ... occupied space and watched the doors.

Tagan came back inside followed by the Firethorne team, who entered into the lobby gazing around like they'd never been in a fine museum or visited an old English manor. Some of them carried duffle-bags, others sported backpacks. One pulled rolling luggage that was missing a wheel and squeaked loudly.

I began to feel even more sorry for them, exchanging uncertain glances with Brooke and Tomio as the team shuffled in to stand in a ragged line on the marble. They gaped at their surroundings more than they seemed to notice us. A couple of them had the haunted look of refugees. Which begged the question: what kind of set up did these mages train with and live in?

Someone whispered at an inopportune moment, "This'll all be ours soon, can you b'lieve it?"

My pity vanished. I sat back in one hip and crossed my arms as Harriet and I exchanged a look. Hers said, *it's like that is it?*

"Welcome to Arcturus Academy," Basil said in a near bark.

A couple of the Firethorne kids actually jumped, like they only now realized they weren't alone in this fine, upper-crust foyer.

"Is it safe to presume your headmaster meant to be here and has been waylaid?" Basil's tone was thick with sarcasm.

They exchanged uncertain glances.

Now that Basil had addressed them, their eyes roamed across us like fingers over a rolodex, weighing us, picking us apart. Was it just me or had the temperature in the lobby dropped?

"Ms. Barbara said she'd meet us here." A petite woman with a high, shining black ponytail lifted a hand in greeting. "I'm Liu Xiaotian. Shall we introduce ourselves?"

Basil invited her to proceed with a sweep of his hand.

I found the wheat-blond bob again. She stood at the far end. As Liu went down the line introducing her teammates, I found myself unable to look away from the young woman.

"Liam Walsh, Kristoff Skau, Serenamen Hall," Liu was saying, but the names became a drone in the background.

She was perfect, and that was saying something, because up until I laid eyes on this woman, I'd always though Georjayna was the most beautiful woman I'd ever seen. But it wasn't just her beauty that captured me, it was something else, something I couldn't put my finger on. I wanted to shake her hand, see if there was a flash of fire between us, hear her speak. I hadn't felt so entranced by someone since I'd first met Targa's mum. It was disconcerting and uncomfortable.

"Sean Pilterman, Axel Bell, January Jaques—"

She stood there demurely, making that horrible pale green uniform look good. Her hair lay in shining layers, bluntly cut and framing a face that couldn't be described as anything other than doll-like. Finely arched blond brows framed thick, dark lashes (if they were naturally that black I'd eat my fireproof socks) framed glacier-blue eyes. Generous, petal pink lips curved in a polite smile. Her cheekbones glowed with a pearlescent sheen. She was average height, every joint was aligned, every feature perfectly symmetrical and elegantly formed.

Liu came to the blond but made no indication that she was about to introduce anyone special. And, why would she?

"Eira Nygaard."

I stole a glance at my teammates, wondering if they felt the same urge to study Eira. To my amazement, no one was paying her any extra attention, at least not this second. Not even the men.

"Saxony Cagney."

I gave a start as Basil addressed me. "Yes?"

There was a titter and I realized he'd just been introducing me.

The headmaster gave me a weird look and moved on. "Cecily Price, Peter Toft—"

Heat flushed from the base of my neck to the roots of my hairline. I wanted to crawl behind the nearest sofa. I cast my gaze to the carpet and gave myself a talking to. *She's just another fire mage you have to defeat. Put her out of your mind.*

"Ah, all the competitors are here?" Guzelköy's voice jarred me out of my private pep-talk as he appeared from the direction of Victory Hall, Davazlar trailing behind with a stack of tablets in his hand.

"All here, Zafer," said Basil, "with the exception of Babs and Mr. Bunting. I guess they're running late."

"No worries, we don't need them for this part." The game-makers came to stand side-by-side as the group faced them. "Everyone? Welcome to Chaplin Manor. I'm Zafer Guzelköy and this is my partner, Demir Davazlar."

The big game-maker briefly looked up from the top tablet which he'd been fiddling with, smiled, and then continued whatever he was doing.

"Before Dr. Price shows you to your rooms," Guzelköy announced, "we'll need to complete the intake forms. Dates of birth, contact information, next of kin and so on, as well as the release form. Davazlar will help you. Let's start with the guest school, shall we?"

Guzelköy had the Firethorne competitors arrange themselves in a relaxed line along the wall. Davazlar handed out four tablets and got the students inputting their information.

Tomio appeared at my shoulder. "Look at them. Signing away life and limb," he joked. "Suckas."

"If that makes them suckas, then we're suckas too," I whispered back.

He waggled his eyebrows and gave me a cheesy, exaggerated wink. "We're not suckers. Suckers lose. We're going to win."

PART TWO
THE GAMES BEGIN

TEN

CHALLENGE THE FIRST

At eight-fifteen the following morning, after an early breakfast, the competitors filed into Lecture Hall A for their briefing. It was smaller than Lecture Hall C, split down the middle by an aisle. Rows of wooden bench seats and desks glistening with a high-shine finish sat on graduated platforms. The first row was at ground level, and each row behind that was higher by roughly a foot.

We took the central aisle to the front and broke into two groups. Arcturus students took the seats on the right side of the room and Firethorne took the ones on the left. Basil and Christy surprised us by sliding into the front row, taking a seat on the bench like they were students.

Seated between Cecily and Tomio, I leaned forward and shot the headmaster and Dr. Price a questioning look.

"This is just as much the unknown to us as it is to you," Basil said. He crossed one leg over the other and sat back against the wooden bench.

Taking their direction from Basil and Christy, Babs and Mr. Bunting sat with the Firethorne students as well. This was the first time I'd seen them since the committee meeting.

"Nice to see they finally showed up for their team," Tomio whispered out the side of his mouth.

I nodded, barely listening. Clouds of butterflies fluttered around in my stomach. I couldn't tell if they were from anxiety or excitement. Guzelköy and Davazlar were at the front of the room, standing on the dais and talking quietly. Davazlar's bulk blocked out much of the chalkboard. His head was bent low to listen to his much shorter partner. Guzelköy's neat, quick hands flashed around as he spoke. Davazlar had a hand over his mouth in a thoughtful posture, nodding at intervals.

When everyone was settled, Guzelköy stepped in front of the lecturer's desk, rubbing his hands together. His eyes sparkled. I was certain this man loved his job. Davazlar remained in the background, leaning against the desk with the backs of his thighs and keeping that same pensive posture.

"Welcome to the Arcturus Academy versus Firethorne Collegiate Games." Guzelköy opened his palms and bounced on his toes. "After much hard work, some inventive construction and days of testing, our first challenge is ready. We will begin within the hour."

Whispers swept through the lecture hall. It sounded like wind stirring the tops of summer grain.

"We call the first challenge *Traps, Tools, and Time*. It's an obstacle course but not one you've seen before, unless you've competed in one of our designs previously and I never forget a face, so I know none of you have."

He pointed a finger around the room, eyeballing the faces.

I shifted on the bench and fought to keep my knees from bouncing up and down. I loved obstacle courses. Not that I'd done many, but our elementary school had had a challenging one, which I'd loved, as part of the playground. In grade ten I'd taken part in a muddy obstacle course event to raise money for multiple sclerosis. The day had been full of laughter and feel-good moments when our team had come together to master the course.

"Each competitor will run the course alone," Guzelköy said.

My legs relaxed. That didn't sound like near as much fun.

"This briefing is to prep you, but I can't give you much information so listen carefully. The course has been built to test fire mages specifically. It consists of ten obstacles which tests six main skills. Some obstacles will require you to combine skills to complete them, some will take a lot out of you while others will require more brains than brawn."

Davazlar cleared his throat and Guzelköy looked back at him. Some silent communication passed between them. Guzelköy swung back to face us, looking contrite.

"Enough about the course. The only metric that matters is time, so just get through it as quickly as you can. You'll get no extra points for creativity. This course is not like the ones you've seen naturals doing. There won't be monkey bars or rope ladders."

Davazlar cleared his throat again.

Guzelköy blushed. "Anyway, moving on. There will be no observers, but you will be monitored and recorded at all times. When you're finished, someone will escort you away from the gym. Those who have completed the course will be kept separate from those who have yet to run it, to avoid information leaks. No one goes in with any extra information. Once every contender has run the course and the times have been registered, we'll reconvene as a group to reveal which of you have won, and which of you is ... well, suddenly dead, since this is sudden death."

Someone from the Firethorne side called out, "This is a single-elimination, right? One Firethorne competitor against one Arcturus competitor. How do we know which competitor we are up against?"

Guzelköy swung to look at Davazlar and then swung back again, presumably after some telepathy. "You won't."

A confused murmur swept through the group.

"The clock is your main opponent but there is another factor at play behind the scenes. Your respective headmasters have furnished us with detailed information about your strengths and weaknesses. That information has been converted to data and that data has been uploaded to a custom algorithm, into which we also load metrics from our game's structure. The algorithms then supply an Arcturus name against a Firethorne name, but the pairings won't be revealed until the end. We'll reveal your opponents and the times all at once. You'll have no specific preparation beyond what's said here today, and you'll take nothing into the course with you beyond clothing and shoes.

Water will be provided along the course. Any further questions?"

Tomio put a hand up.

Guzelköy nodded. "Yes, sir."

Tomio spoke in a voice loud enough for the room to hear. "I don't understand what the custom algorithm is designed to do, exactly. Can you elaborate?"

Guzelköy gestured to Davazlar that he should take this question.

Without moving from his post at the desk, the other game-maker answered. "Without the algorithm, this kind of game structure comes with a high probability that one team could win the whole tournament in any given round, eliminating all competitors from a single team at a single event. The algorithm spits out pairings that *should* mitigate this problem since our aim is four full rounds, but the algorithm doesn't just make pairings, it looks at the data as a whole and predicts outcomes. I say 'should mitigate' because there's no guarantee, your performances still determine the outcome, but our algo is sophisticated and has proved itself reliable in many other tournaments of this nature."

There was a murmur of quiet amazement at this explanation.

Tomio had a second question. "Will we have access to the footage when the challenge is over?"

Guzelköy answered this one. "Not before the games are completed. Your headmaster will have access for coaching purposes, but competitors will have to wait until the conclusion of the games."

Tomio settled back, satisfied.

"Anyone else?" He swept the room and found a few

hands raised in the Firethorne crowd. "Yes? The lady at the end."

"Have you run the course yourselves?" asked Liu.

"Of course we have," Guzelköy replied. "Multiple times. There's no other way to work out the kinks."

"Then I was wondering if you could tell us what a good performance time might be. Something to aim for?"

That stilled the room but Guzelköy shook his head. "I'm sorry but we can't. First, because we don't know. We've run the course but we also designed it, so we don't know how long it might take someone who tackles it for the first time. Second, even if we knew, we wouldn't say. If we said 'x' time would be considered strong, you will try to keep an internal clock and if it takes you longer, there's a risk you'll become demoralized, or go more slowly because you think it's a lost cause. Worse, that might happen to someone who may in fact be ahead. We don't want that."

There was a pause as Guzelköy eyed the crowd, but no one had any more to ask.

"Okay." Guzelköy slapped his hands together, which triggered Davazlar into action. He picked up a cardboard box that had been sitting behind him on the desk and moved toward the crowd as he opened the flaps. He pulled an item out of the box and looked at it. Scanning the group, he approached Tomio and handed him a small plastic disk.

Tomio took it. "Thanks."

I peered at the disk as Tomio turned it over in his hands. It had a label on the back with Tomio's name and school name printed on it.

Davazlar rifled through the box, pulling out another that looked the same. He handed it to me.

"Thank you." I took my disk and looked at the back. It had my name printed in small neat letters next to Arcturus Academy. One side of the disk was slightly raised. I'd seen similar devices given out by restaurants to patrons who had to wait for a table. It was a buzzer.

Davazlar moved through the lecture hall, digging through the box and matching a disk to the competitor whose name was on the back. I marveled that he seemed to have everyone's name and face memorized. The only Firethorne students I knew on sight were Eira and Liu.

"Davazlar is handing you a buzzer with your name on it. This is your own personal starting gun, keep it with you at all times. When your buzzer goes off, you'll have twenty minutes to get yourself to the main doors of the fire-gym. Your game clock will start after exactly twenty minutes, whether you are there or not, so please consider punctuality your first obstacle."

After distributing the last of the buzzers, Davazlar returned the box to the desk and resumed his relaxed posture.

"The game will pause from 11pm to 8am. No one will be buzzed overnight. But you'd all best be up and ready to go every morning before 8, in case you're the first competitor of the day."

I looked up, blinking with surprise. Every morning?

There was an unsettled murmur in the room, but Guzelköy noticed my expression first.

He templed his long fingers in front of his lean stomach. "Ms. Cagney? Question?"

"This challenge could take days?"

The game-maker's expression turned smug. "Not *could*, Ms. Cagney. *Will.*"

There was the sound of bodies shifting against one another and wood creaking as we absorbed this.

"We're almost done here, just a bit of housekeeping." He beckoned to Dr. Price.

She slid off the end of the bench and stepped up on the dais, facing the opposing team. "Firethorne competitors have been designated the first-year lounge on the first floor. We'll have meals brought to the lounge while the games are in progress. Once you've run the course, you'll be escorted to a lounge on the second floor. Pack an overnight bag, as where you sleep will be determined by whether you've finished the course or not."

The doctor turned to address the Arcturus students. "The same instructions go for you, only you'll start in the lounge on the third floor. Once you've run the course, you'll be escorted to the professor's lounge, where you'll wait out the remaining time. Likewise, have an overnight bag ready." She looked at Guzelköy and nodded, then returned to her seat beside Basil.

"If there are no more questions," Guzelköy said, now grinning like the Cheshire Cat, "then let the games begin. Good luck to all, and keep an eye on those buzzers."

He turned and strode over to Davazlar and they resumed the tableau they'd started with. I watched them, fascinated, wondering how they'd come to have the professions they had, and if we might be allowed to hang out with them casually at any point in time.

A tap on my shoulder by Tomio made me realize that half the students had left their seats already. Gripping my buzzer, I slid along the bench, hopped into the aisle and followed the group out.

DR. PRICE ESCORTED the Arcturus students to the third-floor where she stood by the door of the lounge and waited until the last of us had gone inside before following us in. We lined up our overnight bags along one wall and then spread out. I gravitated toward the window seat, hefting my buzzer absently as I shoved a pillow against the frame and sat down. Tomio joined me there while the rest of the team collapsed on the sofas and chairs.

Dr. Price stood by the door, resting a hand on the knob.

"Lunch will be at twelve-thirty," she said.

"Is Lars cooking?" Harriet asked, polite but clearly hoping not.

"He'll cook for the Firethorne team," Christy replied, "since he's Mr. Bunting's contact. We'll be catering in your food."

"Hallelujah," Felix murmured under his breath.

Dr. Price ignored him. She picked up an empty basket sitting on a side-board. "We've loaded the lounge with movies, books, games. Please use only the third-floor toilets. Also, you must surrender your cell phones until the challenge is completed." She pointed at the basket, indicating where we were to put our phones.

There was a collective groan at this. One by one we approached Christy, dropping our phones into the basket before returning to our seats.

"I'm sorry." Dr Price said to our moping faces.

"Game-makers rules. No outside communication is allowed."

"Can we go outside?" Cecily asked as she pulled a magazine from the stack on the coffee table onto her lap.

"Only with an escort, I'm afraid."

There was a communal groan. These early summer days in England were the finest we'd seen.

Dr. Price gave us sympathetic look. "I know, I'm sorry. I'll be monitoring the games as they progress. While the Firethorne students are running the course, I'd be happy to go outside with you, as long as Basil doesn't need me."

"Are we going to see him?" Felix stretched his extraordinarily long legs out before him, hooking a heel on a coffee table.

"He's juggling matters of his father's estate while this is going on, as well as some agency business. He'll be in as often as he can."

A disappointed look flitted around the room like a bird.

"He didn't even give us a team pep-talk or anything," Brooke grumbled.

As though summoned by her complaint, Basil appeared behind Christy. "Hello, troops."

He looked tired, but less weary than he'd looked all semester, and there was an electric air about him. I supposed the worry about his father had passed now and he'd had to shift into survival mode. The games were unexpected, but he looked as though he'd come to terms with them.

He passed Christy and took a seat on the ottoman next to the cold fireplace. He palmed his hands between his knees, fingers pointed to the floor. "Thank you for what you're doing for me."

"Maybe don't thank us yet, Boss," Cecily murmured.

"I can accept failure," Basil said, startling everyone in the room as he adjusted his glasses and gathered his thoughts.

This wasn't what I would expect a coach to say to their team before any kind of tournament.

"What I can't accept is not giving it our all. Just promise me you'll do your absolute best and whatever happens, happens. Okay?"

We agreed.

Tagan suddenly leapt up from his seat by Peter, dancing in place and reaching for his back pocket. "Oh, oh, oh!"

Christy put a hand over her heart. "Tagan, what on earth—?"

He whipped his buzzer out of his pocket, fumbled, caught it, then held it up for everyone to see. His disk vibrated quietly against his hand, the small plastic light on top blinking a robin's egg blue. He looked around the room, then at Basil, the whites of his eyes visible. Given that he'd not bothered to run comb through his hair that morning, he looked like a loon.

"It's me! I'm first." He was breathless, but I didn't know why. Aside from fumbling his buzzer, he hadn't done anything yet.

"Right." Basil got to his feet. "I've never been a sporty person, but I see this in movies sometimes."

He put a hand out, palm down over the floor at waist height. He adjusted his spectacles with his other hand, and it was only because of that gesture that I noticed his hand was shaking.

We swarmed in close to the headmaster, dodging furniture. Dr. Price came too. Putting our hands in a layer-cake, we looked at Basil expectantly.

He looked lost for words. Then, uncertainly: "Go, team Arcturus?"

There was a pause, then Brooke began to chant. "We're fired up, we're sizzlin' hot! We've got the heat, we will not stop! We're fired up, we're sizzlin' hot! We've got the heat, we will not stop!"

Everyone added their voices, picking up speed as we bopped our hand-cake to the beat of the chant. When it got too fast and we could hardly go any louder, Brooke slipped her hand to the bottom of the pile where she began to drone in a low voice: "Gooooooo..."

Picking up the cue, the team joined in, stooped over and slowly raising up to standing. Our wail lifted along with our hands until we broke at the top with, "Team Arcturus!"

Basil looked delighted, even clapped twice, eyes shining. "I say, that's very clever, Brooke. How very clever. Bravo."

We broke into laughter at Basil's old English gentlemen impression, which wasn't an impression at all. Tagan began to high-five every team member. He almost fell over when Cecily bowled into him with a hug.

Dr. Price eyed Tagan's outstretched hand with suspicion.

"Come on, doc." He laughed. "Don't leave me, hanging. It's bad luck!"

Christy gave Tagan's hand a resounding smack,

looking quite pleased with herself but also relieved that he'd moved on to someone else. Felix loosed a deafening whistle as Tagan headed for the door, followed by Christy (carrying the basket of phones) and Basil. Giving us a last shining look and a wave goodbye, Tagan disappeared, the first of the Arcturus competitors to face the challenge that awaited all of us.

ELEVEN
TOMIO'S SECRET

After an hour of sunshine in the back yard, monitored by Dr. Price, we were served a catered lunch of soup and sandwiches. With full stomachs, we settled into the lounge to wait for the next buzzer to go.

Tagan had been gone for three and a half hours. Maybe he was finished already and the first Firethorne competitor had started. No one knew, and no one would tell us.

Tomio moved to take the other end of the window seat where I'd resumed the crossword puzzle I'd begun before lunch. He set his buzzer on the cushion by his hip.

"There hasn't been time for you to bring me up to speed about Gage and Ryan," he said, settling with his back to the wooden paneling and drawing his knees up. "What's the story?"

I put the crossword puzzle and my pencil down. "Gage is still in Italy with his mum. He says they've met with Ryan once but couldn't get much out of him other than he's got business to attend to. He doesn't have any interest in going home yet, or coming back to Arcturus."

"But he won't give them any details?"

I shook my head. "I've got an impressive collection of photographs of the Amalfi coast, though. It seems they've taken the opportunity to turn it into a bit of a work vacation. Gage says it's been nice that it's been just him and his mum. They've been antique hunting together. He says his mom booked a whole shipping container and wants to fill it."

"They must not be stressed about Ryan, in that case."

I shrugged. "I haven't been thinking about Ryan at all, with all this going on." I gestured to the situation at large.

His head bobbed, his thick, black hair bouncing. He hadn't had it cut in a while.

Giving me a weighty look and lowering his voice, he said: "I've been meaning to talk to you about the conversation we had the other night. The one we had a group?"

I lowered the volume of my voice as well. "You mean the one where everyone dumped the responsibility to win this thing on me?"

He either missed or ignored my sarcasm. "Exactly. You can't go into the challenges assuming you haven't got what it takes to win."

I glanced at Felix and Harriet who were the closest to us. They appeared to be deeply absorbed in a game of chess.

I worked to keep my frustration out of my tone and didn't entirely succeed. "It's not fair to put it all on me. No one has any idea what the game-makers have come up with, aside from the fact that the first challenge is an obstacle course. Assuming that I'm the best chance we've got is putting the cart ahead of the horse."

"No, it's not." Tomio spoke patiently, confidently. "You didn't spend that much time as an Unburned mage. You underestimate the difference between us." Tomio let out a sigh and cast his own sideways look at Felix and Harriet. He started to say something, then stopped. His discomfort deepened as he hesitated.

"Spit it out, we haven't got all day," I whispered with a half-smile. "Your buzzer could go at any moment. If you have advice, I want it."

Tomio looked out the window, chewing his cheek. "It's not common knowledge, even Basil doesn't know, but I received my fire by plenary endowment, too."

My mouth drifted open. I'd been expecting him to say something about the games. "Why didn't you say so sooner?"

"I was embarrassed."

"Why?"

He looked sheepish, rubbing his stomach in an absent gesture. "I didn't want to be thought of as counterfeit. It wasn't until Basil told the whole school about you that I realized that no one seems to care."

"Wait, don't the registration forms ask applicants for specific history?" I knew they did because I'd had to give a brief explanation of the facts when I'd gone through the formality of filling out the forms.

Tomio turned red. "I lied."

"So Basil *still* doesn't know?"

"No one at Arcturus does, except you."

Was I hiding my astonishment well? I couldn't tell.

I didn't want Tomio to feel judged but I was shocked. "How did it happen? When did it happen?"

"I was nine and already an MMA phenom. I was small, but strong, mentally as well as physically. My sensei—I was his uchi-deshi at the time, a live-in apprentice—knew a mage with a baby girl. Her fire was developing but as it grew stronger, she grew weaker. They were concerned it would soon kill her, and she was in pain all the time."

I shifted closer to Tomio, tucking myself into a cross-legged position and leaning my elbows on my knees. "That's how it was for Isaia as well. His fire was going to kill him, it was only a matter of time."

Tomio studied my face, his eyes wide. "How old was he?"

"Six. Yours?"

He winced. "Only three. It was awful. Her parents begged my sensei to find someone worthy to accept her fire. They didn't want just anyone to have it and they trusted my instructor. In the beginning, I couldn't figure out why my sensei was asking me all these weird questions."

"Like what?"

"I can't remember specifically anymore but he wanted to know if I believed in the supernatural, or if anything supernatural had ever happened to me. He wanted to know my heritage, which was tricky because I had been adopted. I never knew my birth parents."

"What?" I squeaked, tucking a lock of hair behind my ear. "You're a deep well of secrets."

He smiled. "My sensei became obsessed with finding them, caring about it even more than I ever had. I'd been adopted by really nice people, I loved them. I didn't feel the need to know about my biologicals. Eventually, I learned that it wasn't my genetic heritage he was after, it was where I had been born and spent my life up until I'd been adopted. Something to do with the earth's grid and supernatural energy."

"Ley lines," I whispered.

His dark eyes shone, wide and bright. "Exactly. He didn't share all this with me, but he sure was invested in doing his homework. What he found seemed to satisfy him because he introduced me to Junko and her family, and explained the opportunity. He said there was a risk involved, as well as pain. But I was already a fighter. Risk and pain was my life. So I agreed." He sat back and spread his hands as if to say, *that's the end of the story*.

I stared at him, questions surfacing like bubbles in soda. "Why are you ashamed of that?"

"It's not the circumstances I'm ashamed of. After receiving Junko's fire and surviving, her father trained me how to manage it before I returned to my sensei. He'd warned me to keep it a secret, especially among other fire mages. He didn't want me to be looked down upon for not having been born with it. It wasn't until you were outed that I realized that his warning applied within Japanese culture, it wasn't universal. Over here, no one cares."

My head swam as I imagined Tomio at nine years of age, accepting a dying girl's fire, bracing himself for the pain, knowing it was coming. I had known squat. It wasn't like Isaia had been able to warn me or ask my permission. The strength of character Tomio must have had at such a young age was staggering.

"Did your parents know?"

He shook his head. "They still don't."

I arched a brow. "Where do they think you are right now?"

"Well it's just my mum now. My dad died of a heart attack on his way to work three years ago."

I closed my eyes in horror but Tomio spoke matter-of-factly, with no hint of grief or self-pity, which was typical Tomio. I'd hardly seen him without a smile on his face, let alone looking down in the dumps.

"It's okay. Mum thinks I'm studying law in London. She's pretty deaf these days and hates to wear her hearing aid, so the less I say the more she likes me." He chuckled and raked his thick strands upright. He gazed out the window for a moment, where lamps circled the fountain. The sky was overcast now and dark enough the lamps had turned on, casting a pale, geometric design across the driveway. Pulling himself back to the present, his sharp gaze returned to mine. "Anyway, that's a bit off topic. The point I was trying to make was, you can't go into these games without the right mindset."

I struggled to see how Tomio's story had anything to do with the games, but humored him. "Well, being an MMA champion, competition is nothing new to you. What's the right mindset?"

Tomio launched into a stream of consciousness, moving his hands as he spoke. "You have to trust yourself, be confident in your ability to perform when the time comes. If you go in not owning that you're Burned and that makes you a front-runner, you're selling yourself short— therefore selling your team short. Focus on the task at hand, walk into the ring relaxed but ready, then let your instincts take over. That's what instincts are for. I've trained with numerous women over the years and I've coached them, too. Consistently, their fatal flaw is that they underestimate themselves and they over-analyze everything. Don't think so much. Be in the moment. Failure is acceptable but don't accept it before you've actually failed. In fact, don't even think about it."

I blinked, wondering if I should ask him to write it all down. His little pep-talk was giving me goosebumps because he was right. I did think too much, I did over-analyze, and I did underestimate myself because I didn't want to be arrogant and then fall on my face. I knew I was good enough to coach first-year Unburned magi, but facing Firethorne's best was the unknown. I'd be facing magi who'd been born with the fire, and some of them would even be Burned. But Tomio had just admitted he'd been born without fire and he won Top Marks this past year, relegating the assumption that time-with-fire meant an advantage to the realm of myth.

"Anything else?" I asked.

His black eyes sparkled. "Play to your strengths and, when face-to-face, make chaos for your opponent."

"Right." I wasn't sure what my strengths were, I had no other Burned peer to compare myself to.

"Oh, and try to enjoy yourself. I know the outcome is big for Basil, but this wager is not of your making. Try not to dread it. Competition is so much a part of us that when the time of the gladiators passed, both humans and supernaturals invented other excuses to compete, other ways of opening those primal outlets again."

Tomio studied my face. His brows pinched and I knew he was mirroring my expression. "What did I say about thinking too much?"

I laughed, he was right, there was a frenetic conversation going on inside me.

"Find the calm in the storm, Saxony. Take it from someone who has faced a thousand opponents. You're strong, smart, Burned, and have home court advantage. You can do this."

"Thanks."

Tomio grinned good-naturedly and slapped both of my knees. "You're welcome."

TWELVE

ALCHEMY'S ENTRANCE

By the time supper had been served and consumed, the atmosphere in the lounge had grown tense. It was nine fifteen and no one's buzzer had lit up. All conversation had ceased. Peter, Cecily and Brooke, who had at one point had a raucous game of Hearts going, had separated and gone quiet. Brooke was stretching on the carpet along the far wall, Peter was staring into the dead fireplace while Cecily had taken a post at the window seat and was watching the darkening sky. Tomio lay stretched out on one of the couches, a ratty looking John Grisham thriller open but face down on his chest as he stared off into space.

I slouched in a wingback, feet propped up on an ottoman, contemplating reaching for the sudoku book on the bottom of the stack of books on the coffee table.

Harriet held a cup and saucer, but paced back and forth along the library shelves looking at the titles, not drinking her tea. Felix was doodling in a sketchbook, the only one of us who still seemed somewhat relaxed.

"It's been nearly twelve hours since Tagan left," said Tomio to the ceiling.

Brooke let out an exasperated breath, like she'd been waiting for someone to bring it up. "Exactly! I mean, I know the game-makers told us the game might last for days, but I didn't fully believe them. It's going to take ages if everyone takes this long to get through the course. What are they making us do?"

"Hang on." Felix set his sketchpad on the arm of the chair and spoke with a calm I wished could be bottled. "Tagan could have been done by lunch time. We don't know how long it takes for them to reset the course for the next competitor. It could take hours. The first Firethorne kid could be a dodo, stuck on a single obstacle for ages. We don't know anything and shouldn't make assumptions. Stop worrying so much."

We fell silent and the grandfather clock in the corner ticked on, marking time in a relentless rhythm.

A soft buzz began. We grabbed frantically for our buzzers, except Felix, whose buzzer was sitting on the table in front of him. Its light was not flashing.

"You see?" He relaxed against the plush chair-back, making the springs groan. "No reason to fret."

Harriet lifted her blinking buzzer, her face pale but set. "Right. My turn."

"Well, don't look like that." Tomio rolled off the couch and onto his feet, graceful as a cat. He put his hands on her shoulders. "You're not going to a firing squad. You're going to play a game."

Harriet smiled and nodded, her shoulders inching downward in an effort to relax.

We gathered around her and repeated the spirit chant Brooke had taught us, with a little less vigor this time. We sent Harriet off with cheers and good wishes, but after she'd left the atmosphere turned gloomy. It was rotten luck. No one was at their best after a long day of lounging around and eating.

THE FOLLOWING MORNING just before lunch, Tomio's buzzer went off. He left us looking like he was headed to a buffet, eager and hungry. Then it was Brooke's turn, her buzzer went off the next day at nine fifteen. She popped off the bench we were seated at in the back garden with a whoop, pronouncing that the waiting around was killing her.

Peter taught me, Cecily, and Felix how to play Bridge and we kept ourselves distracted by running a marathon tournament. Our buzzers never left our sides and Peter's went off shortly after seven in the evening.

It wasn't until late-afternoon the following day that my buzzer lit up. My heart gave a surge of relief and anticipation. If Brooke thought it had been hard waiting around for two days, she should have tried four. Not knowing how our teammates had done, or even being able to see them or text them, was slowly driving us all mad.

Cecily and Felix hugged me good luck and I met Dr. Price outside the lounge door, my backpack slung from one shoulder.

"Nervous?" She asked as we crossed the archway and took the steps down into the fire-gym's lobby.

I nodded. "A little. More excited to get at it though. It's brutal being toward the tail end of this thing. I don't suppose you can tell me how the others are?"

She smiled as we approached the doors where Guzelköy stood waiting for me. "You'll see them yourself soon enough. Good luck, Ms. Cagney."

She put her hand out to take my bag and I handed it over. Thanking her, I turned to face the game-maker.

Guzelköy had one hand on the fire-gym's door and his eyes on his watch. "Just one minute." He flashed a look up at me. "How do you feel?"

"Like I'm about to visit the dentist … but at Disneyworld," I replied, stretching my arms overhead.

He chuckled. "That's the most unique answer I've ever received to that question."

"Something to remember me by."

He nodded, then pulled the door open. "You can go in now. Good luck with the Disney dentist."

I took a deep breath and stepped forward, ants of nervousness marching in circles around my stomach. A strange pink glow emanated from inside. I'd expected to at least recognize the gym, but that was not the case at all.

The door closed behind me but I hardly noticed, wrinkling my nose at the stench. It wasn't as offensive as rotten eggs but it was awfully close.

I was in a small, closed off room. In front of me stood two statues, identical but mirror images of one another. They were made of gray stone, probably concrete, and set far enough apart for a person to pass between them, arms outstretched, without touching either of them. Except that passing them was impossible. There was a wall in the way. In fact, there were walls on all sides. I was boxed in with these statues and a bad smell.

The statues were female and dressed in flowing

robes and head coverings. They each held a hand outstretched. Looped over each palm was a chain from which dangled a lantern, hanging at the height of the statue's knee. For me, that was chest level.

The lantern on the right was lit with pink flames. This fire was the only source of light. The statue on the left held a lantern that was not lit.

The task was clear enough, I thought. Light the other lantern to move to the next obstacle.

I approached the unlit lantern and found a dry wick ready. Lighting the end of my finger, I started to bring it to the wick when the difference in the colors of the flames stopped me. My fire was the usual garden-variety amber, the color found in fireplaces and wood-stoves worldwide.

The color of the flame in the other lantern had to be chemical, which explained the smell.

I pulled my hand back, feeling my armpits grow damp. What would happen if I lit the other lantern with fire that didn't match?

The pink flames shifted in color, settling into a very fetching violet. The rotten-egg stink shifted as well, the smell became sharper, more pungent.

"Well, damn." I pulled my hand back and let the flame on the end of my finger go out.

I wasn't off to a good start. Matching the color required alchemy, and I had no clue how to do it. Tension built in my body. I bit my lip, trying not to imagine the look on Basil's face when I couldn't pass the very first obstacle of the entire games.

The violet flame shifted to blue. The pungent smell sweetened. It became a cloying perfume that made the back of my throat clench. My thoughts picked up speed.

Guzelköy and Davazlar designed this game to challenge our fire-skills. They knew that there would be some of us who might not know alchemy. Perhaps the colors were shifting through levels of difficulty. If I could have matched the pink, I would have been on my way a long time ago. The violet would be slightly easier, the blue easier yet.

The blue flames flickered, changing to green. The sweetness burned away and the smell sharpened and became metallic, almost burning my nose.

My breathing accelerated as time ticked by. Surely, the very last flame the lantern would produce would be regular old boring amber fire? I watched the lantern, shifting my weight from foot to foot from the nearly unbearable urgency.

The green flames made me think of Ryan's idle, even if his color was totally different. This green was bright lime, his had been a deep emerald.

The green flickered, changing to yellow. With it came the sharp tang of fresh-cut grass that made me feel dizzy. I tried not to think of the time ticking away, the minutes adding up.

The yellow flames flickered to a bright, unnatural red, the color of blood. When they shifted to orange, I lit my finger again, but hesitated. The orange wasn't quite right. It was too tangerine, too-neon-bright to be right, and there was a smell like turpentine in the air.

When the tangerine shifted into the color of my fire, I lit the wick with a shaking hand. How much time had I wasted? Part of me wanted to curse the game-makers, part of me wanted to congratulate them on their cleverness, the remaining third dreaded what was ahead. If this was establishing a pattern, penalizing your clock the less advanced your skill, then I might be in big trouble. I'd only made it through one year at Arcturus, and with less than half the normal course-load.

The wick flickered to life, throwing back the shadows. The sound of stone grinding against stone echoed around me as the wall between the two statues moved back and then slid to the right, revealing a dark corridor.

Heart thumping, I wiped the sweat away from my brow and stepped through the opening. I took a deep breath of unscented air as the stone wall slid closed behind me.

There was no going back now.

THIRTEEN
TRAPS, TOOLS & TIME

My eyes adjusted to the gloom of the corridor as the light from the lanterns faded away. A strange dim light —as if from the glow of some hidden exit sign like you find in cinemas—came from high above my head. Looking up, I realized there were steps ascending before me, steps that had been constructed with a giant in mind. Each stair was twice my height, but it wasn't the height of the steps that concerned me. I could clear them using detonation, which this obstacle was modeled specifically to challenge. It was the fact that the ceiling followed the stairs, keeping the same height consistently. The construction resulted in a zigzag pattern, it was more like a tunnel full of right angles than a set of steps.

I could only make out three of these huge steps, what was beyond that was blocked from view. If I detonated too little, I wouldn't clear the step. If I detonated too hard, I'd smack my head on the ceiling, or even knock myself out.

I blew out a breath, firing up along my muscles and joints.

With measured explosions, I vaulted high enough to hook my hands over the lip of the first step. Slow-burn energy hardened in my knuckles as I swung a leg up and over the edge. I had to roll like a log a few times before I had enough clearance to stand. I got to my feet and approached the next step.

I repeated this process five more times, narrowly avoiding the roof and rolling like a log each time. At the fifth step I saw the source of light. It was an actual exit sign, backlit with a white halogen bulb and positioned over top of a black doorway with no visible knob. A stenciled sign read 'Stage Door'.

I studied the door. Running my hand along the jamb, I pressed against the edges. On the right side it didn't budge, but on the left it swung open. The moment the door opened, the sound of crickets chirping began. I stepped through and looked around.

Artificial stars glittered down from the fire-gym's ceiling several feet above my head. Before me was a plain black expanse with even blacker polka-dots scattered randomly across it all the way to the far wall some sixty meters away.

An owl hooted and the sounds of rodents running in invisible underbrush made my forearms prickle. I squinted at the strange, perfectly flat terrain, registering that the black circles weren't polka-dots. They were holes. Holes about the same size as the manhole I'd descended to rescue Ryan.

It wasn't immediately clear what I was supposed to do until a light in the distance turned on. An arrow, blinking and pointing to the right.

I'd been standing here for too long. Pulse picking up, I stepped a foot down onto the platform, intending to beeline past the holes to the other side. The pure darkness of them sent a shot of adrenaline into my blood. I imagined huge toothy worms snaking out of those holes to snatch me and drag me into their den. But, putting my weight onto the 'stage' and taking it off my back foot showed me pretty quickly that this challenge was not about worms.

I loosed a bloodcurdling scream, a combination of fear and exhilaration, as the entire floor moved beneath me.

Arms flailing, I staggered back to the safety of the door where there was a foot's width of solid surface. I had to jump to catch it as the floor swung downward. Grabbing the lip, I hauled myself up, chest heaving as I navigated my way to standing on the narrow ledge.

I let out a shaky laugh of relief as I turned and watched the floor with the holes level itself. Now that I'd removed my weight, it returned to perfectly balanced. The entire stage had to be suspended on hinges or casters. It was just like those old wooden maze games where you controlled the tilt in order to get the marble through the maze without sinking it.

"I get it." I put my palms together and rubbed them vigorously as I eyeballed the blinking arrow. "I'm the marble."

The trick would be ... well, there was no trick. Try to get across the floor without falling into a hole. The fact that I had no idea what I'd land on or in if I did fell added further adrenaline to my bloodstream. My hands were shaking, but my pulse was pounding with excitement.

I couldn't detonate after I stepped onto the maze, that might make the whole floor vertical or even make it turn over completely, dumping me into whatever was below. I could only detonate once, from the solid lip on which I presently stood. After that, detonations would mostly work against me. My first step would have to get me as far on the floor as possible, after that, I'd just have to scramble.

Hinging at the hips, I cocked my arms back for a double-legged jump, and fired.

The sound of wind blew against my eardrums, adding to the backdrop of cheerful crickets and hooting owls, as I vaulted toward the center of the gameboard. I'd aimed to land between two holes, not quite at the center line. Landing in a half-squat, I shrieked as the ground dropped when my weight came down, but it didn't swing as wildly as it had before. Still, I staggered for balance as the board tipped me toward a hole. The black, yawning space made my stomach leap into my mouth as I tried to step away from it.

It was impossible to stay upright. I hit the floor, unable to stop myself from rolling. Lifting my legs as I slid along on one hip toward a hole, I stretched my toes out and cringed, reached across space. The soles of my shoes caught the far edge of the hole as my outstretched arms braced either side. The ground beneath my hip vanished, my torso hung suspended by my limbs. Slow-burn lit through the back of my shoulders and in my hips as I made my body taut to keep from falling. The floor swung, slowed, then settled, not flat but at an angle.

Panting, I eased myself so I could balance on my toes on the lip of the hole. The blinking arrow was out of sight now as the floor had tilted up and covered it, but I knew where I was headed.

Only now I was in a bind. How to get off this hole when there were no holds or anything other than a slick neoprene surface all around me. I craned my neck, scoping out the next closest hole. I'd have to detonate after all, if I wanted any chance of reaching it.

The cricket sound lulled me into a state of concentration as I focused on the lip of the next nearest hole. Aiming to hook my fingers on it and ride the floor back to some approximation of level, since the next hole was nearer the middle of this crazy obstacle, I detonated.

Hands outstretched like a flying squirrel, the floor moved away as my weight left it. Hooking the edge of the next hole with my fingers, I rode the floor down, my stomach forgetting it was part of me and remaining suspended. My weight settled against the neoprene as the floor tilted further, in the other direction this time. I'd overshot center.

I slid straight for the hole on my belly, letting out another scream. I hadn't known that I was such a screamer, but this obstacle had the adrenaline level of the Tower of Terror ride at Disneyworld. It seemed impossible *not* to scream.

Flailing for a grip as the hole loomed under my torso, my fingers clutched at air. Wishing wildly for Felix's long limbs, I slipped into the hole just like the marble in the game. Then I was falling, but I hit something much sooner than I expected to. Too bad it was a surface just as untrustworthy. It was a large ball and I landed on it with a harsh 'oof.' My torso hit first and my legs followed, falling lower than my upper body. My weight caused the ball roll underneath me. With nothing to hold on to, I was dumped off and dropped onto a second ball suspended just below the first.

I scrambled for a grip but even a fire mage can't hang on to a smooth slick surface, a perfectly round ball larger than the largest fit-ball I'd ever seen. I rolled and slithered as I failed to get control, dropping from ball to ball and fighting off panic as the faint light from those artificial stars got further and further away.

Helpless, I tumbled like a ragdoll through a set of cartoon gears, all the way to the bottom ... the floor of the fire-gym. I landed on my back. Winded, discouraged, and a bit giddy from the pure looniness of this obstacle, I lay catching my breath.

Like a thick cloud of jellyfish, the cluster of balls I'd just fallen down hung suspended above me. It was easy to see which ones I'd struck on the way down, they were still spinning. If I squinted, I could make out a network of iron forks and pins, suspending the balls in space. If I wasn't so disappointed about having failed the life-sized marble-maze, I would have marveled at the pure engineering genius.

I sat up and looked around. There was no visible exit, but there was light emanating from a strange construction off to the side.

Unsure if I was supposed to try and climb my way out—an impossible task, even for a Burned mage—or if there was another obstacle I had to deal with down here, I got to my feet. Brushing myself off, I headed toward the construction, feeling heat baking off it.

It was a water-feature of sorts, with seven masks lined up in a row over seven basins. Liquid poured from the mouth of each mask, but it wasn't water, it was molten metal. Even before I stopped in front of the feature, I had identified three of the metals from their color alone.

A streetlamp stood on either side for illumination, and beyond the one on the right stood a little table like the one in Basil's office. On it sat a carafe of water and a glass. Thankful, I went to it and poured myself a cup of water. As I set down my empty glass I noticed a drawer beneath the tabletop. Cautiously, I opened it. Inside were several pieces of metal, all the identical shape but slightly varied in color. I took one out and held it up in the light of the lamp. Wrinkling my nose, I realized it was shaped like a human tongue.

"Yuck."

But even as I shuddered, I realized what I had to do.

A subtle whirring sound began somewhere behind the walls. A gentle breeze licked at the hot skin of my cheeks. I looked around and realized that the jellyfish-balls had begun to rotate. All of them. That complicated things further.

I took a breath. One problem at a time. Grabbing the metal tongues, I went over to the masks. Holding one tongue up in the light, I looked at the liquid metal pouring from the mouths of masks and compared their color to the tongue in my hand. The variances were minute, but I'd done a lot of this work with Basil. He'd even told me I was gifted with metals.

I stepped to the third mask, whose drool matched the tongue in my hand, and slipped the tongue into its open mouth. The flow of metal from its mouth ceased.

Encouraged, I moved along the masks, matching tongues to molten drool and sliding each tongue home. When I slid the last tongue home, two things happened simultaneously. The distant engine quit its drone and the wind stopped. I looked up, confirming that the spinning of the balls had slowed and was slowing further even as I watched. There was a loud clank, like a bolt sliding home, and the balls suddenly froze in place.

Below the line of masks, a drawer popped open. It looked like a lockbox at a bank. The box inside had a little handle. I hooked a finger and pulled it out, feeling its considerable weight. Taking it over to the table with the carafe, I opened the latches on the front and lifted the lid.

Inside were two very thick bracelets, like Viking vambraces, which looped over the thumb and covered from hand to mid-forearm. Spikes jutted from the sides. Sliding one over my right arm, I cinched three thick leather straps with metal buckles. Quivers of energy vibrated in my gut as I pulled on and secured the other one, and approached the nearest ball.

Drawing my hand back, I made a fist and slammed it flat on the ball. THUNK. The tooth at the side of my hand buried itself deep in the ball. It didn't pop or cave in, just accepted the spike into its side without sacrificing its integrity as a solid object. Pulling on it, I confirmed that the ball was indeed locked in place.

I began to climb.

FOURTEEN

A LONG DROP, A SUDDEN STOP

By the time I reached the gameboard near the ceiling, I was panting and my clothing was damp with sweat. Tendrils of hair stuck to my cheek, making me itch. I craned my neck, looking up from the underside of the holey landscape. I'd climbed aiming for the blinking arrow, but as I was still underneath, I couldn't see it. I hoped it hadn't moved.

I could hear the crickets chirping and the odd hoot of an owl as I hooked one of the spikes in my gauntlet on the edge of the hole above me. Keeping myself balanced on the ball beneath my feet, I pulled and the whole floor tilted down easily. Pulling further, my head emerged and my torso followed it. The lip of the floor against the far wall, struck something and stopped. I tugged, but it had hit its limit.

Crawling the rest of the way out through the hole, I slid flat-footed down the slope toward the wall. The ledge running the circumference of the gameboard was a little too far over my head to reach, so I detonated to catch it, then used slow-burn to pull myself up. The floor swung upward as my weight left it.

The ledge wasn't wide, so bringing myself up to standing was a slow process. As I straightened, I found the blinking arrow. Wiping at my face—making sure not to stab myself with the spikes—I shuffled along the ledge toward it.

When I reached it, the swinging gameboard came to an end, and a platform was before me. An arch made of square-cut rocks spanned the width of the platform. The rocks making up the arch itself had wooden wedges between them, the plinths holding the curve together. Stepping off the narrow ledge and onto the platform after testing to see if it was solid with a tentative toe, I came to stand beneath the arch.

Along the wall nearest to where I stood, to halfway across the gym where it ended, sat a long rectangular pool filled with black water. The water was completely opaque. I had no idea if it was shallow or deep. Where the pool ended was another blinking arrow pointing down, into what, I had no idea, but clearly when I reached it, I'd find out.

I knelt at the edge of the pool and sniffed. There were no strange smells, it really did seem like water. But what if it was something less friendly? I was about to get on my knees and reach down when a low hum began behind me.

I squeaked with surprise as an unseen force grabbed both of my wrists and yanked me backward. It was so powerful it pulled me back through the arch. With loud clanks of metal on metal, both of my wrists slammed against something solid, pinning me with my hands up by my ears in a gesture of surrender.

Struggling to pull my hands away, I realize that I could still lift my head and bow my body away from the surface I was stuck to. Only my wrists were fastened tight.

It was a giant magnet, and my vambraces were the only metal things on me. But now I was stuck. I took a breath and detonated in my shoulders and back, trying to yank the cuffs away from the metal. They juddered and slid a little along the magnet's surface, but didn't come away. I tried something similar but moved more slowly, using slow-burn.

With a grimace of effort, I detached my right wrist, but the energy required to keep it away from the magnet drained me so quickly that I soon gave up. My wrist snapped back against the magnet.

Panting, I looked from one wrist to the other. I needed to get out of the vambraces, but the buckles were too far away for me to undo with my teeth. I'd have to melt my way out of them.

Stoking up enough heat to melt what I'd determined was iron, I sent it into my right wrist.

Liquid iron drooled onto the floor as I slid my wrist free. My right hand flew to undo the buckles of the gauntlet around my left wrist, and I stepped away from the magnet.

Immediately, the hum of the magnet ceased. The gauntlets dropped to the floor, one of them landing on my toe. I hopped briefly with my injured toe in the air, but forgot all about the pain when a loud crash made me whirl around, the whole platform shaking beneath my feet.

The stones making up the arch had fallen to the floor and landed in a heap amidst blackened wood and ash. I'd been sloppy with my heat pollution, allowing it to burn up the wood holding the arch together. Oops.

I hadn't yet studied different woods, but whatever this was, it had burned easily and quickly. A stone had fallen into the black water, answering the question of depth.

Stepping over the pile of blocks, I came to stand at the edge of the pool. The square-cut rock sat in just six inches of black liquid, sitting proud of the surface by three inches, making a kind of square lily-pad large enough to step on.

Kneeling at the edge, I dipped a hand into what I hoped was water. It felt like water, cool and the same density, but I had never seen water so black before. In theory, I could walk across this pool, if it was all the same depth, but I had a feeling it wasn't supposed to be that easy.

I went to pick up another of the square blocks and grunted when I couldn't get it off the pile. It was impressively heavy. No wonder it had shaken the floor when the arch fell.

"What is this made of? Lead?"

With a grunt and a combination of detonations in my lower body and slow-burn in my upper, I lifted one up to standing. Even with the fire, this block was not easy to carry. It weighed a lot more than even Ryan's dead-weight.

Staggering over to the pool with my burden and wondering if it might be compressing my spine permanently, I gathered my fire and stepped onto the block that had fallen into the water. Panting and with sweat pouring down my face, I let the stone drop into the black liquid just beyond the first one. Once I'd been relieved of my burden, I felt as light as a plastic bag floating on the wind.

A sizzling sound reached my ears and I looked down to see holes appearing in my fireproof pants from the splashes that had struck my legs. Even the hard neoprene boot encasing my left foot had taken a droplet and sustained a steaming dimple.

What kind of water didn't hurt my skin but ate through fireproof clothing? But I didn't have time to stand around contemplating the game-makers' devices. I had work to do.

Stepping back onto the platform, I picked up another ridiculously heavy block and carried it, grunting and sweating, until I was standing on the last stone I'd dropped.

But I couldn't just drop them or my clothing would be in ruins by the time I got to the blinking arrow. Squatting, I slowly lowered my burden into the pool.

Returning for the next block, my heart fell as I realized how much effort and how long this was going to take. There were enough stones to get across the liquid, of that I was certain. But by the time I was all the way across, I was going to be a quivering pool of jelly with red ringlets. This was a test of pure strength.

There was nothing else to do but get to work. I just hoped there was a huge glass of water waiting for me below that blinking arrow.

There wasn't.

What was waiting for me was a long drop into darkness. My heart pounding from my exertions and my muscles throbbing, I stared down a straight square shaft. Presumably, it ended on the floor of the fire-gym, since I was currently somewhere up near the ceiling. But if I jumped without being able to calculate the distance to a landing, even the fire might not keep me from busting my legs.

I chewed my cheek and took deep, calming breaths, feeling mutinous about the cheerfully blinking arrow telling me that straight down was where I had to go next.

The shaft wasn't very wide but it was about the right width to shimmy down like a sweating, deranged Santa Claus, bracing myself with my hands and the soles of my shoes.

I swung my legs out over the shaft and braced my weight with my hands. Fire lit along my limbs as I reached a foot to the other side and braced it well enough to take my weight.

Suspended over nothing, I began to shimmy my way down the shaft. It wasn't so bad until my head got so far from the edge above that I could no longer reach it. My heart sped up and I fought off claustrophobia as the sides closed in and the top grew distant.

Down and down and down I shimmied. Some five minutes of shuffling and my muscles were aching with weariness. I'd just carried what felt like thousands of pounds across the pond, it was enough of a challenge after that just to carry my own weight.

A light came on below me, startling me badly enough that I almost let go. I'd gotten used to being a creature of the dark. I looked down and saw a smiley face painted on the floor of the gym. Now I could drop, and I did without hesitation because I worried that the lights would go off again.

Cushioning my landing with small detonations, I straightened and looked around. A corridor lay before me, going back under the pool, naturally, since the rest of the gym was taken up by the shifty-shifty floor.

At the end of the corridor was something that looked like it had been taken straight out of a submarine. I raked a forearm against my forehead and strode forward on wobbly legs to inspect it. A wheel protruded from the center of a dome-shaped brass door. I'd tried to spin the wheel, but it was locked. Of course.

Stepping back to look at the hatch from a distance, I studied the details. It was a handsome door, shining brass with silver dials and a gleaming black wheel, with black studs encircling the frame. It looked like something out of a steampunk comic.

To the right of the wheel were the rotating numbers of a combination lock, the kind you might find on a briefcase, only this combination wasn't just three or four digits. I counted twenty dials. At the left side of the dials an alpha symbol had been engraved into the metal. At the right side was the omega symbol. So, start at the left and work to the right. Very helpful.

A set of bolts led straight up the wall from the center of the hatch-cover. My eye followed them, until it was drawn to something dangling from the ceiling. Something very small hung in the air by a wire or fishing line, some filament too thin to see.

I stood directly beneath this hanging thing and squinted at it. It was circular, about the size of a quarter, and had three little concentric rings of colors I could hardly make out, and a dot in the middle.

Good grief. It was the world's smallest bullseye.

I looked around for a projectile but there was nothing but the submarine hatch-door itself. Fire was the only projectile I had. If I could throw a fireball straight up and hit that tiny bullseye, something else would happen, something that would help me crack the code and open the door.

I cocked an arm back, fueled up a fireball, and hurled it at the bullseye. It sailed past, missing by an inch, then plummeted back toward my head. I stepped to the side and let it splatter on the floor in an explosion of sparks. Watching the sparks bounce across the neoprene gave me an idea. Maybe I wouldn't have to have perfect aim, if I just...

Cocking my arm back, I drew tight that fiery elastic within, and released a snapping fireball. I smiled as my ball exploded within range of the hanging bullseye.

A dark shape fell and I caught it. It was a little metal cylinder with a tiny hinge. Opening one end, a red button popped out, the kind I'd seen in movies about fighter jets.

Wincing and not sure what to expect, I depressed the button.

To my right, a panel dropped open and a tray of rounded handles slid forward. I approached, recognizing them as the pitch spindles we used in skills classes. Before my eyes, they lit up and began to glow with varying levels of brightness. I stood looking at them, baffled, until I noticed a small alpha symbol to the left of the row of spindles. The right side had the omega. My confusion parted like clouds moving away from the sun.

Grasping the first spindle, I closed my eyes and narrowed in on the temperature. Keeping it in my mind, I went over to the combination dials and flicked through the first four, putting the combination at 1292, the same temperature in Fahrenheit the spindle had given me.

I stepped back, wondering if I should be using Celsius instead. The answer would become clear as I worked, because what was four digits in Fahrenheit could be three in Celsius, resulting in a shorter code. If I got through several of the spindles and ran out of dials, I would have to start over.

Walking back and forth between the spindles and the dials, I worked my way down the line. Fahrenheit had been the right choice. As I put in the last number, my heart thudded with hope and my head and eyes throbbed with exhaustion.

I grasped the wheel. It spun easily under my hands. When it reached the end of its rotation, I pulled. The heavy door swung toward me. Stepping over the door's threshold, I found myself in a hall that led to my left. It was lit by normal bare lightbulbs and ended some twenty feet before me at a plain wall. I began to walk, wondering what new obstacle might present itself.

"Footsteps," said a disembodied voice. I froze.

The head of Zafer Guzelköy appeared from around a corner up ahead. He saw me and smiled. "Well done, Ms. Cagney."

"Thank you." I started to walk again. My throat was burning and my muscles were made of sod, but I was finished.

He looked at someone behind him I couldn't see at said, "She's out."

When I rounded the corner, I saw Guzelköy and Davazlar along with Christy and Basil. The game-makers stood by a small folding table with steaming coffee cups in their hands.

"What did you think? Did you enjoy it?" Guzelköy

asked in a rush, looking like he had a million more questions to pepper me with when I got through those two.

"Very ... nice," I croaked, feeling dazed and like stringing more than two words together was beyond me just then.

Davazlar admonished his partner. "Come, Zafer. She needs a rest, not an interrogation."

Christy came forward and hugged me. "You look shattered. Come on."

Basil looked like he wanted to hug me, too, but he was too appropriate for hugs so he shook my hand instead.

"How'd I do?" I rasped, desperate for some clue as to whether I'd been faster than those who'd gone before.

"Just fine, dear." Christy said, putting an arm around my shoulders and leading me away. "Just fine. Come on, let's get you some water. Are you hungry?"

I nodded, disappointed in her answer but not surprised. I let her escort me in silence, feeling too tired to push for more details.

FIFTEEN
COMMISERATION

As Dr. Price escorted me to the professors' lounge, I lifted my hands out in front of me, watching them tremble a little. My quads, calves and back were so tired they were burning. Christy carried my backpack and refused to hand it over when I'd tried to take it. I was grateful.

"May I shower before you take me to the lounge? I smell terrible." I did stink of smoke, but even more than a shower, I wanted to be alone to relive what I'd just been through. My brain wanted to chew on it for a while before I could let it go.

"There are showers in the professors' lounge," she said as we climbed the carpeted stairs to the third floor. "You must be starving. The caterers have just delivered a spread of curries. I hope that takes your fancy."

I hardly ever came up here, in fact I hadn't been on the top floor of the villa since chasing the thief. "Thai sounds great."

"It smells more Indian to me, but what do I know? I grew up on leek and potato stew."

"How are the others?" I asked, at real risk of not making it to the top of the stairs without having to use the banister. A muscle beside my right knee had begun to twitch and I desperately wanted to scratch an itch on the sole of my left foot.

"You'll see for yourself in a second or two. Here we are." She pushed through a swinging door with a brass label engraved with 'Professors Lounge' in a curly script.

"Wow!" I stopped dead, then lurched forward before the swinging door could hit me in the back.

Dr. Price gave me a tired smile. "You've never seen the profs' lounge either? I guess it's technically a library and a lounge in one."

I shook my head, finding my legs as Dr. Price led me through the ornate library. Dark wooden shelves hand-carved with foliage, flowers and vines stood in neat rows on the parquet floor. The ceiling was high in the middle but fell steeply on either side. At the end of the library shelves was a collection of shiny wooden tables, each with a green, glass desk lamp dangling a golden chain. Six dormers, three on either side of the library, sheltered more tables, these were round and with thick hand-carved legs that matched the bookshelves. In the center sat a large model of the universe. In the next section was a huge golden globe suspended in an ornate wooden cradle. Along one wall, between bookshelves, sat a case containing what looked like samples of rocks, minerals and gems.

Passing the library, Dr. Price led me to a narrow, arched passageway at the far end of the room. The smell of Indian spices and fresh-baked naan bread boffed me in the face and made my mouth water and my stomach growl.

Harriet, Tomio, Brooke, Tagan and Peter were seated at a round table that was overlooked by a stained-glass window I'd often seen from the outside of the building. They were almost finished their dinner. A spread of takeout containers sat on top of a sideboard next to a coffee machine, a tall jug of steaming tea and a collection of canned soft drinks and juices. Harriet's fork paused halfway to her mouth and she straightened. She elbowed Felix, who looked like he was about to pick his plate up and lick it.

"Saxony's finished."

Christy handed me my pack. "Give her time to shower and eat before you bombard her with questions." She directed me toward a closed door on the left. "Ladies' showers are through there."

I gave my teammates a tired smile and lifted a hand in greeting. A smile spread across Tomio's face as he got up and came over, his arms opening to hug me.

I cringed away from him. "I smell like a barn fire."

His smile never faltered as he walked in a little circle with his arms pumping comically as he headed back to his meal. "You *do* smell like a barn fire."

I laughed and hitched my bag. "There'd better be some naan left when I get out."

"No guarantees," Peter called through a mouthful of food.

The ladies' washroom was just as interesting as the rest of the lounge, with an air of old-fashioned shabby chic. A chaise lounge sat between a set of frosted glass doors, beyond that were three white ceramic pedestal sinks with golden swan's heads for taps. The floor was a mosaic of tiny glass tiles in lavender, pink, and gray, matching the upholstery of the lounger. Three more doors, white and saloon style, hid the toilets.

Opening one of the glass doors I discovered a small changing area in front of the shower. Dropping my backpack on the lounger I dug out my toiletries and pajamas. I stared at the soft fabric of my sleep shorts and t-shirt. I wanted to fall into bed right after I ate, but no one else was wearing pajamas yet.

"Screw it," I muttered, unearthing my bathrobe too.

I emerged fifteen minutes later with my wet hair turbaned up in a towel, wearing a robe and slippers. Shuffling over to the food, I fixed myself a plate. My teammates had broken up and left the table. I couldn't see any of the guys and guessed they'd ducked into the library.

Harriet got herself a cold drink and joined me at the table while Brooke made herself some tea.

"So how was it for you guys?" I asked, shoveling a forkful of rice and curried vegetables into my mouth. My gaze narrowed on Harriet. "Yours started so late in the evening. Were you tired?"

"I was, but I have this weird quirk where I actually perform better under pressure. I muddled through. Let me bring you up to speed, since only Tagan was here before me. I've heard all the stories." Harriet pushed her chair back from the table to give herself room to sit cross-legged.

Brooke set her tea on a side-table and collapsed into the loveseat closest to the table, pulling her feet up under her. She propped an elbow on the armrest and her chin in her hand. She'd heard all this before, too.

"First off, did you fall through the tilty gameboard?"

I nodded and rolled by eyes, still chewing.

"Well, don't worry. Nobody made it past that bloody thing without falling through."

My second forkful froze on the way to my mouth, momentarily forgotten. "No one?"

Brooke tugged on a coil of long brunette hair. "No. But, we figure no one was meant to."

"Otherwise how would you discover the masks in the bottom?" Harriet tapped her fingernails against her glass.

Brooke nodded. "Yeah. If a Firethorne kid actually got past the board without falling, they would save a ton of time, so we're thinking that part of the game wasn't meant to be beaten."

I nodded, hoping they were right. It would have taken a lot of practice to get across that board without falling down one of the holes, practice no one had had.

Harriet sipped her drink. "The game-makers said time was the only metric that mattered. Figuring out the tongues and climbing those balls took me longer than anything else. It would have cut off an hour not to have to deal with all that."

"Not for me." Brooke dragged a hand across her forehead in a gesture of frustration. "For me it was the pool. Figuring out how to release those ropes—"

I paused again. "What ropes?"

Brooke and Harriet exchanged a look before Harriet's calculating green eyes swung back to me. "How did you get across the pool if you didn't find the ropes?"

"I used the blocks." I set my fork down. There had been ropes? So ... what, they had swung across the pool like Tarzan?

"What blocks?" Brooke and Harriet asked together.

"The ones that made up the arch. You mean you didn't have to use the arch?" My mind had started to whirl.

Brooke's eyes narrowed. "*How* exactly did you use the blocks?"

"I burned the wood getting out of the vambraces, which caused the arch to fall down. So I used the blocks to make stepping stones across the pool." I picked up my fork again but only because my stomach had given an embarrassing growl.

Harriet's jaw dropped. "The pool was that shallow?"

I nodded. "Wish I'd found the ropes though. Carrying those blocks was exhausting. By the time I reached the shaft, I was pudding."

Brooke and Harriet absorbed this, then Harriet asked, "Which obstacle was the worst for you?"

"The hardest or the one that took the longest?"

"They aren't the same?"

I shook my head and dabbed at the corner of my mouth with my napkin where I felt a stray bit of sauce. "I haven't learned any alchemy yet so I had to wait for the lantern at the beginning to change to normal fire. It felt like it took forever. I was stressed about how much time I'd lost at first, until I tumbled down those balls. I'd say the climb out took me the longest."

Brooke had a long thumbnail between her teeth. "Not the masks or the sub door?"

I shook my head, breaking off a piece of buttered naan. "Basil has drilled me a lot about metals, and pitch is one of my stronger skills, so I was okay with those. How about you?"

She sighed and let a foot dangle over the floor. "The submarine door took me forever. I'm okay with pitch but if you weren't bang on accurate, it didn't work. I started out using Celsius and had to do the whole thing over again, converting to Fahrenheit and making guesses a few degrees either side of the right temperature."

"Me too," said Harriet. "But those gigantic steps were the worst for me. I tend to over-detonate and whacked my head twice." She put a hand up to the crown of her head, wincing. "It's still tender."

"Sorry." I gave her a sympathetic smile. "How did the guys do?"

Brooke filled me in with her charming Spanish accent. "Peter figures he aced it, even if he fell through the floor. He agrees that no one was meant to get across the gameboard. Everything else, he figured out. Tomio stalled on the masks, the lanterns, and the tiny bullseye. That's to be expected since you've both just finished first-year. Tagan says he loved it but hasn't told us which ones stumped him, if any, I think he's keeping quiet until we get the results."

A burst of laughter from the library drifted through the archway. However the course had gone for them, the boys sounded pretty happy.

"They've taken up a game of Hearts," Brooke explained, getting to her feet and stretching. "I think I'll join them."

Harriet looked like she wanted to go, too. "Do you know it?"

"Hearts? No. I've never played."

"We can teach you. It's good fun." She waggled her brows in invitation.

"Thank you but I'm going to fall into bed. I'm exhausted."

Harriet nodded and got up to follow Brooke out, then paused. "Did you get your key from Dr. Price?"

I shook my head.

She went to a side-table and picked up a woven bowl, raking through its contents. She pulled out a room key attached to a disc by a thin chain. She slid it across the table to me. "It's just down the hall beside mine. Number forty-five. I mean, you're forty-five, I'm forty-three."

"Thanks."

She smiled and headed for the arch.

I took another bite of my curry, chewing slowly but not really tasting it. I marveled at how I could have missed the ropes the girls found. I couldn't recall seeing any clues or triggers. I wondered if the guys had found the ropes or if they'd had to lug a zillion pounds of stone back and forth like me.

Only Cecily and Felix were left to go of the Arcturus crew. That meant there'd be two Firethorne students left as well. If everyone did the course within an hour or two of one another, surely this challenge would be over by the end of the day tomorrow.

SIXTEEN
DEATH METED OUT

My stomach jangled and tumbled around like a dryer full of socks and coins as we marched into Lecture Hall A and took our seats on the same sides of the room as before. It was early afternoon on day six and the first challenge was completed.

Davazlar and Guzelköy stood at the front of the room, but instead of talking, they watched us come in, keen eyes passing over every competitor, pausing on a few. I thought Davazlar's watchful gaze lingered on me a little longer than anyone else, but that could just be my fire-engine red hair. Mom used to kiss my head and tell me I could stop a cruise ship a mile away.

When we were seated, Guzelköy took his place at the edge of the dais, the spokesmen of the odd couple. Davazlar stood near the blackboard.

"Before we get to the results, Davazlar and I would like to congratulate you all on your performance. It was a very close game with many of your times coming within minutes of one another. Thank you for your patience as we ran this first installment. It required quite a bit of fiddling between rounds to ensure you all had the same quality of course to run. Some of you did quite a bit of damage to the game." He chuckled.

I could have been imagining it but I thought his eyes lingered on me the way Davazlar's had. I fought the urge to shrink in my seat. Had I caused more damage than anyone else?

"Davazlar will first reveal who the algorithm paired against whom." Guzelköy gestured to his partner and stepped to the side.

Davazlar slid the blackboard in front to the side, revealing the list. People leaned forward to read it. The names were listed in the neat printing of a first grade teacher.

1. Tagan Lyall VS Kristoff Skau
2. Harriet Ashby VS Sean Pilterman
3. Tomio Nakano VS Liu Xiaotian
4. Brooke Ortega VS Serenamen Hall
5. Peter Toft VS Axel Bell
6. Saxony Cagney VS Liam Walsh
7. Cecily Price VS January Jaques
8. Felix Kennet VS Eira Nygaard

I wracked my brain to try and remember which one of the Firethorne kids was Liam Walsh. I'd been so distracted by Eira that I hadn't paid enough attention.

Competitors on both sides looked across the room to locate their matches. Others remained facing front.

Guzelköy cleared his throat, pulling a folded piece of paper from his pocket. "I have the performance times here, Davazlar would you mind?"

Davazlar grabbed a piece of chalk, pinching the little white thing between thick digits.

"Starting at the top and going to the minute since

the seconds didn't matter for any of these matches, in the end." Guzelköy unfolded the page. "Tagan Lyall clocked in at three hours and two minutes while Kristoff Skau finished in two hours and fifty-five minutes."

Davazlar scratched out the times beside the names as this first announcement registered among the teams.

The Firethorne kids burst into applause and whistles. Some of them turned to a slender kid in the middle row, high-fiving him. Kristoff blushed, bringing to attention the impressive crop of pimples on his forehead. He definitely wasn't out of his teens, and he wasn't cocky either. He smiled, but kind of slouched down in his seat and crossed his skinny arms over his narrow chest. Looking at him, you'd never guess he'd be much competition for Tagan, but that was the world of fire magi. You couldn't tell what kind of firepower one might have banked beneath even the littlest ribcage. I doubted Kristoff was Burned, because Tagan wasn't and their times were only 7 minutes apart.

Tagan rubbed his face, disappointment apparent in the gesture. Felix, who was seated behind him, thumped him charitably on the shoulder.

"Well done, Kristoff. Moving on," Guzelköy lifted the sheet. "Harriet Ashby came in at three hours twelve minutes."

There was a disappointed murmur from the Arcturus side. It seemed like the Firethorne kids were holding their breath, getting ready to loose another cheer.

"While Sean Pilterman clocked in at three hours fourteen minutes."

Two seconds of silence passed and then the whole

room groaned, even us, in spite of Harriet's win. Our groan was in relief, though. She'd edged out Sean by a hair.

"Two minutes," Peter said as he wrapped an arm around Harriet's shoulder and gave her a congratulatory squeeze.

There wasn't time to figure out who Sean Pilterman was before Guzelköy was reading off the next set of competitors.

"Tomio Nakano finished with a time of two hours, thirty-two minutes," the game-maker said, his gaze flicking up to find Tomio.

I gasped and squeezed Tomio's bicep. He put a hand over my knuckles and his body went tense. His time was the best so far. I was sure he had it in the bag.

"Liu Xiaotian clocked in at two hours, eleven minutes," Guzelköy read.

The Firethorne side of the room lost their collective minds as the Arcturus side froze in a tableau of disbelief. Liu had knocked Tomio out of the games. Tomio dropped his head in disappointment, then leaned back and looked up at the ceiling as the Firethorne kids loudly congratulated Liu.

A glance at Liu kindled my ire. She nodded and smiled smugly, like she'd known all along that she couldn't be beat. Surely she was Burned to have knocked an impressive competitor like Tomio out by almost twenty minutes.

Basil turned to give Tomio a sympathetic smile but Tomio didn't seem in the mood for sympathy, and let himself slouch in his seat, his gaze on the floor. Tomio was not accustomed to losing, but this wasn't an MMA tournament. He'd been schooled.

"Quiet, please," Guzelköy said, directing this to the Firethorne side who were still laughing and talking with excitement. I caught Babs sending a sidelong glance at Basil and my blood threatened to boil. I closed my eyes and took a breath. We still had the results of five matches to go.

The room went still.

"Brooke Ortega," Guzelköy began, finding his place on the page, "finished with a time of three hours and one minute, while Serenamen Hall completed at two hours and fifty-eight minutes."

I let out a groan and covered my eyes as the Firethorne kids celebrated again. My heart had begun to drop toward the region of my pelvis. Arcturus, one. Firethorne, three.

I opened my eyes and put an arm around Brooke. "It was that bloody submarine door and those masks," she murmured, her voice tight. "I'm sorry."

"Don't be sorry," I whispered as our teammates reached out to touch Brooke, if they couldn't reach her they gave her a sympathetic smile. Basil didn't turn around this time, his shoulders seemed locked back against the chair. I saw Dr. Price's arm move, maybe she had taken his hand.

"Moving on." Guzelköy cleared his throat. "Peter Toft clocked in at two hours fourteen minutes, and Axel Bell finished with a time of four hours and four minutes."

This time it was the Firethorne side who fell into a shocked silence. Our team didn't scream or clap, it didn't seem right to celebrate a win with such a wide margin of time but there was a collective feeling of relief on our side of the room. I wondered what had gone wrong for Axel.

I looked over at the Firethorne side but no one was moving. Liu shot a venomous glance at the back of a boy in the front row who didn't turn around. His ears were red, but we didn't have time to study their reactions. My name was next. My fingers trembled against my leg and Tomio took my hand and squeezed. I shot him a grateful look, happy to see that he'd bounced back from his loss quickly.

"Saxony Cagney finished with a time of two hours and three minutes," Guzelköy announced.

Everyone in the room froze, then our side exploded into applause. My knees were slapped, my shoulders whacked, my body jostled from side to side. My jaw was on the floor. I had the best time listed so far, even better than Liu by a whole eight minutes and that felt pretty damn good. My body went into a kind of weak state of relief edged with shock. I reminded myself that Liam's time hadn't been announced yet, and stiffened up, holding my breath.

"Liam Walsh came in at two hours..." Guzelköy paused and frowned at the page. Guzelköy went back to Davazlar, showed him the page and whispered a question.

Tomio's hand tightened on mine and I squeezed back just as hard. It seemed the whole room was holding its breath. This was how I was going to die, from pure stress and anticipation.

Davazlar whispered something back to Guzelköy, Guzelköy nodded and returned to his place at the front of the room. Without explanation, he cleared his throat and began again. "Liam Walsh finished with a time of two hours, twenty-three—"

An explosion of whistles, screams and applause from our side of the room drowned out the last of Guzelköy's announcement. I grinned, my lips trembling against my teeth.

"Simmer down, ladies and gents," Guzelköy called over the din. "Simmer down. We're not through yet."

Team Arcturus found their seats and settled into them, buoyed by the latest results.

"Cecily Price performed with a time of two hours, thirty-seven minutes," Guzelköy said, with a raised voice this time. "While Ms. January Jaques finished with a very close two hours and thirty-eight minutes."

Groans from the Firethorne side mingled with an Arcturus cheer. We were back on track now with four Arcturus wins, three Firethorne wins and one to go. Felix was a force. There was a sense on our side of the room of confident anticipation.

"Felix Kennet clocked in at two hours, two minutes," Guzelköy announced.

Another explosion from the Arcturus side of the room. Felix had beat my time, and held the record thus far. He got smacked around with congratulatory beatings and looked like he enjoyed every second.

"And Eira Nygaard finished with a time of one hour, five minutes," Guzelköy finished, a strange gleam in his eye as he glanced at the ice-blond Firethorne competitor. "Well done, Eira."

Our side of the room went numb with shock, even some of the Firethorne competitors looked startled. Some of them clapped but many of them turned and began to whisper questions at her. Basil and Christy leaned their heads together and exchanged quiet words. Babs sat in the front row of the Firethorne side, next to Mr. Bunting. She glanced back at Eira and gave a nod of approval. She didn't even look surprised at the woman's performance, as if she'd expected Eira to clean house.

I glanced at Felix who looked like someone had sucker punched him in the back of the head. No one spoke, but everyone must have had some version of the same question running around in their minds. How had she done it? How had she bested the next fastest time by almost an entire hour?

"Well done, competitors." Guzelköy lifted his voice above the Firethorne group's storm of whispers. "Davazlar and I need a week to prepare for the next round. If there are no questions, we'll release you and get to work."

There was a spattering of applause.

The Firethorne students left their seats and began to file out one by one. The Arcturus group remained seated, watching our opponents leave the lecture hall. Liu shot me a triumphant glance but I barely noticed, my eyes were on Eira, but the blond kept her gaze demurely on the floor as she left the room.

Challenge one was over. Each team still had four competitors in the running, evidence of the algorithm at work, resulting in the improbable tie match the gamemakers wanted. So why did it feel as though we'd been roundly beaten?

SEVENTEEN

A LOOPHOLE?

It was spitting as the Arcturus teammates, both current and former, stood in the driveway in front of the villa. After the *Traps, Tools and Time* game was over, the disqualified Arcturus competitors, with the exception of Tomio, made arrangements to leave. A taxi with all its doors open waited patiently for its cargo. Tagan, Brooke and Felix would share the cab to the train station where they would then go their separate ways.

Tagan and Felix gave a round of hugs and got into the vehicle but Brooke lingered, eyeing the fire-gym's exterior as she pulled her hood over her hair. Small drops of rain spattered against her jacket.

"I wish I were a fly on the wall in there," she murmured.

Babs and Basil had joined the game-makers in the observation pods to view the footage from the first challenge, which was being guarded more closely than state secrets.

"Do you know," Brooke was saying to Harriet and

me, "I overheard the Firethorne students talking about her?"

There was no point in asking which 'her' Brooke was referring to. Eira Nygaard had become the star of the show, though none of us knew how she'd done it.

Brooke drew her eyes from the gym to look at us. "They call her 'The Doll'."

Harriet shook her head and scoffed. "What a silly nickname. Just because she looks like one? No matter what a woman can do, if she's beautiful, that's what she's known for, not her abilities. She deserves a nom-de-plume based on her skills, not her face."

"Yeah, yeah, yeah," Tagan called from inside the car. "You can carry on with that feminist bullshit another time. I've got a train to catch."

Cecily and I exchanged a look. Tagan had been unpleasant since he'd been knocked out of the games. I liked him most of the time, but truthfully, I was glad he was leaving. His overly competitive attitude sometimes had me on edge. Tomio had elected to stay and support us until the games were over. That was a relief but I was still gutted that he was out.

Brooke threw her arms around my neck, squeezing hard. Her cucumber shampoo wafted into my nose. When she pulled back she kept a hand on my shoulder, her gaze flicking from me to Cecily, then to Harriet and Peter, the remaining Arcturus competitors. "Good luck, everyone. Make Basil proud."

Peter hugged Brooke, waved to Felix and Tagan one last time and then disappeared into the villa. Harriet and Cecily hugged Brooke in a squishy threesome, then followed Peter into the villa as Harriet told Cecily she was dying for a coffee. Tomio and I waited for Brooke to get into the taxi.

Before she shut the door, her dark doe-eyes caught mine. "When you find out what Eira did to get through the course so fast, will you text me? I won't sleep properly until I know."

I told her I would, shut the cab's door and stepped back, accidentally stepping on Tomio's foot.

"Sorry," I murmured as we waved goodbye.

He appeared not to notice, his gaze fixed on the car as it made its way up the steep drive. "I still think she cheated."

I took him by the elbow and turned him toward the arch. A wispy, blue-gray sky was gathering thunderheads and growing darker by the second. "Come on, a storm is coming. Look at those clouds."

He followed me toward the fire-gym doors, our feet crunching on the gravel. We passed through into the fire-gym's lobby and headed for the stairs leading up to the arch. A sign taped to the double doors leading into the gym proclaimed it off limits in big bold letters.

Halfway through the archway, we paused to watch the storm clouds gather over the Channel. We stood there for so long that my hips and back began to ache. I was still a little sore from the course. When I sank onto the carpeted floor into a cross-legged position, Tomio joined me.

Heavy raindrops spattered the glass, blurring our view of the sky and making the ivy shudder. Being in the arch during rainstorm made my stomach give a wistful twist for Gage. Thinking of Gage made me think about the last overheated make out session we'd had, which made me feel sad.

"What's wrong?" Tomio's eyes were on my face.

I leaned back, rested on the palms of my hands. I wouldn't have minded talking about my problem with Gage with someone, but not Tomio.

"Nothing," I replied, letting my thoughts go back to Eira. "I don't think she cheated."

His black brows arched. "No?"

I shook my head. "How could she? Every move we make in there is recorded. Plus Guzelköy and Davazlar are supposedly incorruptible. If Basil trusts them, then I trust them. They're legally bound to run the games fairly and they are impartial about who wins. Mr. Pendleton, the lawyer, even had them polygraphed to make sure they didn't have any conflicts of interest."

"So I heard." Tomio leaned back on his hands and mimicked my posture. "I guess we can see how she did it for ourselves, after the games are over."

Yeah, I thought sourly. After we'd lost Basil's property to someone known as The Doll.

Tomio said, "Don't let her intimidate you."

I snorted, wondering how anyone, Burned or not, *wouldn't* be intimidated by Eira's exceptional time.

The sound of the fire-gym's doors slamming open echoed up the stairs, making both Tomio and me jump.

"This is an outrage!" It was Basil's voice. I'd never heard him sound so angry.

Tomio and I shared a wide-eyed look and Tomio lifted a finger to his lips.

"Calm down, Basil." That was Babs. Her voice was pitched at a normal level. She sounded cool and confident, a little smug. "No one has broken any rules."

"That's complete and utter hogwash," Basil sputtered, then barked at someone else. "Tell her."

"I'm afraid she's right, Mr. Chaplin," Guzelköy replied, but he sounded sorry about the fact that Babs was right. "We set the rules together and we all agreed to abide by them. They're legally binding, and none of them have been broken."

Basil wheezed. "How can you—"

There was a break of silence during which no one said anything.

"How can you side with her? You know what she's done is devilry. The girl is some kind of hybrid."

Babs sighed, sounding both petulant and pleased. "How many times do I have to say it? Eira is a fire mage."

There was the sound of paper ruffling before Guzelköy, sounding perfectly calm and rational, stated: "Even if she is half something else, the rules don't explicitly state the competitors have to be fire mages."

"*What?*" Basil's voice came out under so much pressure I cringed for his vocal chords.

"It says right here. All competitors must be either graduates of the past school year or registered students at either Arcturus Academy or Firethorne Collegiate to be eligible to compete."

There was the sound of paper being snatched, then everything went quiet. Rain splattered against the arch above Tomio and me as we sat there, holding our breath. I felt sick for Basil, sick and confused. A hybrid?

"This is impossible." Basil sounded hollow now, defeated. "It's implicit. These games were entered with the understanding our schools teach exclusively fire mages. It wasn't necessary to explicitly state that the competitors have to be fire elementals. Guzelköy, back me up! Surely, you can see—"

"She *is* a fire mage, Basil," Babs repeated, still with that infuriating patronizing tone.

"She may be, yes, at least half of her," Basil spat, his voice rising. "Where did you dig her up and what did you pay her? I want to see her registration papers and all of her history. Medical records—"

As Basil continued to kick up a fuss, his voice receded. The lobby doors slammed open and storming footsteps crunched over the gravel beneath the archway.

Tomio and I rolled onto our stomachs and army-crawled across the floor of the arch to press our noses to the glass. I caught a glimpse of Basil's jacket through the ivy as he disappeared around the front of the villa. Babs and Guzelköy walked after him, Guzelköy clutching a bunch of damp papers.

"It doesn't matter, Headmaster," Guzelköy's distant voice drifted through the sound of pouring rain. "She is a registered Firethorne student. She is eligible to compete. I am as upset as you are, but Ms. Chaplin is correct. No rules were broken."

"Rules *you* helped make," Babs added helpfully as she too vanished around the corner.

Their voices faded away to nothing, leaving Tomio and me sprawled on the carpet on our stomachs, absorbing what we'd overheard.

Tomio rolled onto his back and I flopped over beside him. We stared at the ceiling of the ivy-draped arch, watching as water poured down the glass and raindrops shook the vines. After several minutes had passed, Tomio looked over at me.

His dark eyes gleamed with indignation. "He thinks she's some kind of hybrid."

I nodded, my mind spinning like a top. Maybe that was how she'd gotten through the course so quickly, she had additional supernatural skills. It could explain it, though if Basil had some idea of what Eira's other half might be, he hadn't stated it. To me that indicated that he wasn't sure, that whatever it was he'd seen Eira do, it wasn't starkly obvious.

"Sounds like it doesn't matter, even if she is," I said, rubbing at my eyes. I suddenly felt very tired. More than tired, world-weary. It was apparent that Babs had pulled one over on Basil, used a gray area to her advantage, created a loophole for herself. And maybe Basil had been sloppy, but you wouldn't think it necessary to explicitly state that all the contenders had to be pure fire mages, just being students would mean they had to be.

"Bullshit it doesn't matter," Tomio hissed. "I trust that woman like I'd trust a rabid dog. Something stinks."

I agreed. "What can we do about it?"

Tomio chewed his cheek thoughtfully before his gaze narrowed on me. "*You* aren't going to do anything other than focus on the next challenge. *I'm* going to do a little reconnaissance."

He got to his feet and reached down to help me up. My back twanged like a stringed instrument. I was moving at half my usual speed, without any desire to move faster.

"Come on. Let's get lunch then go to the CTH for a workout," Tomio said, already at the other end of the walkway.

I put a hand on my backside for a little stretch. Something popped unpleasantly in my tailbone.

Tomio brightened at the thought of putting me

through my paces. "We need you sharp and firing on all pistons. You need to lean into this business."

I groaned but followed, grumbling under my breath that I didn't want lean into anything, I wanted to lie down on my bed.

FIVE DAYS later I still felt like a stringed instrument, but a finely tuned one. While the game-makers worked on the next challenge, Tomio had put me through daily paces. Each team was given access to the CTH for five hours every day to train, but with an hour between the training times. It seemed like a lot of effort was being made to keep the teams from running into one another. We saw the Firethorne team in the cafeteria during meals, but even there, they were given a table on the opposite side of the room to ours. And we had to alternate which group got served first.

"Who do you think is behind the strict rules to keep us apart?" Harriet murmured one lunch hour over a ham and pea soup that was straight out delicious. Either Lars' cooking had improved, or we'd become accustomed to it. Maybe a bit of both.

"Babs, obviously," Tomio said, tearing his bun in two and dipping into his bowl. "Do you think Christy or Basil would care so much?"

"I don't know, maybe it's the game-makers," Peter suggested, his cheek bulging. He looked into his bowl. "This stuff is growing on me."

Cecily put her spoon down. "It could just as easily be Basil. He warned us against making friends. Or it could even be the lawyer. What did you say his name was, Saxony?"

"Mr. Pendleton," I said, blowing on a steaming spoonful more from habit than from any desire to cool my food. It wasn't like hot soup could burn me. "But it's not him. He didn't make the rules, he just facilitated the meeting and drew up the contracts. I don't think he cares about the details as much as everyone following the rules. I think Tomio is right."

He nodded. "It has to be Babs. She doesn't want us to mingle with her students." Tomio leaned into the table, eyeballing our faces one by one, his tone full of implied meaning. "She's afraid of what we'll discover."

"We all know what *you're* trying to discover," Peter's brows waggled lewdly. "Got rejected again, didn't you lover boy?"

The whole team knew by now that Tomio had taken it upon himself to dig for intel on Eira, since Basil and Christy wouldn't tell us anything. They were bound by the agreements they'd signed. The whole team also knew that Tomio had gotten exactly nowhere.

"My interests are purely professional. I promise. She'll crack. Just you wait. No one can resist these charms." Tomio gestured to his flat abs and rounded pectorals.

The table laughed.

I looked over at the Firethorne foursome, stooped over their food and talking quietly. Eira was on the end, not appearing to engage in conversation with her teammates. She sipped small spoonsful of soup and took small bites of buttered bread, chewing slowly and thoroughly before swallowing. I took advantage of her lack of awareness to study her profile. The button-nose, generous lips, rounded cheekbones and gently sloping jaw. Her hair reflected the cafeteria's lights, gleaming like it was sprayed with lacquer. She really was fun to look at.

She paused mid-chew, then turned her head, as though she'd felt my inspection. The blue of her irises was vivid enough to make out even across the big cafeteria.

I gave her a small but genuine smile.

She dropped her gaze into her soup.

Mr. Bunting appeared in the cafeteria door. He headed toward the kitchen but didn't get a tray. Instead he pulled a chair over to where the hardwood met the linoleum and, wheezing, got up to stand on top of it.

"Attention, please," he said, hiking up his pants and puffing from lifting his bulk onto the chair.

Everyone stopped talking.

"Tomorrow morning, be in Lecture Hall A for eight a.m. The game-makers will address you about the next challenge before breakfast. That will be all."

When no one looked away, Mr. Bunting made a 'go on' motion with his hand. A moment passed and he flushed red when he realized that we were more interested in watching him get down from the chair than we were in returning to our soup.

He put a hand on the chair's back and lowered a foot toward the floor, teetering a little before finding the floor. Puffing, he dragged the chair back to its place and scurried out of the cafeteria mumbling under his breath.

Everyone in the cafeteria laughed when he disappeared but I knew Mr. Bunting could hear it and almost felt sorry for him. I glanced over at the Firethorne kids. For a moment they looked so young, so carefree. Just a bunch of classmates giggling over the embarrassing antics of an authority figure.

Eira glanced up and we exchanged a look while everyone was still laughing. We shared a proper smile this time, though hers was partially covered by her fingers, like she felt guilty for laughing. She dropped her gaze to her lunch and the moment was over.

I went back to my soup, wondering if I might have a better chance of getting her to talk than Tomio had.

EIGHTEEN
RUDE REDHEAD

Just before eight the following morning, the teams filed into Lecture Hall A. Like a group of trained seals, Arcturus went for the right side of the room, and Firethorne sat on the left. I followed Harriet along the bench seat of the front row, Cecily followed me. Peter and Tomio brought up the rear.

"The group is so much smaller with half of each team gone," Harriet said as we settled on the wooden bench.

"Yeah." I stole glances at the remaining Firethorne competitors. Leaning toward Harriet, I kept my voice low. "Remind me who is who? I know Liu and Eira, but I can't remember the other two."

"The tall guy is Kristoff Skau," she answered under her breath. "I suspect he's Burned. And the other one is Serenamen Hall. I overheard her talking, she has a strong Jamaican accent."

I studied Kristoff as the game-makers entered the hall and headed for the dais. He was tall and lean, slender as a shaft of wheat. Somehow, even with hardly any bodyfat, he still managed to have a babyface. Maybe it was the flat-top haircut.

Serenamen reminded me of a mouse. Cute, and a little on the fidgety side, with bright black eyes that missed nothing. Her hair was a springy nest well on its way to afro-hood. Serenamen had finished the first challenge at just over three hours. Decent but not a threat, although just because someone did well in *Traps, Tools and Time* didn't mean they wouldn't dominate in a different challenge.

"What makes you think Kristoff is Burned?" I asked Harriet. Kristoff had finished under three hours but he'd still been bested by nine other competitors. "I'd be more worried about Liu."

"Oh she's *definitely* Burned." Harriet spoke with respect. "I just have a suspicion about Kristoff. It's his voice. A little froggy, you know."

"Good morning." Guzelköy addressed the group as Davazlar took up his usual position, leaning on the desk.

There was a murmur of good mornings from the students.

Out of the corner of my eye, I spotted Basil and Christy sliding into the seats behind us. Mr. Bunting was already here, seated on the far side of his competitors. There was no sight of Babs. It was remarkable how the woman found so many other places to be at critical moments in these games.

"I trust you're well rested and ready to tackle our next challenge. This won't take long, as not a lot of prep is necessary for this game." Guzelköy rubbed his long, tapered fingers together with barely concealed glee. "Our first competitor will begin at eleven o'clock today

—to be determined by random draw before you are dismissed. For this challenge, we have utilized Headmaster Chaplin's wonderful VR technology. This challenge is structured as a quest game and is titled *Save the Music*."

I exchanged a cocked eyebrow with Harriet. What music had to do with fire magi, I couldn't guess. Although I'd never been a gamer, if I had been, quest games would be more my style than combat games. The combat exercises Professor Knight and Basil had taken me through were enjoyable enough. I hoped that meant this would be fun.

"The entirety of the fire-gym has been converted to the setting of our game. If you were to see it right now, it would look pretty odd, but when you put the VR visor on, everything makes sense. You'll be interacting with the game mostly digitally, but there will be a few features you'll have to interact with physically. It may not always be obvious, but that is part of the charm of the game. We think, anyway."

We listened quietly, absorbing Guzelköy's description. The game-maker went momentarily blank, fumbled at a pocket, and retrieved a crumpled piece of notepaper. He studied it for a second, then looked up, enlightened once again.

"The VR equipment, meaning the visor you'll be required to wear, is robust but sensitive enough that you should be careful. If you have fire or heat in your hands, please don't touch it. Wait until your hands are cool. We have spare visors, but each one is valuable and we don't want to break them. You'll also have high-tech dots fixed to your hands, but those are specially made to withstand high temperatures."

The Firethorne kids whispered and stirred. Their expressions had taken on a veiled excitement. I doubted any of them had been exposed to such state-of-the-art equipment, if the bus they'd arrived in and the uniforms they'd been wearing were any clue.

"The objective of the game is to complete the quest as quickly as possible, but how you tackle each challenge will be graded. A time bonus can be awarded for efficiency in dealing with problems, while penalty minutes can be tacked on to your finishing time for blunders or incomplete tasks."

Guzelköy looked back at Davazlar, who shrugged.

"I believe that is all. And now for the drawing of our first competitors." Guzelköy beckoned to Davazlar, who produced a jar containing folded bits of paper.

He held it up for Guzelköy to pluck from. Guzelköy gave us a sheepish smile.

"Our selection system is not as sophisticated as our algorithm," he joked.

No one laughed, we were too busy holding our breath.

A folded paper was plucked, and Guzelköy drew it open and read the name. He looked up. "Saxony Cagney, you'll be the first player."

There were a few sighs from the group, whether they were in disappointment or relief, I couldn't tell. I nodded and smiled as my pulse picked up the pace.

"Meet me in the fire-gym's lobby just before eleven. That'll give you enough time to digest your breakfast."

"Okay," I replied. "Thanks Mr. Guzelköy."

He nodded and scanned the room. "Any questions?"

"How will the next one be determined?" asked Liu,

shooting a hand into the air. "Will you draw that one from a jar too?"

"No. Saxony will choose a Firethorne competitor, and that competitor will choose an Arcturus student. And so on until the challenge has been completed."

All glanced my way.

"And what about who we're pitched up against?" Harriet asked.

"Our algorithm has already determined that, but once again it will be revealed at the end. Anything else?"

When no one else spoke, he dismissed us with a final instruction. "Please wait in your respective lounges, the next competitor to go will be fetched from there."

We waited for the Firethorne students to file out, since it was their turn to get their food first. I watched Eira as she left but she kept her eyes down and trailed out ahead of the rest of her team, who were talking quietly among themselves. To an outsider, it looked as though she wasn't really friends with her own schoolmates, but maybe she was just very shy. Her behavior fit the bill for that, too.

Following Tomio and Peter as we filed out of our row, we trailed through the halls toward the cafeteria. The Firethorne group lined up at the food station where a sweating Mr. Hoedemaker stood ready to serve.

We gave a collective inhale as the scent of something baked and buttery reached to our noses.

"What is that glorious smell?" Tomio breathed. "Pancakes? Oh man, it's like Victoria Falls in my mouth. Wish we could have gone before them this time."

I agreed but my response trailed away. Eira had been the first to get served. She'd already set her tray at the team's usual table and was heading for the coffee machine next to the drinks fridges. Deciding there wouldn't be a better time, I headed over to the hot drinks counter.

I came to stand beside her, making a show of trying to decide between the flavored coffees, none of which I actually liked. Fake hazelnut flavoring in my coffee? Ick.

Eira noticed me at her elbow but didn't speak. She looked up, tucked a lock of hair behind one ear, and reached for a cup from the stack. She mused over the coffee flavors and picked a cappuccino, but she didn't put it in the machine, she studied the label instead.

"The other one is better, in my opinion." I gestured to the other cappuccino option. "That one is Spanish. The Italian one is nicer."

"Is it bitter?" she asked, her voice timid and soft.

I smiled, pleasantly surprised that she'd even spoken with me. "No. The Italian is very smooth."

She nodded, now studying the stainless-steel jugs sitting beside the coffee machine. "I see skim, one percent, and two percent. There was cream here yesterday."

"Ah, the English don't really do cream, but there's probably some in the fridge. Dr. Price likes cream, so she brings her own. She won't mind. Shall I take a look for you?"

She looked at me, blue eyes wide. "Would you mind? I can't stand regular milk."

"Sure." I left the coffee counter, passing the Arcturus team, who were now being served by Mr. Hoedemaker. Tomio glanced up with an inquiring look as I walked by. I winked at him. So far, so good.

Going to the fridge that held the dairy products, I rooted through the containers and found no regular cream, but I did find a carton of whipping cream. I checked the date, hoping it would make Eira happy. With a wave to Lars on my way out, I took the carton over to the coffee machine where Eira had chosen an Americano instead of a cappuccino. When she saw the carton, she lit up.

"Whipping cream?"

I handed it to her. "Sorry, it's all there was."

"No that's perfect. The fattier the better. I like to eat keto as much as I can, though it's almost impossible with all this Dutch food."

I didn't really care about her diet, but it was an opening, so I pounced. "What's keto?"

Opening the carton with deft fingers, she added a generous dollop of whipped cream to her coffee. She plucked a spoon from the jar and stirred. "You've never heard of the ketogenic diet? It's amazing. It's helped my mum lose a bunch of weight. It trains your body to burn fat instead of—"

"Eira!" Someone screeched, clearly incensed.

She jumped at the sound of her name, sloshing coffee over her thumb.

We looked over to see Babs charging toward us, glowering. I half expected to see steam come out of her ears.

Eira visibly cowed then moved away from me

without saying anything more. She headed for the Firethorne table where her team was watching.

Babs glared at me, putting her fists on her hips. "What were you talking about?"

Anger flared and my fire rumbled, heating me several degrees. "Nothing. It was just two coffee lovers chatting about our favorite drink. Why? Is there a problem?"

Babs raised a finger, not quite pointing in my face, but too close for comfort. I bristled.

"I've got my eye on you," she sneered. Gone was the Marilyn Monroe voice. She sounded like a chronic smoker, a furious one.

She swung her finger around at the Arcturus team, who were watching from near our table. Tomio, Harriet and Peter hadn't even sat down yet, and held their trays in a big-eyed tableau of surprise.

"I'm watching all of you. You leave my students alone. I'll not have you fishing for information, or intimidating them, or using any of that insidious neurolinguistic programming on my team."

I exchanged a baffled look with Tomio. What was she talking about?

My tone walked the line between respectful and sarcastic. "It was an innocent conversation, Ms. Chaplin. Relax. It's not like we were about to sign a blood pact."

It was the wrong thing to say, but I knew that when I'd conjured the words and said them anyway.

Her face turned red. "You will not speak to me in such a way. You are my inferior in every way, and when I am headmaster of this school, the first thing I'll do is teach you some respect."

"If you become headmaster of this school, the first thing *I'll* do is drop out," I shot back.

"Saxony!" Dr. Price stood just inside the entrance to the cafeteria. I hadn't noticed her come in. "That's enough."

Trying to hide the fact that I was so angry I was shaking, I walked past Babs and headed for the stack of trays. My cheeks were burning. Mr. Hoedemaker had been watching the exchange with interest. I set a tray on the rails, took a plate, and slid over to the food.

"Hello, Lars."

"Pannenkoek?" He asked, buttery spatula poised to serve.

"You bet," I said, forcing a smile even as my heart still thundered. "Load me up."

By the time I faced the tables with my tray, Babs was seated with her students, her back to me. Either she was going to wait until I had moved away from the food to get some, or she'd already eaten.

Dr. Price gave me a warning look as we crossed paths, me en route to our table and her en route to the food.

I set my tray beside Harriet's and sat down. Picking up my fork, I cut off a piece of the pancake, which did look and smell amazing. If I'd had more presence of mind I would have congratulated Lars on his baking.

My first forkful paused on the way to my mouth as I realized the team's eyes were on me.

"What?"

"That was so immature," whispered Peter through a huge grin, "and bloody brilliant."

My teammates expressions told me they agreed.

I flushed and took a bite but didn't smile.

Cecily studied my face for a moment before leaning over to whisper: "What are you thinking?"

I chewed and swallowed, glancing over at Babs, who was speaking sternly at Eira.

"I'm thinking that only extremely untrustworthy people are that paranoid."

NINETEEN
SAVE THE MUSIC

At eleven, I met Guzelköy in the lobby of the fire-gym. He was waiting with the VR visor in one hand, and a small square of paper with four glittery, circular stickers.

"Put this on before we go in, Ms. Cagney." He handed the visor to me.

Taking the expensive piece of equipment carefully, I fitted it over my head and pressed the button. It gave a little vibration as it conformed to my bone structure.

"Have you used the VR before?" Guzelköy asked, as he fixed two of the high-tech stickers to each of my hands, one at the base of my wrist on the inside and the other matching its position on the outside.

"Yes, most of last semester in fact. I used it multiple times a week." I grinned. "Why, will that give me an advantage?"

"That depends. What were you using it for?"

"Combat training."

"Ah. Well, there won't be any of that in *Save the*

Music," he said, then seemed to rethink his statement. "Not much anyway. Ready?"

I nodded.

He opened the door and my vision turned a shadowy dark green. Guzelköy became just a dark silhouette.

"Put a hand on my shoulder if you need to," the game-maker said.

"I'm ok." Following Guzelköy's dark form out onto the fire-gym's huge floor, I could barely make out any details. The observation pods were dark shadows near the ceiling.

"Stand here." Guzelköy stopped and turned, putting his hands on my upper arms to guide me to the precise spot. "Davazlar will begin the game in a few seconds. I'm just here to escort you safely to your starting block. I'll leave you now. All good?"

"All good."

"Bonne chance, Ms. Cagney." The sound of Guzelköy's foot falls receded.

A few moments later, the scene of a clearing in a jungle opened before me.

A bright, sunny sky arched overhead. Hard, penetrating daylight illuminated thick foliage. Vines looped and drooped through the canopy. Impossibly bright butterflies flitted from fantasy foxglove blossoms as long as my arm to bobbing daisy heads and butter yellow coneflowers. Whistles and caws of jungle birds and the buzz of insects provided a rich soundscape.

Before me, sitting chest-deep in ferns was a little boy with messy black hair. His posture was stooped and little neck bent as he looked into his lap at something I couldn't see. He sniffed and rubbed his nose. He hadn't noticed me.

"Hi, there." I took a step toward him, parting the ferns with my legs.

The child looked up, startled, then scrambled to his feet. He had something in his hand but put it behind his back before I could make out what it was.

"I'm not going to hurt you." I took another step.

Now that most of his body was out of the ferns, I could see his details. He was naked except for a loincloth. Skinny, dirty, maybe six years old. He looked up at me with eyes a little too big for his face. They were the color of cinnamon bark.

"Can you help me?" he asked, still keeping his hands behind him and staring at me fearfully. His wide eyes gave a computer-generated glimmer of unshed tears.

"I think I'm supposed to." I took another step. "I'm Saxony."

"I like your name," he said. "Saxony."

"Thank you. Do you have a name?"

The child—in a move so realistic it made my heart turn over—rubbed a hand under his nose and sniffed again. The other hand remained behind his back. "Everyone has a name. Mine is Kanvar."

"Nice to meet you. What have you got behind your back, Kanvar?"

The boy reluctantly brought it forward, revealing a stick with five shallow, unfinished holes bored into its side. "It's my toy, but I broke it."

I reached for it, but Kanvar pulled it back, squinting at me with mistrust. "I'll only let you play with it if you agree to help me fix it. When it's fixed, it makes music."

I was at a loss to see how this stick would ever make music. The holes weren't deep enough or large enough to make the stick a flute or even one of those cheap wooden recorders, but this was a game, so... "Okay, how do we fix it?"

He pointed a grubby finger at the half-finished holes. "Things go here. I've lost them."

"Where did you lose them?"

"In there." He turned and pointed.

Like lights coming up in a Broadway play, the face of a temple ruin emerged from the undergrowth. Crumbling stone steps, broken pillars, the roots of massive trees entangled the old bones of the building, well along in the process of swallowing it completely.

Beneath a pillar that had fallen to rest on the side of its still-standing neighbor was a dark, triangular hole. The only visible way in.

I walked forward for a better look. The VR background swung around along with my vision, pixilating a little before resolving into perfect smooth detail again. I headed for the entrance, then paused, looking back at the kid.

"Are you coming?"

A frightened gleam passed over one of those big brown eyes and he winced. "Kanvar is afraid of the dark."

I smiled. Not just because he'd referred to himself in the third person, but because his phobia reminded me of Gage. My heart gave an ache of longing. I wished that he would be waiting for me when I got out of this game.

Kanvar gave another of his patented sniffs. "Be careful in there."

"Thanks, little buddy." I ducked to pass through the small opening.

Inside, was a circular, dome-shaped room. The ceiling was cracked in places, broken up by plant-life and time. Tree roots protruded, winding their way around the stones and choking the windows. The distant call of birds came in from outside. Shafts of light penetrated here and there, lighting what was obviously the first challenge of the quest.

Angular blocks of stone sat throughout the room, the tallest of which came up to my waist. I counted twelve all together, positioned around the perimeter like the numbers of a crooked clock. The top of each block came to a sharp angle, but each angle was unique. Each block had been draped with a piece of canvas. The canvas didn't touch the floor, only covered the top half of the block. The base of each block was a perfect circle. What looked like purple felt had been stuck to each bottom. They were like modern chess pieces, but too similar to function properly for a game, plus there weren't enough for a game of chess, and no checkerboard pattern on the floor.

The floor was perfectly smooth and shone like a brand new, stainless-steel countertop. It didn't go with the temple ruin atmosphere at all, it was too modern, almost space-age.

As I looked down, my own reflection looked up at me. When I reached the center of the room, I rotated in a slow circle, studying the set up and trying to figure out what the task was.

An electronic sound drew my attention to the wall, where between the trunks of two gnarled roots was a recessed shelf. Coming closer, I saw that a small box sat in the shelf, but when I reached out to take it, another electronic sound told me that I didn't have the right to take the box. At least, not yet.

Just above the cubby was a curious round button or panel. It was the size of the face of a large wristwatch, and it had concentric circles leading to a central point. It looked like a bullseye with a strange shimmery quality.

Continuing my turn about, I noticed another strange feature directly across from the box in the wall. Outside the ring of blocks with canvas coverings was something I recognized easily. It was a spindle for quenching or pitch.

It had been set to stand freely in a shelf of stone and beside it was a rectangular box, much taller than it was wide. I picked up the box and inspected it. The bottom of the box was open, and the inside was hollow and full of zigzags of light. A tiny hole in one side let in light that reflected back and forth inside the box. It had to be lined with mirrors.

Frowning, I put the box down, standing it on end. It was a little taller and a little wider than the spindle. I picked up the box again and slid it over the top of the spindle. It covered it completely.

Moving back to the center of the room, I gave it another going over. Aside from the covered stone blocks, the shimmery bullseye, the untouchable chest in the wall, and the spindle and mirrored box, there was nothing else in the room.

Walking over to the nearest angled block, I touched the canvas to see if I could take it off. It lifted easily away with a digital sound, then vanished, revealing that the top of the angled part of the block had been fixed with a mirror.

I moved to the next block and took that canvas off. It too, had a mirror fastened to its angled top. My pulse sped up as I glanced at the shimmery bullseye. I thought I understood.

Circling the room at a fast walk, I yanked the canvas coverings away one after the other. Giving one a test push, I discovered the blocks slid along the floor easily with a satisfying whooshing sound. They even went a short distance on their own, like tall curling stones.

I rubbed my hands together and stoked up my fire as I returned the quenching spindle. It could give heat, but it could also receive heat, and that's what was needed here. Putting my hands on it, I poured heat into it until the metal began to glow a dim red. I increased the temperature until it was glowing a bright, supernova yellow.

Moving quickly, because the moment I let go the light would begin to fade, I put the mirrored box over the spindle. A beam of light as fine as a laser shot from the hole in the box. It hit the stone wall and a black circle began to expand upon contact, accompanied by a sizzling sound.

Kicking the nearest block into the path of the beam, I spun it so the beam hit the mirror. The laser snapped to a right angle and began to burn a hole in another wall.

Soon I was sweating as I ran around the room trying and discarding the mirrored blocks as they shot the laser around at crazy angles. Ordering the blocks to send the laser into the bullseye was the goal, but it became apparent that there was only one order that would work. I lost track of time as I rotated each block through the light, analyzing the direction it sent laser in. I had to return to the spindle when the light became too pale, take off the box, heat it up to brighten the light, replace the box exactly the way it had been placed, and go back to work.

When the light beam finally struck the shimmery bullseye, I held my breath. A crack reverberated through the room as a spiderweb fracture appeared in front of the chest. The virtual glass crumbled and I reached in and grabbed the decorative box.

Flipping it open, I discovered a chime, the sort found dangling from the wind chimes on millions of porches throughout the world. It dangled on a thin chain connected to a screw. This must be one of the broken parts of Kanvar's toy, then. It was meant to screw into the stick. For a moment, I wasn't sure what to do with it.

Did I return to Kanvar? Did I pocket it? I drew the chime toward my pocket and it blinked out of my hand, but appeared in the top right hand corner of my vision, hovering there and slowly rotating.

When nothing further happened I turned my attention back to the box and found a little slip of ribbon jammed into a seam. I tugged on it and a false bottom lifted away.

Holographic shapes drifted into the sky before my face, transparent and rotating slowly, just like the chime. They were symbols, but crude ones, and not any that I recognized. They consisted of right angles only, like the letter H or E, but they didn't make letters.

I reached up to see if I could grab one, but it zipped up into the left hand corner of my vision. I guessed they'd be important later. They settled into a string of five icons in the corner of my vision and triggered the next step. A stone-on-stone grinding noise drew my attention to the wall, where cracks had formed. The fissures started slowly and began low, at floor level. Then the fractures sped up, sending chunks of broken rock skittering across the smooth floor and revealing a narrow passageway.

Approaching the entrance, I ducked inside.

THE SOUND of crackling fire reached my ears before the visual reached my eyes. Emerging from the short, narrow passageway into the next room, I immediately recognized it as an old-fashioned forge. It was cute and fantastical, with an asymmetrical brick arch over flickering, banked coals. The fire danced and crackled, hovering over the coals but not touching, as if levitated by magic. A large red bellows with fine black trim gleamed from a peg on the wall. Overhead hung unfinished pieces of armor, weapons, handles, horseshoes, even what looked like wrought-iron bed posts. A half-built suit of armor graced one of the corners, while opposite it was a matching set of armor for a horse, majestic in its size.

Along the wall to the left of the fire was a bank full of drawers. Instead of handles, each face had a blank rectangle depressed into its surface. Beyond the drawers was a thick-barred gated door, the kind you'd expect in a medieval jail. Crossing to it, I gave it a tug. It didn't budge but there was a keyhole.

I explored the room further, charmed by the off-kilter design, but feeling urgency growing in my gut. The task was not yet clear.

I went to the wall of drawers, discovering a small black shape imprinted on the top right hand corner of each drawer. They were silhouettes. One outlined like a blade, another a throwing star, another a scythe. Every shape was a weapon except for one. One was a simple line, stamped onto the wood at a slight angle. Squinting at it, I could make out the thin chain with the tiny screw on one end. It was a chime.

When I touched the drawer, the blank rectangular recess flipped over to reveal glowing words: *What is it that when given one, you'll have either two or none?*

A riddle.

I tried the next drawer. Its panel flipped over as well, reading: *It cannot be seen, it cannot be felt, it can't be heard, nor can it be smelt. It lies behind stars, it lies beneath hills, it ends life, and laughter kills.*

I flipped a few more panels. Each of them had a unique riddle. I couldn't find a place to input an answer. Fingering the edges of the drawers, I felt for buttons, notches, grooves or tiny levers, but there was nothing but smooth faces and the flippy panels with the backlit letters. Perhaps I only needed to speak the answer.

Returning to the drawer with the chime stamp on it, I reread the riddle. Hopefully I wouldn't have to solve all these riddles, because that might take days. I wasn't particularly good at riddles, but I'd had a teacher in elementary school who had loved them enough to spend a whole week trying to teach us the kind of out-of-box thinking required to solve them.

I read the riddle aloud, which was the first step the teacher had assigned us. She'd said there was often something in the phrasing itself, a collection of words which would sound familiar, especially when spoken, that might trigger the answer.

"What is it that when given one, you'll have either two or none?"

My mind shuffled through possibilities and rejected them just as quickly. It couldn't be something tangible, it had to be something metaphorical or abstract. A concept.

I gnawed at my lip. My armpits felt damp. An answer seemed so far away. If I didn't get this riddle, then I wouldn't get that chime.

I closed my eyes and read the riddle aloud again. The words 'when given one' were close enough to another familiar phrase: when given a choice.

"A choice," I said aloud.

The chime's drawer popped open and I grinned, some of my anxiety diminishing. Progress felt good.

Pulling out the drawer, I found it removed from the wall completely. Carrying it over to the anvil on the workbench in the middle of the room, I set it down and opened it. There was a chime tucked inside. I picked it up and brought it close to my pocket. It flew to join its rotating fellow in the top right corner of my vision.

I examined the box for a false bottom or secret compartment, but there was nothing else inside. Putting it back into place, I looked around the room to see if anything had changed. At first it seemed like nothing had changed, then I noticed another set of drawers beneath the forge itself that hadn't been obvious before. These drawers each had an icon as well. They were lit up with a blue glow, and the shapes were familiar. A glance to the top left side of my vision confirmed these shapes were from the same alphabet as the holograms I'd taken from the first room.

There were five symbols in the top left hand corner of my vision, but many more drawers and symbols available to choose from. So the ones I'd been given told me which drawers to open.

I found a drawer that had a matching symbol and opened it. It slid open smoothly to reveal a mold. The depressed cavity matched the symbol on the outside of the drawer. Glancing between the top left hand corner of my vision and the bank of drawers, I pulled out all five.

Laying them side-by-side along the top of the workbench, I studied them. Three had grooves which ran right off both sides of the mold. If I were to pour molten metal into them, the liquid would dribble out. But the other two only had grooves on one side. When I lined up the grooves they looked like the teeth of a key.

I sucked in a breath as it became clear. I had to forge a key to open the gate. I looked for a chunk of metal to use, and grabbed a horseshoe. Heading back to the forge to put it into smelting pot, I paused. Was I supposed to melt the metal for real or as part of the game? There were digital flames here, as well as a bellows, but I was also in the fire-gym. It would have been easy enough for Guzelköy and Davazlar to set up a hafnium basin for the purpose of melting. But if there was a hafnium basin, I couldn't see it because my vision was obscured by the VR. I decided to ask the game.

"Am I supposed to make this key for real?"

In answer, the digital fire flared brightly.

"Okay, then."

I tossed the horseshoe into the smelting pot and set it in the coals. Pulling the bellows off the wall, I set the mouth into the coal and pumped oxygen into the fire. It growled and flared, liquifying the horseshoe much more quickly than I could have done in real life. A satisfying bubbly sound effect came on when the iron turned liquid.

Carrying the smelting pot to the molds, I poured it slowly into the cavities, watching as it ran through the grooves of one mold to the next until it filled the last mold, the square key-fob. I returned the smelting pot to the forge and came back to watch it cool. I didn't have to wait long. The key hardened with a little audio accompaniment that sounded like a cartoon bubble bursting.

Dumping the key into my hand, I went to the gate and put it in the lock. With a click then a grinding sound, the gate hoisted itself upward.

I walked through, feeling rather proud of myself.

The sound of wind wailed above my head as I emerged in a very tall, crumbling gothic structure. Sort of like a cathedral but without religious paintings or stained-glass windows, pews or pulpit. There were a lot of dark shadows and cobwebs drifting back and forth in a breeze I couldn't feel.

I shivered as my footsteps echoed on a flagstone floor made of octagons. The honeycomb pattern spread before me, huge and broad. Countless pillars stretched high overhead, arranged in a scattered and disorganized way and connecting overhead like the ribs of some huge animal.

Something caught my attention way up near the ceiling, glinting and sparkling. It was difficult to make out a such a distance, but it couldn't be anything other than a chime. It was so high that couldn't reach it, even detonating my hardest. I adjusted my visor, wondering if there was a way I could magnify what I was seeing. Pressing the little button on the side did nothing.

I'd answered the riddle with my voice, maybe I only had to ask?

"Magnify view," I said aloud.

A hundred thousand tiny red eyes appeared—in every dark shadow, in the narrow darkness between every pillar, and beneath every lopsided curve and arch. I gasped and my hair stood on end.

Suddenly, the air was filled with flapping, screaming creatures. Sharp little teeth flashed as they dive-bombed my head.

Bats! Zillions of them.

I swung at them as they attacked. While I couldn't feel them, I knew they were hurting me as a life-bar appeared in the bottom left hand corner of my vision, flashing red and diminishing in size.

Punching out at the bats knocked out very few and only by luck. They were so fast and there were so many of them, I would soon die a digital death at this rate.

Panting, I ran back to the safety of the forge. As I ducked into the short passageway between the forge and the eerie cathedral built by a drunken architect, I was relieved to see the bats couldn't follow me. They threw themselves against the invisible wall dividing the forge from the cathedral, screaming and gnashing their horrible little teeth, red eyes glowing. But they soon gave up and flew away, leaving me panting and holding a hand over my pounding heart.

I'd need a weapon after all. Those drawers and riddles weren't just there for show. Feeling humbled and sheepish, I returned to the forge to face the riddles.

TWENTY

HOODED STRANGER

I stood before the drawers, contemplating the options. While I was more knowledgeable about weapons now, thanks to Alfred, I was still no expert. Some were more tools than weapons, like the pick-ax and the sledgehammer. Others were more obscure, like throwing stars in a variety of shapes, long-handled broad-swords, hunting knives, and axes. Drawn to a medium length Roman-looking sword, I flipped the panel for the riddle, and read: *Different lights do make me strange, thus into different sizes will I change. What am I?*

After a minute's consideration and coming up blank, I stuck my tongue out at the riddle and flipped the panel for a set of brass knuckles.

Only one color, but not one size, stuck at the bottom, yet easily flies. Present in sun, but not in rain, doing no harm and feeling no pain.

The phrases 'stuck at the bottom' and 'present in sun but not in rain' flicked the answer out of my brain like a tiddly-wink.

"Shadow," I said aloud.

A sound effect like a bolt sliding back accompanied the riddle panel flipping over by itself, exposing a handle. I pulled the drawer out of the wall. Inside was not a set of brass knuckles, but the mold to make one.

I left the mold by the forge to scan the ceiling for a piece of metal. Selecting a gauntlet, I returned to forge, melted it down in the smelting pot, and poured the liquid into the mold. When the first set was finished, I repeated the process.

Sliding them over my fingers, the digital knuckles triggered the life-bar to re-appear in the bottom corner of my vision.

I ducked through the gate, knocking the knuckles together as I emerged in the cathedral. A metal-on-metal clink sent a shower of sparks onto the cathedral floor. A loud clank made me whirl as the gate crashed to the floor. I didn't have time to be frightened at the prospect of being locked in here because the clank woke up the legion of bats. The red eyes appeared, the screaming began.

Hands clenched into fists, I brought them up into a fighting stance and glared at the oncoming mass of wings and teeth and sharp little claws. Swinging wildly and with abandon, my vision flashed with red and digital blood splatters. It was a little on the gruesome side, but satisfying all the same. My own blood was up, my heart pumping as I used little internal detonations to speed up my attack. Flying around like a tornado, fists with gleaming brass knuckles glinting in the dim digital light, I sent bat bodies everywhere, splatting against pillars, dropping to the floor, even exploding into shards like the shadow-men in the capture-the-flag game. My own life-bar shrank a little, but the weapon I'd ended up with did the trick.

When the aerial attack diminished, I swung around, panting and sweating, looking for more of the hideous little creatures. They'd vanished, even the bodies and blood, but something new emerged in the middle of the room: an octagonal cylinder had risen out of the floor. It stood almost as high as I was tall.

My vitality bar disappeared, and so did the digital knuckles, as I approached the cylinder. This was a modern gadget, an octagonal tube made of something transparent. Peering through the transparent side, I realized it contained a liquid—that looked a lot like water, and that the container descended far enough below the floor that I couldn't see any bottom.

No instructions or hints about the purpose of this cylinder appeared. I examined it for cracks, buttons, panels with riddles, anything I could interact with, but there was nothing.

I lay a hand on its side, then pulled back with a startled cry. The cylinder wasn't a graphic, it was real.

Putting a hand on its side, I drew heat down my arm and sent it into the cylinder, slowly and gently, not pushing too hard. The liquid inside didn't appear to change, but jets of digital steam shot from the cracks between the octagonal stones in the floor. I yanked my hand back, startled at the outcome. Then I applied heat with fresh vigor. The water inside the cylinder began to bubble.

Steam hissed from the floor, jets of it sprouting up like a fountain in front of a Vegas hotel. A few of the stones lifted, protruding from the floor. When I withdrew heat, these settled back down to level. When I increased the heat, the stones jutted up further. A staircase was being revealed.

With renewed heat, I boiled the water and kept the temperature high. Octagonal-shaped steps emerged from the floor, leading to the sparkle near the ceiling. It was the most treacherous and narrow staircase I'd ever seen, tall and without much surface area, but it would be enough.

Only, when I took my hand away from the cylinder and there was no steam to keep the steps aloft, they began to sink. To succeed would require exceptional speed. If I'd been more skilled with tele-combustion, maybe I could have kept them aloft for longer but I'd have to do the best I had with the skills I'd developed.

Pouring the heat on to give as much steam as possible, I gathered myself to sprint. Body tense, I eyed my target, then took off, fire detonating in every joint. Taking the narrow steps at high speed and feeling them shake beneath my pounding foot falls, I loosed a cry as the steps at the top dropped. The gap between the last step and the chime grew by the millisecond.

I met the falling steps and took the last one with a giant leap and a powerful detonation. I flew toward the chime, hand outstretched, grabbed it, then plummeted toward the floor. My stomach lurched as I fell, then bounced as I cushioned my landing and dropped into a roll. I popped up and landed on my feet, breathless but triumphant.

I brought the chime to my hip and it went spinning to join its fellows.

A low arch appeared in the cathedral wall, an unseen light source glowing from within. Ducking my head to pass through, I emerged in a primitive throne room.

An old wooden bench overgrown with vines circled the deteriorating wall, facing a pedestal in the center. Over the pedestal hovered my prize, another chime. A glass bell-shaped lid sat over top of it. I went to the pedestal and took the handle to remove the dome. My eyesight faded and turned red. When I let go, my vision returned.

Stepping back, I examined the pedestal more closely. Vines twisted and gnarled up its sides, but between the leaves I could make out something metallic. The leaves and vines came away easily, littering the floor with greenery. Removing the plants revealed flippy panels with riddles on the underside, just like the ones in the forge. Below each panel was a series of dials with numbers and letters on them.

I sighed, hoping I wouldn't have to solve all the riddles in order to get at the chime. There five panels altogether.

Homing in on one panel, I counted eight dials beneath it. Each dial ran through the numbers from 0 to 9 and the alphabet from a to z.

The riddle read: *I conduct electricity and heat like a boss. Over time, I grow green as moss.*

If I'd been as digital as this game, a eureka bubble would have appeared over my head.

"Thank you, Basil, for making me memorize the properties of metals until I was blue in the face," I said as I rotated the dials one by one to the atomic number 29. Following that, I rotated the dials to spell copper.

The moment I put the r into place, the sound of a

crack echoed through the room. A spiderweb fracture appeared in the glass over the chime.

Moving to the next panel, I flipped the panel to read: *I am necessary for all life, including batteries.*

This answer also had eight dials. I'd already used copper as an answer, so I doubted it would be required twice, but just to check, I set the dials to 29 and copper. Nothing happened. Lithium wasn't necessary for all life and it was too long anyway, but cobalt would fit. I wracked my brains for the atomic number. Cobalt wasn't a metal I had focused on as much as others, but the answer eventually came into my mind and I ran the dials into place.

Another crack appeared in the glass.

If all these questions were about metals, then I might be through this challenge faster than expected. Cracking my knuckles, I moved to the next question. This one had eleven dials. The question read: *I am beloved by astronauts, but depleted by stars.*

Aluminum and titanium were both used in spacecraft manufacture, but while aluminum fit the dials with an atomic number of 13, titanium didn't fit and didn't have anything to do with stars. Beryllium was a possible option, but with an atomic number of 4, it didn't fit the dials either. Since no other metal came to mind, I turned the dials to read 04 beryllium, and grinned when another crack appeared.

Two riddles to go.

The answers to both flew from my fingers with ease. The first (*I am noble*) and the second (*I make rainbows*) might be difficult for the average person to answer, but not for someone who'd been working closely with platinum and bismuth for a whole school year.

As I entered the last letter, the glass shattered apart. I grabbed the chime and put it into my pocket. It flew up to rotate beside its three fellows.

Kanvar's stick had had five little holes in it. I had four chimes, so one left to go.

Nothing changed about the room, but the sound of echoey footfalls started low and grew loud. A man's legs appeared beyond the arch.

He ducked under to pass through and when he emerged and stood up straight, my neck creaked looking up at him.

He was a huge. Broad, muscular, and wearing a cape with a hood. The hood was up and obscured his face completely. All I could see of his features was the tip of a black beard, the rest was swallowed in shadow.

He wore a tunic, a thick leather belt, and gloves that went halfway his elbow. A pouch hung from his belt. dangling along one thick thigh. Tall black pirate boots came up to his knees.

He folded his hands in front of his belt buckle and looked at me, or at least, pointed his hooded face in my direction.

"Hello," I said, butterflies swirling in my gut.

"What are you doing here?" His deep voice reverberated.

"I'm looking for something," I replied, wishing those brass knuckles hadn't vanished.

The man hadn't made any offensive moves but his presence was aggressive and more than a little sinister. I hoped I wouldn't have to fight this character. I had no weapons, and neither did he, at least none that I could see, so that had to be a good sign.

He lifted one gloved hand toward the pouch at his

side and produced the last chime. "Is this what you're looking for?"

I gulped. "Yes."

The chime disappeared back into the pouch and he resumed his relaxed stance. "Tell me my name and I'll give it to you."

I gave a start and my mind began to scamper back through the game. Why would I know this character's name? There had to have been a clue somewhere along the way that I had missed, perhaps back in the cathedral? The forge had closed but the cathedral was still accessible, only I'd have to go around the hooded man. I didn't want to try that if I didn't have to.

"Can you give me a clue?"

"No name. No prize," the giant rumbled.

I walked slowly toward him, heading a little off-kilter, just to see how he'd react. His shoulders and the black hole of his face kept square to me, turning as I walked to his right, and turning back when I headed to his left.

"What's my name?" he repeated.

"Adam?" I guessed, taking a few steps closer.

The hooded figure threw his head back and laughed. Some light penetrated his hood and I caught the glint of an eye and a row of straight, white teeth. His laughter faded and as he straightened and closed his mouth, all that remained in view was the tip of his beard. I saw nothing that triggered any memory. He didn't look like either of the game-makers, even Davazlar, but maybe it was worth a guess. If I made him laugh then maybe I'd catch another glimpse of his features.

"Demir Davazlar," I ventured.

The hooded man didn't laugh this time. His voice was a glower. "Are you making fun of me?"

"No." I replied hastily, eyes on the pouch.

If I couldn't think of his name, then maybe I could snatch the chime out of the pouch. I was only six feet away now. Peering up into the stranger's face only gave me a black hole. He had to throw his head back for me to see any detail at all.

I thought of a name that I'd always found amusing, maybe it would make the character laugh again, give me a better look at his face.

"Mortimer?"

He lifted a gloved finger and cocked his head. "You are wasting my time. Do you know my name, or not?"

I came to stand within reach of him, my body tensed to jump back or duck if he took a swing at me. If I kept guessing, I'd soon be in trouble. I needed to go back and scour for the clue I'd missed.

"If you wouldn't mind stepping to the side," I said, politely, "I'd like to get by."

The figure bent at the waist, bringing his black hole of a face almost level with mine. He raised his hands to his waist and fisted them there. "Make me move, little girl."

I was startled by a sudden idea. Little, popping detonations flew along my arm as I snaked out a hand. Grabbing the back of his hood, I yanked.

He gave a startled roar and I jumped back, lifting my hands in a fighting stance. His hood fell back, revealing a handsome pirate face. Thick black hair, high cheekbones, tanned skin, that black beard and ... eyes the color of cinnamon bark.

He cocked a fist back to hammer me.

"Kanvar!" I yelled.

The figure paused, his fist in the air, then he vanished with a faint 'pop.' His cloak and clothing, gloves and boots, landed in a lumpy heap. Beneath the cape, something moved.

Heart thumping, I yanked the cloak away.

The little boy version of Kanvar huddled there. He was crouched in a ball, wearing that same dirty loincloth. He looked up at me with a sad face, those big eyes shining with tears.

I fumbled in the heap for the pouch and retrieved the final chime. The moment my fingers touched it, Kanvar's face transformed and he got to his feet. The chimes in the corner of my vision swept forward to hang in the air before us. Kanvar produced the stick, and we arranged the chimes on the stick in order of the smallest to the largest.

"You fixed my toy!" Kanvar danced in place with a child's glee. "Do you want to hear its music?"

"Absolutely," I replied, smiling at the digital boy who looked almost but not quite real.

Kanvar ran a finger along the chimes, making them knock against one another. The sound of wind chimes came and the boy dissolved away.

The fire-gym came into view as the digital background faded. Lifting the visor off my face, I blinked around, adjusting to a drearier atmosphere than the one I'd just left.

I could see the steps and platforms I'd walked on during the game as well as the honeycomb pattern in the floor, the octagonal cylinder and the pitch spindle, but all the other details had been the result of the computer.

Guzelköy approached, hand out for the visor. I handed it to him and held out one hand, then the other, as he removed the dots.

"Well done, Ms. Cagney. Dr. Price and Headmaster Chaplin will escort you to the professor's lounge where you can clean up and rest. Who would you like to go next?"

"Eira Nygaard." Her name came out of my mouth before I even stopped to think about it. The anticipation of waiting for one's turn to arrive was worse than the actual games themselves. After this morning's painful interaction, I wanted to spare Eira that small discomfort. If Guzelköy had asked me why her, I couldn't have explained it.

But the game-maker didn't ask for an explanation. Just said, "Very good."

He escorted me to the door where Dr. Price was waiting.

I thanked Guzelköy and sent a wave up to Davazlar, whose huge hulking shape was visible through the window of the first observation pod. He lifted a hand in response.

Two challenges down. Would I make it through this round to see the third?

TWENTY-ONE

HALF-TIME

"Ready?" Cecily poked her head into my room as I finished trading my slippers for sneakers. I joined her in the hall, seeing the backs of Peter and Harriet as they headed for the stairwell.

"Are you nervous?" I asked as I twisted my hair into a low bun and wrapped an elastic around it. Cecily had been the final Arcturus competitor, so we hadn't had a chance to chat yet.

"Not really. I don't expect I'll have made it to the next round to be perfectly honest. All that metals trivia did me in—it's never been my favorite subject. It was a fun game, though. The effects were amazing. What a great investment for Arcturus, or Fireth—"

"Don't say it," I snapped. "Sorry, I don't mean to snap. Just a little on edge."

"Fair," Cecily replied. "I would be too in your position."

I considered whether I wanted her to elaborate on what she saw as my position, but we'd reached the lobby where students were gathering. The game-makers had moved us out of the lecture hall and into the big lounge area in the foyer to announce the results of the quest. Maybe they preferred the more casual atmosphere. They had erected an easel in front of the fireplace upon which rested an oversized pad of paper.

Basil and Dr. Price leaned against the wall near a front window, while Babs and Mr. Bunting stood behind the couches. Serenamen, Kristoff and Liu had taken one sofa while Eira sat cross-legged on an ottoman. Harriet and Peter occupied a loveseat facing the window so Cecily and I took the two wingback chairs in front of Basil and Christy. I sent Tomio a smile where he sat on the stairs.

"Morning, everyone," Guzelköy began.

A few of us muttered a reply.

"The results of the quest have been tallied. As you know, both time and tactics were important for this game. Each task was assigned a value in points, against which you were given a grade. The grades you were assigned resulted in either time being knocked off or time being added. Just like the first game, an Arcturus competitor was pitted against an unknown Firethorne competitor. We'll reveal those first."

Davazlar lifted the first page off the pad to reveal the list of competitors.

Though we could read them all for ourselves, Guzelköy read them out loud.

"Harriet Ashby went up against Serenamen Hall. Peter Toft against Kristoff Skau. Saxony Cagney against Liu Xiaotian and Cecily Price against Eira Nygaard."

I glanced at Liu, who winked at me. I looked away. Coming from her, the gesture nettled me. It would be very satisfying to wipe the smug look off her face. If

Liu and I had been at the same school, I didn't think we'd be friends. The thought drew my eye to someone I thought could have been a friend under other circumstances. Eira's eyes were on the game-makers, her hands folded neatly in her lap, her doll features serene.

"On to the results." Guzelköy produced a thick black marker from a pocket inside his coat and handed it to Davazlar.

"Harriet finished with a total time of three hours, four minutes."

Davazlar scratched out the times next to Harriet's name, looking oddly charming scribbling on a pad of paper like a preschool teacher.

"Serenamen Hall finished slightly ahead of Harriet—"

There was an intake of breath.

"But lost points in the bat cave and closed out at three hours and twelve minutes."

There was a sigh of disappointment from the kids on the Firethorne couch. Peter took Harriet's hand and lifted it into the air. She yanked it down, blushing but smiling.

"Peter Toft finished with no time added or removed at three hours and eleven minutes," Guzelköy continued. "While Kristoff Skau finished slightly behind that, but had time knocked off for his excellent handling of the mirrors. His final time was three hours and seven minutes. Congratulations, Mr. Skau."

The Firethorne kids applauded. This time Harriet took Peter's hand to comfort him.

"Next we have Saxony Cagney, who, thanks to performing very well at metals, knocked five minutes off her time. She finished at two hours and forty-nine minutes."

There was a smattering of applause.

"Liu Xiaotian gave us a record-breaking performance but took penalties in the mirror challenge for a final time of two hours and fifty-three minutes."

Liu gave a hiss and I covered my mouth to hide a smile. She'd had a better time than me, but thanks to spending so much time on metals this past year, I'd edged her out.

"And, finally. Cecily Price took a penalty in the bat cave to finish at three hours, thirteen minutes. While Eira Nygaard gained points in the forge to complete the quest at three hours, eleven minutes."

So, Cecily was out and Eira was in.

A collective breath eased the tension in the room and the defeated shifted in their seats, no doubt wanting to get back to their summer holidays. The victors were still, hoping for details about the next challenge.

"Well done. Even those who were disqualified performed well." Guzelköy said. "For the third round, we have finalists Harriet Ashby, Eira Nygaard, Saxony Cagney, and Kristoff Skau. The rest of you are dismissed, unless you want to stick around and hear about the next challenge."

Liu got up from the sofa like someone had pressed an ejection button. With her nose in the air, she disappeared down Victory Hall. No one else moved.

Unbothered by Liu's rude departure, Guzelköy crossed his arms. "The details of the next challenge are mostly finalized, all that remains is to build it. It will run in five days and will be an escape room."

I pressed my lips together as my nerves twanged. I'd never been a fan of enclosed spaces. The escape room craze had exploded without any participation or appreciation from me. Now I regretted never having done one with my friends. I wasn't entirely clear on what it entailed, but I had time to do some research.

"We'll have two identical rooms constructed. You will begin at the same time as your competitor. Whoever escapes first, wins. Very simple. The title is: *What Waits for No One.*"

He let that sink in before continuing. "You'll notice laborers and craftsmen coming in and out of the school over the next couple of days. We've advised them to use only the fire-gym entrance so they won't be in your way, and we'd appreciate it if you would stay out of theirs. Speaking to you is a breach of their contract and will result in their immediate dismissal."

We agreed not to speak to their construction team, and were released.

PART THREE
UNEXPECTED OUTCOMES

TWENTY-TWO

A BLAST FROM THE PAST

I had just finished drying off after a shower and was wrangling my hair up into a topknot when a knock came at the door. I was in underwear and a tank top so I hollered that I'd be right there, grabbed a pair of jeans and wiggled into them. I zipped up my fly and opened the door to find Dr. Price with a take-away cup of coffee in her hand.

"There are a couple of surprise visitors in the front lobby for you." She gave an enigmatic smile. "Don't ask me who, I'm not supposed to say."

My heart leapt. Could it possibly be Targa or Georjayna? It was unlikely to be Georjie, since I'd seen her a couple of weeks ago, but I hadn't seen Targa since last summer. She had access to a pilot and a private jet and it would be like her to drop in unannounced. If there were two visitors, maybe I'd finally get a chance to meet Antoni in person.

I thanked Christy and grabbed a button-up sweater from where it lay on the bed. Pulling it on over my tank top, I slid my feet into a set of cheap flip-flops I'd bought in Dover. Since I hadn't planned to be here over the summer, I hadn't had much in the way of summer clothes or shoes.

The flip-flops thwacked out a staccato beat on the bottoms of my feet as I took the corridor at a fast walk and descended to the lobby. I emerged with a hopeful smile but came to a dead stop, recognizing the woman looking out a front window, even from the back.

"Elda!?"

The lady I had au-paired for in Venice last summer turned, revealing her youngest where he'd been hidden in front of her.

"Isaia!" I smiled and crouched, opening my arms wide.

A grin overtoook his face. He ran across the carpet and wrapped his arms around my neck, his cheek pressed against my ear. He was still small, but he felt so much more resilient than when I'd first met him.

Tears pricked behind my eyelids. Seeing the boy who had passed his fire to me was a shock to my emotions. I'd become good friends with the family last summer, but had only exchanged a couple of emails with Elda since then. I never really expected to see any of the Baseggios again.

"What a surprise." I stood and met Elda's eyes as she approached, shifting her designer bag from one shoulder to the other.

We hugged over top of Isaia, and when I released Elda, he slid his fingers into mine, sending a look of adoration up at me. He hadn't said anything yet. Part of me was frightened for a second that he'd lost his voice again.

"How are you?" I asked him. "Comé stai?"

"Cristiano went to Trentino with Dad," he replied in his soft Italian accent.

I laughed. "And you came to England with your Mum. How do you feel about that?"

Isaia gave a shy smile and looked at the floor.

"He's been talking about you a lot lately," Elda said, then directed her next words at her son. "You can see she's fine now, can't you? You don't have to worry."

I knelt in front of Isaia. "You've been worried about me?"

His gaze flashed to my torso and up to my face again.

"The fire doesn't hurt me anymore," I said. "Is that what you were worried about?"

He nodded.

Kristoff and Eira passed through the lobby, studying us.

"Come on, let's move into the lounge where it's quiet." I led them into the nearest lounge. "Can I get you something to drink?"

Isaia wanted water and Elda asked for tea so I directed them to sit at the couches close to the windows while I fixed the drinks at the sideboard.

"What are you doing here?" I asked, setting Elda's tea and Isaia's water on the coffee table. "How did you know where to find me? Even I didn't know I was going to be in England this summer."

Elda stroked Isaia's hair. "I had meetings scheduled in London and since Pietro and Cristiano are in Northern Italy for the week, I thought I'd bring Isaia with me. He's been asking when we would see you next. Enzo told me about this place and I called ahead to see if you were still here."

I looked at her with alarm at the mention of Enzo.

Attending Arcturus had been Enzo's suggestion to me when we'd made our deal, but I hadn't known that he'd been in touch with the Baseggios. Enzo had told me he would leave Elda and her family alone.

"Has he been bothering you?" I gripped the edge of the sofa.

Squirrel-chatter from outside drew Isaia to the window. Elda leaned over and touched his back. When he turned, she pointed out the library shelf across the room.

"Why don't you see if there are some nice books on that shelf, darling?"

He moved away, going for a little expedition on his own.

When he was out of range, she answered sotto voce. "Not bothering, exactly. But he did give me a bit of a fright. Possibly he didn't intend to frighten me."

I frowned. "I highly doubt that."

Enzo was head of the oldest and most powerful family in Venice. He wouldn't admit to being mafia, not even to his own men, but if it walks like a duck and sounds like a duck...

"He came to the villa," she said in a small voice.

My nostrils flared. Enzo never did himself what he could send a man to do for him. Visiting Elda's home bordered on an act of terror in my opinion. "What for?"

"He wanted to see Isaia. I think he still doesn't fully believe that there's no fire left in him."

"That's ridiculous." It took effort to keep my voice

down. "How can he think Isaia has fire when I'm here at fire mage school?"

She shrugged. "We non-supernatural folks are clueless when it comes to these things. He wanted to see Isaia for reasons beyond my understanding, but my guess is that he wanted to remind me that if you don't come through on your part of the bargain, I'd still be on the hook. It put pressure on me, to put pressure on you, I'm sorry to say."

My tummy shriveled. "Why? I understood that he'd cash in his chit after I'd graduated. I still have another two years here." I kept to myself that I had hopes to graduate in one. I wanted to delay paying this debt off for as long as possible.

She sighed. "I don't know what goes on in that man's mind, but when Enzo shows up at my door with his eyes on my son and his mouth running off small talk, something is up. He didn't look good. He's aged. Whatever is going on in his life, it's a rough patch. Maybe he's considering you for something, and wanted to make sure what we owe him hasn't been forgotten."

"What *I* owe him, Elda," I reminded her, not liking the worry on her face. "Our deal was that he'd forget he ever knew Isaia as long as I did him a favor. He won't go back on that, it wouldn't even make sense for him to go back on it. Isaia has nothing to offer him, Nicodemo's son or not."

Elda nodded and took a sip from her teacup, glancing at Isaia. He'd taken an atlas from a bookshelf and was flipping through it, the big book balanced on his lap, feet sticking straight out on the sofa.

"Is that why you came? To tell me that Enzo is gearing up to cash in?"

"I don't know, Saxony." She sighed and rubbed at her forehead. "I came because I was close by, and because Isaia wanted to see you. It wasn't enough to tell him that you're fine, that you're no longer in pain. He wanted to see you with his own eyes. Now that he has, maybe he'll stop nagging me." She raised her gaze to mine. "And I wanted you to be aware that something is going on in Enzo's life. I don't know what, but it might spill over into yours and I wanted you to be forewarned. I think that's why he came to our villa. He'd rather *I* gave you a heads up. It's not his style to do it himself."

I chewed my lip. I didn't have time to be concerned about Enzo right now. We were halfway through the games. I had to focus on getting Arcturus clear of Babs.

"How are you, really?" Elda asked. "How is"—she rolled her gaze around the lounge— "this place? Is it good for you?"

"Yes. I'm mostly happy here."

I told Elda about my classes and the developments leading up to the games, watching Isaia with one eye. When he was finished his journey through the atlas, he wandered around the room, looking at the paintings. He seemed especially drawn to the ones featuring fire. I wondered how he felt about fire now that it wasn't part of his life. When he'd made his circuit of the room and came back to us, I asked him if he was happy.

He nodded, leaning into his mother's side.

"Do you ever think about your fire?" I asked, laying a hand over my rib-cage.

He nodded, dropping his gaze to my hand.

"Do you ever wish you still had it?" I held my breath while he thought about his answer, but I wanted the truth.

I wondered if one day, a grown-up Isaia might have regrets about giving away his fire. But then, if he hadn't given away his fire, he'd never have become a grown up. Still, the mind had a funny way of looking back through rose-colored glasses. Maybe he'd forgotten how close to death he'd come and missed his flickering companion.

Eventually, he shook his head. "It's better if you keep it."

"So you're happy you gave it away?"

"I'm happy because Mum and Dad are happier now. I can do more things. I can play football," he said stoutly. "I'm as good as Cristiano."

I grinned, knowing well that Isaia was nowhere near as talented as his older brother with a football. Just the thought of Isaia running around after a ball was startling. I'd only ever seen him play with Lego, do puzzles, read or draw. Now he was living the life of a healthy seven-year-old.

As long as Enzo stayed away from Isaia, the Baseggios' life was perfect.

Almost perfect.

As Isaia moved away again, drawn by voices coming from the lobby, I asked Elda how things were between her and Pietro. She'd had to admit to her husband that Isaia was the result of an affair. An affair with a now deceased fire mage, Nicodemo. Poor Pietro had had no idea why his son was so sickly or why he'd lost his voice, until Elda made a full confession. After a period of uncertainty, Pietro chose to stay in the relationship. They'd agreed to counseling, but I was sure it was still a bumpy road.

Elda told me that their marriage was up and down, that there were days Pietro had locked himself in his office and wouldn't speak to her, or where he didn't answer his phone all day. But most of the time he seemed okay. She didn't think he'd fully forgiven her but she had hopes that one day he would. Her concern was that when the boys grew up and left home, Pietro might leave too.

"It keeps me focused," she explained, watching as Isaia leaned on the doorjamb and observed the goings on in the lobby. "Relationships take effort. In the beginning, everything is easy and exciting, but time passes, and soon real work is required."

I nodded, thinking of Gage with a stab of longing and dismay. We were supposed to be enjoying the exciting phase, but we couldn't with the fire coming between us. If it was this difficult already, how could we last long enough to reach the hard work phase?

"Hey there little man." Tomio appeared in the doorway, looking down at Isaia. He smiled at me, then Elda. "This one is yours, I take it?"

"Hello. Yes, that's Isaia. I'm Elda." She waved.

Tomio waved back and Isaia ran to his mother's side, suddenly shy. Tomio grinned and disappeared.

"Friend of yours?"

I nodded.

Elda cocked a brow. "More than a friend?"

I laughed. "No. He's more of a sparring buddy."

"Have you *got* a more-than-a-friend?" Elda squeezed Isaia in to her side, he melted into her and yawned.

I nodded. "But he's not here right now. Funnily enough, he's in your country."

"Really?" Elda's interest kindled.

"Not in Venice, though. In Naples."

I told her a little bit about Gage, editing out the details of why he was really there, and telling her that he was on working holiday with his mum. Elda was charmed. She thought the idea of a guy in his late teens going on holiday with his mum was the most adorable thing she'd ever heard and that she hoped Isaia and Cristiano would want to holiday with her when they were older.

We spent another hour chatting and then Elda stood and stretched, looking at her watch. "I have a dinner meeting somewhere in Angel and I'm not sure about the navigating the tube. Also, I need to get Isaia back to the hotel and settled with the babysitter, so I'd better catch the next train."

I walked her and Isaia to the front door and hugged them both goodbye, feeling weighed down by the feelings their visit had triggered, not to mention the questions. After their cab drove away, I sat on the front step of the school, listening to the birds and lost in my own thoughts. I don't know how long I was there before Tomio found me.

"What was that all about?" he asked, sitting down beside me.

"That was the boy who gave me his fire," I replied, pressing my hands between my knees. "His mum says he's been wanting to see me and she was in London for business, so they popped out to Dover. I haven't seen them in almost a year."

"That was him, huh? What a cutie."

I nodded.

"How did it feel to see the original host of your fire?"

I tucked a hair behind my ear and looked at Tomio.

"I'm just glad he's healthy and that he doesn't want it back."

"You babysat him for a summer, right?" Tomio's brow wrinkled in the glare of the noonday sun.

"Yes."

"So you got pretty close?"

"Somewhat."

He looked down at his sneakers. "Still, it seems a little strange. You're not family or anything. You haven't talked to them for ages and suddenly she's here at the school?"

"It's more complicated than that. We're still ... entangled."

"What do you mean?"

I let out a long breath. "Elda cheated on her husband with a fire mage named Nicodemo. That's how Isaia came to be. He was an accident."

Tomio absorbed this in silence.

"Her husband, Pietro, had no idea what was wrong with their little boy. When Isaia passed his fire on to me and started to speak again, Elda had to tell Pietro the truth."

"Sounds complicated."

I pulled out my topknot and raked it back up again with quick, almost violent movements. I hated thinking about what the Baseggios and Isaia had been through.

"Before Isaia was born, Cristiano, Elda and Pietro's oldest son, was kidnapped while Pietro was out of town. They're pretty well off, the Baseggios, so some wise guy thought to hold Cristiano for ransom. Everyone in Venice knows of Enzo Barberini, and Elda went to him for help."

"Bloody hell," Tomio muttered. "Not the police?"

"In Venice, going to Enzo is basically going to the police, their invisible head, if you catch my meaning."

"Okay. Things are that corrupt there?"

I nodded and carried on, not bothering to say that things were that corrupt everywhere. In Italy, the further south you went, the worse the corruption became.

"Enzo sent his fire mage, Nicodemo, to rescue Cristiano. When he delivered the boy back to Elda, they fell for one another. It all happened very quickly. Her husband was away, and she was emotionally fraught. She accepted ... comfort from Nicodemo."

"That's one word for it," Tomio murmured.

"She wanted to pay Enzo back for his help but he wouldn't take money or even shares in her company. He said he'd let her know what he wanted at some later date. Fast forward to after Isaia was born and Nicodemo died during an attempted Burning. That's when Isaia lost his ability to talk."

Tomio's eyes widened.

I left out the fact that the Burning which had resulted in Nicodemo's death had been facilitated by Dante, Enzo's only son, and that Dante was the one who had locked me in a cell, hoping to bring me close enough to death that I would pass him the fire which Isaia had passed to me, in exchange for water.

"Enzo found out that Nicodemo had a son through these video clips he'd recorded before he died. Enzo went to Elda and told her that's what he wanted."

"The video clips?"

"No, the son."

Tomio blinked. "What do you mean?"

"He knew from the clips that Isaia was Nicodemo's

son, and likely a fire mage. He wanted to take Isaia and train him up. His only fire mage was dead, and in his line of work, which is not exactly clean as the driven snow, he could use a supernatural. So he told Elda he would take Isaia when he was a little older, as payment for rescuing Cristiano."

Tomio shook his head, horrified. "That's barbaric and insane."

"Yep. So when Isaia gave me his fire, I went to Enzo and made a deal. He would forget all about Isaia, who was now useless to him anyway, and I would owe him one favor."

"What favor?"

I shook my head. "I have no idea. I just told him I wouldn't break any laws."

Tomio raked both hands through his hair. "Whoa."

"Yeah. So Elda showing up here isn't just a random visit. Enzo went by her villa. Elda thinks he did it because he might need to cash in his chit, sooner rather than later."

"That's crazy, Saxony."

I wrapped my arms around my knees. "You know what is even crazier? Enzo is the reason I'm here at Arcturus. He said I needed training before I would be able to do any work for him."

"How does he know about Arcturus?"

I shrugged. "Maybe Nicodemo told him, I don't know, but Enzo gave me Basil's card. That's how I came to be here."

Tomio let out a long breath. "That's heavy stuff."

I nodded, thinking that it was only some of the burden making me weary; he didn't know about the problem between Gage and me. I'd never told Gage about Enzo or Isaia but here I was spilling my past to Tomio. A flash of irritation stifled the guilt. If Gage had been back by now, then I'd be sharing this with him, not someone else. So whose fault was it that Tomio and I were becoming closer?

TWENTY-THREE

WHAT WAITS FOR NO ONE

"Here is your blindfold, Ms. Cagney," said Guzelköy, handing me a black silk scarf. Beside me stood Kristoff, taking his scarf from Davazlar.

We stood outside the fire-gym, just the four of us. I fixed the blindfold around my head and felt Guzelköy's hand loop under my elbow. The door squeaked as he opened it and led me inside. He guided me across the neoprene floor and directed me to the left of center.

He stopped me and guided one of my hands up to feel an edge of wood. "You're standing in front of an open door. Step inside, walk forward three paces. When I close the door behind you, you may take your blindfold off. Wait thirty seconds before you light any fire."

I nodded, hearing Davazlar relay similar instructions to my competitor off to my right. Guzelköy released my elbow, and I shuffled forward, finding the door's sill with the toe of my shoe. Stepping over it, I walked forward and felt a whoosh of air as the door closed.

The sound of a ticking clock came to my ears.

I pulled the blindfold off, not that it made much difference in the pitch darkness. Putting my hands out in front of me, I felt only empty air. I took another step forward. My shoe scuffed on what sounded like a wooden surface with nothing below it, a floor over a layer of air. Something brushed against my hip. I brought my hand down and brushed my knuckle against something hard and cold. Grasping it, I felt a round railing, like a ballet barre. I followed that until my hand knocked against a vertical post. Running my fingers up this post I stumbled onto an object; a smooth glass surface with a rounded belly with narrow pipe-like top. The glass gave a soft clink and shifted under my fingers, so it was moveable.

Thirty seconds had surely passed but I waited a little longer just in case before snapping my fingers to light a flame to see by.

The darkness retreated. What I had touched was a kerosene lamp, right in front of my face and fastened to the wall.

Lifting the glass top off, I held my flame to the wick. It flickered to life. As I put the top back on, a whooshing sound accompanied the lighting of a dozen other lamps throughout the box. They lit one by one rather than all at once, illuminating more and more of the room.

I was in a replica of an old-fashioned clock tower. The sound of a ticking clock made sense but it should have been a lot louder considering I was within a few feet of a complicated tangle of gears and cogs.

It had two stories. The bottom floor was connected to the top by a narrow vertical ladder leading up through a small square hole. Four massive clock faces, in reverse because I was inside the tower, surrounded me, one face in each wall, now backlit by a blue-white light. Each face had matching elegant roman numerals, and was ten or twelve feet across. None of the clocks read the same time. As I stood there gawping at the details of my surroundings, the minute hand of the one to my immediate right moved with a click. The other minute hands stayed put.

So, bring all the clock faces to match the one clock that was working? It was a good bet, but I wanted to explore further for more details before taking any action.

In the center of the first floor sat the complicated mechanism. Cogs, gears, chains, pulleys, and a zillion nuts and bolts all came together to make a tinny and quiet ticking noise. Cables ran from the mechanisms to another set of gears and cogs overhead. Through the hole leading to the second floor I could make out the shining curved surface of a bell.

Passing the mechanism to look behind the ladder, I found a little bedroom. A small single cot made up with an army-issue woolen blanket sat beside a collection of furniture. Beside the bed, a crate sitting on its side held a neatly stacked collection of books and vinyl records. On top of the crate sat an antique gramophone with a bright green bell. On the other side of the bed was a sideboard with a set of cupboards and drawers. I tried them and found them locked.

I left the clock-minder's bed to do a full circuit of the bottom floor and found a fire hose behind a locked glass door as well as a wooden panel on one wall, near the floor. The panel didn't budge. Near one of the frozen clock faces, on a thick vertical beam supporting the second level, was a keypad. The keys were distinguished by colors and skimming my fingers over them confirmed that I could depress them. I left them for now and completed my circuit.

Climbing the ladder, I poked my head through the hole to confirm the presence of a large black-lacquered bell with a matching hammer, poised to strike at the top of the hour. Climbing the rest of the way up, I found the platform was connected to a wooden beam about six inches wide. Wide enough to walk along. The beam ran the perimeter of the room, though not equidistantly from the walls. It ran close enough to one clock to reach the minute hand, but too far from the other clock faces to reach without help.

I crawled over the metal railing encircling the bell and inched my way along the beam, arms out for balance. When I reached the clock face whose minute hand I could touch, my eye was drawn to a square patch of color painted on the reverse of the minute arm. It was bright pink and within the pink square was painted a black number one.

I eyeballed the minute hand and reached out, slowly to keep my balance, and applied some pressure. The minute hand did not budge one way or the other. Running my eye down the minute hand to the central point of the clock face, I discovered why. A clamp had been bolted to the arms to keep them from turning. The only way to get the clamp off was to either melt away the bolt and nut or find a wrench of the appropriate size. Either way, I couldn't reach the bolt from the beam, but I might be able to reach it if I stood on the railing of the walkway that ran around the perimeter of the room, a structure that was lower than the beam I was standing on.

I made my way down to the first floor and lifted myself up to stand on the railing of the walkway, tricky, since it was tubular. Stretching up, I could just reach the bolt and found it fastened much too tightly for even fire-mage fingers to turn. I hopped down to continue the search.

Passing a clock face on my way to the inspect the bedroom area more closely, I paused to see if it too had a bolt preventing its movement. It didn't have a bolt, but it did have what looked like a marble jammed into the space between the base of the minute hand and the hour hand. It also had a colored square and a number painted on the back. This one was white with the number zero, or it might be the letter 'O'.

I returned to the bedroom and began to snoop through the books and records, flipping through pages and peeking into the cardboard record cases. Painted on the fabric back of an old copy of *The Time Machine* by HG Wells was an orange square with the number seven. Paging through the contents didn't reveal any secret notes or hidden pockets.

I went through the vinyl records, checking the pockets for clues and skimming the titles. There was *I'll Never Smile Again* by Tommy Dorsey, *Chattanooga Choo Choo* by Glenn Miller, *Rag Mop* by The Ames Brothers. I paused when I found one that stood out, *The Longest Time* by Billy Joel. Not only did it have "time" in the title, it belonged to an era newer than the rest, which were all from the forties and fifties.

I dropped the record out of its case and into my hands. Placing it on the gramophone, I moved the needle to the starting position. Nothing happened, there was no power. I sat back on my haunches with a frown, blowing a strand of hair out of my eyes. There was no obvious way to turn the thing on.

Then I noticed something strange beneath the plate. Small scoop-shaped indents, all with the same concave curve, like little spoons, running around the base of the gramophone's plate. They triggered a memory.

We had a wood stove in our basement back home in Saltford, and while it was great to have wood-fired heat during the cold, damp Atlantic winters, we found that the side of the room with the stove would bake, while the heat wouldn't make the journey around the corner into the rec-room, leaving it too chilly to enjoy. Also, the air near the ceiling would make our foreheads gleam with sweat, while our feet would still be cold. My dad intended to have a ceiling fan installed but it fell down the priority list until finally, in aggravation, my mom had ordered a heat-powered fan to circulate the air in the basement. This turn-table had similar scoops to the ones that ran that fan, only these were smaller and there were more of them.

Pushing heat into the end of my finger, I held it near the turn-table's edge and smiled when it slowly began to turn. Lowering the needle onto the record with my other hand, the doo-wop sound of Billy Joel's hit crackled from the bell in a too-slow, drunken drone.

As I pushed more heat out through my finger, the song sped up. I increased the heat until Billy Joel sounded more like himself. The tune made me smile as I looked around the room, watching for something to be triggered by the music. When a bang went off behind me, I gave a startled scream and then laughed when I realized the sideboard's drawer had popped open.

When I moved away from the gramophone, Billy Joel's singing began to deepen and slur. I pulled the drawer open to find not a wrench, but a crank handle. Even better.

I skipped over to the clock face and crawled up on the banister. Slipping the socket over the bolt, I fired up the power in my right arm and applied pressure to the handle. The bolt came loose. Spinning the handle around and around with a finger, the crank and the nut fell away and into my other hand. The metal clamp slipped off and fell to the floor before I could catch it. The ticking sound increased in volume as the minute hand moved with a click.

Craning my neck to check the time on the only clock face that had been functioning when I first arrived, it read nineteen minutes to twelve. The hour hand of this clock was stuck at six, so I had to make several revolutions of the minute hand to get the hour hand past eleven. Bringing the minute hand up to match the other clock, I jumped off the banister.

Two clocks aligned. Two to go.

I returned to the bedroom to hunt for more clues, inspecting every record and book. There were no more titles alluding to time, neither songs nor stories, and no more items with colored and numbered squares. I stripped the bed and looked under the mattress, inspected the sideboard and crate-table and the little wooden chair sitting in the corner, but found nothing more of interest.

My stomach knotted up as the sound of the clocks began to wear on me, a constant reminder that Kristoff was in the other escape room hunting for clues, just like me.

Returning to the second level, I discovered that I could reach the chains that dangled near the bell. Pulling on them revealed a pulley linked to a track that ran out over the nest of gears. Even so, no clear task emerged.

I needed to figure out what the painted squares and numbers were all about. They had to be connected to the keypad of colored buttons, but those buttons had no numbers on them. So I was looking for something which would give me numbers, or a sequence of colors. Maybe I had to punch the corresponding colored keys in the order each color was given. The highest number I'd found was seven. If there were seven digits in total then I could assume I had four more squares to find.

I'd found two of the colored squares on clock faces, so I descended the ladder and went to a clock face I hadn't inspected well enough yet. Sure enough, on the back of the hour hand was a blue square with the number two. My pulse quickened as I went to the other clock face, scouring it for a colored patch. But there was nothing.

As I stepped back and bit my lip, scanning the room, a glint inside the fire-hose box caught my eye. I knelt in front of the glass for a closer look. The yellow hose had been wound around a familiar metal shape: a pitch spindle. I tugged on the glass door, but it was locked.

Impatient, I decided that it was time to move things along and put my hand against the glass panel. I turned it into goo and watched as it rolled down toward the floor, hissing as it went. Then I reached in and lifted the fire hose. The whole thing came away. It wasn't attached to anything, it was just a prop, but as the last of the hose emerged there was a sliding sound, then a click. The pitch spindle slid forward and began to glow.

I put my hand on it. It ratcheted itself up into the two-hundreds, then the five-hundreds, then past the thousand-degree Fahrenheit mark. It finally settled and stopped changing at 577.7 Celsius, and 1072 Fahrenheit.

I grinned and let out a little whoop. This was my code, it matched the numbers I'd found. There couldn't be any more colored squares to find because the temperature only had four digits.

I crossed to the keypad, flipped up the cover and punched in the sequence of colors. One, zero, seven, two. Pink, white, orange, blue.

There was a metallic popping sound that made me jump as the end of a floorboard flipped up and bounced in the air. Heart thumping, I went over to look in. Lying beneath the floor board was a long-handled, elegant-looking hammer. It had a small brass head and an arched handle as long as an umbrella. Brows pinched, I reached in and picked it up. As I inspected the end, I realized it was exceptionally narrow for a hammer. Just the size of a marble, in fact.

Carrying it over to the clock face with the marble jammed between its two hands, I crawled up onto the banister and balanced myself. Shifting the grip to hold it toward the end, I stretched out and gave the marble a tap. It popped out, flew over the mechanism, bounced off the wooden floor and rolled into the seam between the wall and floor.

Dropping the hammer, I spun the minute hand

around and around until this clock face matched the other two: eight minutes to twelve. With a mechanical click, it began to keep time. The ticking was quite loud now.

I hopped down, eyeballing the final stopped clock. Going to stand beneath it, I craned my neck to look between the two hands to try to see what was keeping it from moving.

There was nothing visible blocking the clock's movements, in fact as I was watching it, the minute hand tried to click forward but succeeded only in vibrating in place.

Running my gaze out to the end of the minute hand, I spotted a wire that stretched to the ceiling. The other end of the wire was too buried in shadow for me to see what it was attached to.

This clock face was too far from the banister for me to reach. But, if I could ride the chains along the track, I might be able to get close enough for a better look.

Climbing up the ladder again, I crawled over the banister and hung on with one hand while I stretched out for the hanging chains. Wrapping my fingers around the cold metal, I gave a tug. It held fast to the track fixed to the ceiling. Gingerly, I transferred my weight to the chains, wrapping my legs around and hooking a toe into a link. The moment my weight had transferred, the pulley squeaked and the chains moved along the track. Very slowly.

Inching my way up to the top of the chains, I reached overhead and hooked a couple of fingers on a rafter to push myself along. The track was not well-oiled, so progress was slow and noisy, but when I hit the end of the track, I was close enough to see that the wire was wrapped over a rafter and twisted back on itself.

Eyeballing the wire, which wasn't very thick, I drew back on that internal elastic, snapped my fingers and sent a bullet sized fireball flying. With a crackle, it struck the wire. Sparks flew but extinguished before they struck the floor. I repeated snapping until a section of the wire began to glow, then I aimed a bigger fireball at the minute hand.

With a snap and a hiss, the wire broke. The minute hand bounced and vibrated. A few seconds later it gave a tick to show me it had been freed.

Using slow-burn in my shoulders and back to combat the fatigue growing in my body as I hung there, I craned my neck to see the time. I only had to move the minute hand three quarters of a rotation to bring it in sync with the others.

Sliding down the chain to where I could swing, I used my weight to pendulum close enough to the minute hand to reach it with an outstretched foot, giving it a downward shove. The hand spun and stopped at the quarter to noon mark—thirteen minutes short.

Sweat beading on my brow, I shifted on the chains and began to swing again. This time I gave the minute hand a kick to send it up to the eight minutes to twelve mark. It now only five minutes behind the other clocks, but now I was out of range. My legs simply weren't long enough.

I blew a raspberry, thinking of Kristoff's long limbs, and eyed the rafters. Some were I-beams while others were basic two-by-eights. An I-beam passed overhead, running parallel to the track. Using slow-burn to shimmy up the chains, I stretched out and hooked my fingers around the narrow flange of the I-beam. There was only five centimeters of metal to grab, but fire oozed into my knuckles and locked them in place as I swung the other hand up to hook the other side.

Releasing my legs from around the chains, I lifted my knees a little and shuffled along the beam, hand over hand. My knuckles locked and unlocked systematically, bringing me close enough to the minute hand to reach it.

Leaving one hand locked on the flange, I reached out and grabbed the minute hand. Hoping for some sign that I'd reached the end of the game, I nudged the minute hand into sync with the other clock faces, then dropped to the floor.

Other than the ticking sound increasing in volume, nothing happened. Frowning, I double checked that all the clocks were in sync. They were, and I counted myself lucky that there was no second hand that needed fiddling with.

I stood there chewing my lip and looking around the small room for more clues. The time was now three minutes to twelve. I'd used the keypad, the fire-hose panel, rifled through all the furniture, and used the gramophone. What else was there? Looking up, I scanned the rafters and balcony, chains and track. My eye fell on the bell as the minute hands clicked over to two minutes to twelve.

Taking the ladder back up, I inspected the inside and found nothing amiss. I ran my fingers over the hammer and up the arm to the inside hinge, discovering a small metal disk wedged there. I couldn't see it, but I could feel it.

The minute hands clicked forward, one minute to noon.

Every clock tower in the world marked the top of the hour. I assumed this escape room clock would be no different, but what would happen if the hammer couldn't move?

Running my fingers over it, the little metal disc felt like a penny. My mind raced as the seconds seemed to grow loud, counting down the time to high noon. The penny had to go and there was no time left to do anything other than melt it away. The bell was cast iron, with a melting point only a few hundred degrees higher than copper.

I felt the penny soften as I channeled all my focus into a tight prescriptive combustion. *Burn the penny, not the bell.* As the liquid copper began to drip, I caught it in my other hand to keep it from dribbling onto the bell. I pulled the heat out of it, cooling into a lump in my palm. The last of the penny oozed away.

Not wanting to risk temporary deafness if I could help it, I vaulted over the banister and cushioned my landing with detonations as the hammer struck the bell.

A shaft of light appeared across the floor as the first bong sounded. Dazed, more from the sudden and unexpected appearance of light than the game-maker's version of the sound of Big Ben, I shook off a bit of vertigo.

The light was coming from beneath the panel. At the second bong of the bell, the panel scraped upward further, thickening the shaft of light. The smell of the fire-gym drifted to my nose and a distant voice came through.

As the third bong lifted the panel further, I dove

forward and crouched in front of the opening. It wasn't big enough for me to fit through, yet.

BONG.

It lifted another three inches.

BONG.

One more and I could squeeze through. Peering into the space behind the panel revealed a square shaft about ten feet long.

BONG.

Head first, shoulders scraping along the sides of the narrow shaft, I army crawled through it. When I spilled out on to the floor of the fire-gym, sucking in air, the bongs of the bell were muffled.

Guzelköy appeared out of nowhere and helped me to my feet. "Well done, Ms. Cagney!"

I got to my feet and oriented myself. The fire-gym was almost its old self, with the exceptions of two black boxes the size of small two-story houses taking up part of the floor.

"Is he out?" I dusted myself off, looking for evidence that a square hole had been opened in the side of the other escape room. I hoped his shaft would be larger than mine, otherwise he'd never fit through.

"No. You've beaten him. But all his clocks are in sync, so he should be out any moment."

"What happens if he doesn't get the penny out before the clock strikes twelve?" I asked as Guzelköy escorted me to the fire-gym's doors.

"Then he has to figure it out before the clock strikes one. Best run along. Dr. Price is waiting for you."

TWENTY-FOUR

HOW IT SHOULD FEEL

"It's because of Babs, of course." I said as I followed Tomio into the quiet gloom of the CTH. It didn't help that it was raining again and the skylights let in a cold, diffuse light like that of a dreary evening, even though it was before lunchtime. I flicked on one set of lights.

"I know, but I thought if Babs wasn't around, maybe she'd loosen up." Tomio rolled his neck and shoulders as we walked into the middle of the nearest dojo. He'd doubled his efforts to get Eira to talk after she'd beat Harriet at the escape room. "I found her by the vending machine at the end of Victory Hall and tried to chat her up while we were alone. When she went down to the beach for a walk, I did my best to appear as though I, too, like to walk the beach in the rain, and oh why don't we walk together?"

I laughed at his impression of himself trying to be flirty and appearing ridiculous.

He smiled, but shook his head. "I've never made such a fool of myself before, even for a girl I liked. She barely even looked at me. Just hurried away like she thought I was going to mug her."

"Babs has really got her scared." I stretched out my shoulders and quads, getting ready to tune up my muscles.

Tomio dropped forward and stretched out his hamstrings, putting his face into his shins and folding himself in half so perfectly it was painful to watch.

I worried my lower lip with my front teeth as I thought about my enigmatic opponent for the last challenge of the games. Guzelköy and Davazlar were neutral and anal with their rules, I trusted them to run a fair tournament. I didn't see how anyone could pull one over on the game-makers. "Do you really think they're hiding something?"

Tomio straightened, his cheeks flushed with blood as he rolled his eyes. "Is a frog's butt watertight? Of course they are."

"But Eira is still in the game, meaning she hasn't broken any rules. So how do I prepare for a fight with someone who might have unknown abilities?"

Tomio swung his limbs into a relaxed fighting stance, his eyes gleaming. He beckoned me with his fingertips. "Do what you do best. Use your strengths."

I blew out a breath and let my body arrange itself into the fighting stance that felt the most natural. Then I moved forward into an attack, unleashing a flurry of punches and kicks, invading Tomio's space.

He blocked them fluidly, always defending, letting me warm up and work myself into a rhythm. As our dance took us fluidly across the floor, I turned off the stream of mental chatter and relaxed into my body, letting my energy flow. The sensitivity of my skin increased, power from my fire became soft and fluid, yet throbbed pleasantly in my joints.

Tomio was a blur of limbs, a flash of dark eyes here, a glimpse of white teeth there. When he took me down, I rolled into it, using momentum to carry me out of trouble. When I took him down, he carried me over with him, taking the lead away from me before giving it back. We circled the mats, swept over every corner, and filled the CTH with the sound of expelled breath, thuds of body contact, and high-pressured sighs. We were heat and thunder, a rolling undertow, flying dancers.

And suddenly Tomio was kissing me, propelling me backward across the mat, all sparring forgotten.

My world tilted and my stomach jumped up to the base of my neck in surprise. A different kind of heat rushed through me, turning the power in my joints into melted marshmallow. The feeling of his lips on mine, his skin on mine, shook me. My mind guttered and whirled. The sensation of being kissed without any fire to numb it lifted gooseflesh across my arms and back. It filled my belly with a liquid warmth that had nothing to do with supernatural flames.

And then I was kissing him back, pressing myself into him as his arms wrapped around me, his hand cupping the back of my head. We shared exhales and inhales and my heart rose and rose and rose. Kisses with Gage didn't feel like this.

Gage.

Tomio broke the kiss. He stepped away and I felt bereft, if my skin could cry out for that touch, it would have keened.

We looked at one another. I shuddered as Tomio's eyes widened. He lifted a hand to his lips, horror rushing into his face. "I'm sorry. My—what have I done?"

I put a hand out and wanted to say that I was sorry too, but I couldn't talk, and was I sorry?

"Tomio." His name came out on a husk of sound.

He shook his head, covered his eyes. "I didn't mean for—"

He backed away, eyes wide and full of shame. His expression was a knife in my gut.

"Wait," I croaked.

He turned, mumbling apologies. Then he was a figure outlined in the open doorway, then he was gone.

My skin prickled. My knees were shaking, my thighs—so full of power a moment ago—felt like pudding. I sank onto the mat, landing on my knees and sitting back on my heels. I lifted fingers to my lips, where the feel of Tomio's kiss still lingered. I had felt everything. Every cell had been awoken. His warmth, his sweetness and softness, his breath. I felt it all, and, while my brain stalled, my body wanted more as I relived how the kiss felt. With no fire in the way, it had been amazing. Or was I just so unaccustomed to the feeling that all it took was a simple kiss from someone with whom I didn't share a bond, to unleash this flood of feelings?

And then the guilt came raging forward, teeth bared.

My phone rang, muffled and distant yet louder than thunder.

The first ring brought me into the present. The second ring had me scrambling to my feet and running across the mat. On the third I had my phone gripped in my hand, thinking wildly that it was probably

Tomio, calling from across the villa. He'd come to his senses and wanted to talk. I was so sure, I didn't even look at the screen. The answer button blazed before my eyes. I slid it to the right and held the phone to my ear.

"Hi—hello?"

"Saxony."

It wasn't Tomio, and my hands were shaking. "Gage?"

"How are you?" He was smiling. I could hear it in his voice.

"Good. Good. I'm great. How are you?" I straightened and my knees popped, scrambling to orient myself mentally. I put a hand to my forehead, wondering if my brain was still there or if it had packed up and gone. Bye-bye, see ya.

Gage chuckled. "Did I catch you in the middle of something? You sound like a stunned arse. Where are you?"

"I'm in the CTH. I was training with Tomio, but he's—he just left, I'm training by myself now." Did that sound as stupid to him as it sounded to me?

I should tell Gage what happened, just put it out there in the open. It just happened. I hadn't intended for it to happen and I didn't think Tomio had either. Our lips just—*just what? Tripped over one another and liked the feeling so they kept on tripping? Is that what you're going to say? Don't be stupid. You can't tell Gage that you kissed Tomio, or that Tomio kissed you. Not now, not over the phone. You're distraught. You're confused.*

You're a cheater, screamed a high-pitched, hysterical voice. *Cheater! Skank! Cheap, tarty cheat!* The voice howled, pointed its long invisible finger with a very sharp nail on the end of it.

I gulped, suffocating.

Gage was talking. "...Pompeii, but it was so freaking hot you could fry an egg..."

The words 'fry an egg' seemed to echo. They came through the phone into my right ear, but then entered a second time in my left ear ... from outside the CTH.

Gage appeared at the door. He put his hands out in a little ta-da gesture, his phone in one hand, still connected to mine.

I dropped my phone, my heart convulsing.

He swept me up in a hug and buried his face in my hair, inhaling. The room spun and, somehow, I gathered my eyeballs and swallowed the shock.

"You're here!"

"I missed you." He kissed my neck three times and little explosions followed every one, flowering under my skin and making the base of my skull feel damp.

"I missed you, too."

He pulled back and smiled into my face. I smiled back, tremulously.

The last ten minutes had been the emotional equivalent of getting hit by a Mack truck. Guilt and shame sizzled in my stomach as I took in the familiar features of Gage's face.

I had to tell him. I owed him honesty. I opened my mouth to begin but didn't know how. I couldn't just blurt it.

"In the end, we had to leave Ryan there. At least for now." Gage wrapped an arm around my waist and led me toward the door. "But it'll be okay, I think. Mom feels better just having seen him, and I do too."

I blinked. I'd missed something. He'd said something to transition the conversation over to Ryan and I'd missed it.

"Really?" I said, just to not be silent and weird.

I stopped to pick up my backpack. Gage began to talk about meeting Ryan at a café outside of some palace called Caserta where they'd filmed scenes for a Star Wars movie.

He took my bag and slung it over his shoulder, chatting, not having a clue about the status that simple gesture raised him to among his kind. Gage was a gentleman, a sweetheart, a selfless and amazing being who didn't deserve to be lied to or cheated on. I had to tell him. I *would* tell him.

Just as soon as I figured out how and when to say it.

TWENTY-FIVE

A DISADVANTAGE

Gage and I walked into the cafeteria that evening for dinner, his arm around my waist. Cecily and Dr. Price occupied one table and the rest were empty. Mr. Hoedemaker stood in front of the food, wearing his signature chef's hat and apron. Bless him, he made such an effort to present himself as a professional, even when there was hardly anyone to serve.

"Where is everyone?" asked Gage, releasing me as we reached the stack of trays.

"The Firethorne students have all gone home." I took a tray and slid it along the rails, walking in front of Gage. "Babs whisked them away the same day they were disqualified. It's been like that since the beginning."

"Do you think they wanted to leave? I'd want to stick around for my teammates, if it were me." Gage's words slowed down as we reached the steaming trays and the smell of fish reached our nostrils.

"I'm not sure Babs cares much what her students

would prefer," I replied before smiling at Lars. "Hello, Mr. Hoedemaker."

"Kibbeling?" He asked, picking up a set of tongs.

"Yes, please." I handed him my plate.

Gage leaned into me and lowered his voice. "What's kibbeling?"

"Battered fish. Holland's equivalent of fish and chips, basically." I'd come to know the dishes Lars made most often.

With our plates loaded, we went over to join Cecily and Christy.

Gage pulled out a seat and sat down across from me. "So the Firethorne kids have gone home, haven't any of the Arcturus competitors stuck around?"

Cecily reached for the salt and pepper shakers in the middle of the table. "Yes, Tomio is still here."

Christy speared a piece of fish with her fork and dipped it in the tartar sauce Lars had made. She sent her daughter a look of surprise. "No, he's not. I saw him leave in a cab only half an hour ago. Maybe he's just off on an errand but I don't think so. He had luggage."

My fork froze on my way to my mouth.

Christy noticed. "You didn't know?"

I set down my bite and stalled for time as I took a sip of water. If I admitted that Tomio hadn't said goodbye, then I'd have to come up with a reason why. Everyone knew we were good friends. If I just told them we'd had a falling out, then that would lead to more questions.

"Yes, I knew," I lied, pressing my napkin to my lips though I had yet to take a bite of my meal. "His mom was expecting him so he had to go. She's lost her eyesight in recent years."

Cecily's lower lip shot out. "He didn't even say goodbye to me."

"Sorry," I told her with a sympathetic smile, even as I cursed Tomio for putting me on the spot like this. "He must have been in a hurry."

I picked up my fork and took a bite, but I'd lost my appetite. My heart ached. He'd just left. How disappointing. How cowardly. I processed this quietly, methodically chewing and swallowing as Gage brought Christy and Cecily up to speed about Ryan. It wasn't until Gage asked about the remaining Firethorne competitor that I dragged my attention back to the conversation.

"So, this Eira. Do I get to meet her?"

Dr. Price swallowed as she set her water down. "Not easily. She eats with Babs and Mr. Bunting in the first-year lounge now that she's their only competitor. Basil's sister protects her like she's made of china."

"She's afraid we'll learn something she doesn't want us to know," I said. I sounded bitter, but it was Tomio I was feeling the most sour about.

"What do you mean?" asked Gage.

I looked at Dr. Price, who knew more than I did, but was keeping her eyes down and hadn't made any move to answer.

"Basil thinks Eira is some kind of hybrid," I explained, eyes still on Dr. Price.

Her head jerked up, eyes wide. "How do you know that?"

"Something I overheard by accident," I said, and made it clear that I had no intention of elaborating. "You've spoken to him about it. You've seen the footage. Is it true?"

She looked uncomfortable. "I'm sorry but I'm not allowed to comment."

Gage stared. "Basil suspects she's a hybrid because of how quickly she completed the first round obstacle course?"

"He didn't seem to react much when Eira's time was announced. I think it's more thanks to something he saw in the video afterwards."

"That's why Mum isn't allowed to say," Cecily explained. "As part of the regulations, the headmasters and their seconds signed an agreement that once they viewed the footage of each game, they wouldn't be allowed to speak about anything they saw."

"That doesn't make sense," Gage sputtered, setting his fork down. "What's the point of viewing the footage if you can't give your own team tips to improve?"

Cecily shook her head. "They can talk to a competitor about their own performance, but they're not allowed to talk about anyone else's performances. Get it?"

"Eira beat Tomio's time by close to an hour," I reminded Gage. I'd told him this over the phone, but hadn't had a chance to discuss the suspicions surrounding Eira yet. "There was an obstacle that none of us overcame, a tilting gameboard with holes in it. You were supposed to cross it and get to the other side, but all of us fell through. If you could succeed at that one, you could cut a lot off your time. Maybe even a full hour."

"You think she did it?"

I shrugged. "It's my best guess. I don't know how someone could get across that thing without falling through, especially on the first try. Even exceptional fire-skills wouldn't help you much, you'd have to have something else, some other ability."

Christy was looking at me with sad eyes.

"I wish you could say something," I said.

"Me too." She looked down at her plate, shoving her food around.

"Draw a picture?" I asked in a light-hearted tone.

She smiled but didn't look up.

"There's Guzelköy and Basil," Cecily said.

Gage and I turned in our seats to look toward the door.

Guzelköy and Basil were not interested in the food, they were headed straight for our table.

"Sorry to bother you over dinner," Guzelköy said. "Davazlar is speaking to Babs and Eira right now. We wanted you to receive the same information simultaneously, so you have the same amount of time to mentally prepare. May we sit?"

"Of course. Zafer Guzelköy, this is Gage Wendig."

"I remember you from the initial meeting, but we never met. Hello." Guzelköy shook Gage's hand.

Gage greeted Guzelköy and said hello to Basil, whom he'd updated about Ryan during the afternoon.

"This is about the final event." Guzelköy settled into his chair, eyes on me. "If you want we can speak privately?"

"That's not necessary," I replied, my pulse picking up its pace. "What about it?"

"Since there are only two competitors left, we're not calling a prep meeting, just keeping things informal. The final event will take place tomorrow. The gym is ready."

I swallowed and nodded. It had only been four days since the escape room. "It's come up fast."

"We have an efficient team," Guzelköy said with a smile. He tapped the ends of his blunt fingers on the tabletop, never still. "I think you already know, since you were at the committee meeting, that this final event pits you and Eira against one another in hand-to-hand combat?"

I nodded, taking a sip of water to moisten my mouth.

"The gym has been turned into a set, of sorts. A varied terrain with features that you can use to gain an advantage. Naturally, you're permitted to use your supernatural abilities throughout, but you must keep all engagement non-lethal. Sorry to state the obvious."

I nodded. "What's the objective?"

"You'll start on opposite sides of the gym; in the middle of the course is a platform," Guzelköy said, tapping on the table. "It's outfitted with four cuffs. Your objective is to get Eira into those cuffs to win the challenge. Likewise, her objective is to get you locked down. We think you'll agree there cannot be a stalemate with this challenge, so there is no time limit."

"Can she use weapons?" Gage asked, leaning his elbows on the table and looking far too relaxed for this conversation.

"No weapons allowed," Guzelköy said with a slice of his hand through the air. "The competitors have plenty of offensive force available to them without bringing weapons and tools into the mix."

"What about parts of the terrain? Could she use something from the surroundings against her opponent?"

"By and large, no," Guzelköy said, "the terrain and features are not to be used that way."

"By and large?" Dr. Price said. "What does by and large mean? Is there an exception?"

Guzelköy wobbled his head back and forth. "When we designed it, we tried to use only materials and features that a fire mage wouldn't use in combat under normal circumstances. Almost everything is fire-proof and fixed. Most of the design features have been ready since the start and could not be altered. It has come to light after the fact, however, that there is one feature that might be utilized as a weapon without breaking game rules."

As he made this little speech, his words slowed down and his gaze shifted around the table. He paused as though needing time to think.

"Are you going to tell us what you're talking about, or are you going to make her find out tomorrow?" Basil asked, shoving his glasses up his nose.

"I'm not sure if I can. Give me a moment to consult with Davazlar? If he's told your opponent, then I can give you that detail as well." He got up and fished a phone out of his jacket. I guessed their telepathy only worked in close contact. Moving away from the table, he dialed his partner.

We waited while Guzelköy murmured into his phone. The call lasted maybe five seconds before the game-maker hung up and returned to us, not sitting down again.

"It's a water-feature," he said.

"Water?" I parroted, feeling stupid. It wasn't immediately apparent to me how water might be used as a weapon between two fire mages. A mage could heat water up, make it boil, turn it into steam, but hot water wouldn't actually harm a mage, whose skin was impervious to heat at temperatures far above that of boiling water. I supposed the steam could be used to cloud the air, reducing visibility.

Basil and Dr. Price shared a look I didn't like, but couldn't put my finger on why.

"Any other questions?" Guzelköy said, sounding cheerful as he dropped his cell phone into its pocket.

"I'm sorry," Gage said. "I'm a little slow. How exactly can Saxony use the water as a weapon? Even hot water isn't much use in a battle with a fellow mage."

"Sorry, I'm not permitted to say anything more about it." Guzelköy's gaze fell on me. "Saxony? Any questions?"

"What time?" I asked.

"Ah, yes. I didn't say, did I? Sorry. You're to meet me outside the fire-gym doors at ten minutes to ten tomorrow morning. Anything else?"

Feeling spaced out, I shook my head, still wondering what the look Basil and Christy had exchanged was all about.

"Then I'll see you tomorrow morning." Guzelköy wished me good luck, dismissed himself and left the cafeteria at a brisk walk.

"Strange," muttered Gage, exchanging a look with Cecily. "I don't get it. Do you?"

Cecily shook her head.

"I think I do, now," I said, my voice sounding dry and looking from Basil to Christy and back again. "You both know what that was all about but you can't say."

"I'm sorry, Saxony," said Dr. Price, looking glum.

Basil dropped his head and sighed, looking into the crooks of his crossed arms.

"Still not getting it," murmured Gage.

"Guzelköy would never have mentioned the water-feature if this fight was between two fire magi, but he had to mention it because Eira is a fire mage and something else. Something that makes it easier for her to leverage water into a weapon than if she were pure fire elemental."

Gage's eyes grew wide, looking from Christy to Basil and back again. "Is she right?"

"They can't say," I said, frowning. "But they know that I'm going into this at a disadvantage, and there's nothing anyone can do about it."

I looked at Basil. "Should I try to call Targa?" Seeing confused looks around the table, I added, "A friend who is a water elemental."

"That wouldn't do much good, I'm afraid," replied Basil, looking miserable.

I took his response to mean that he didn't suspect Eira was a siren. So what *did* he suspect she was?

TWENTY-SIX
THE FINAL CHALLENGE

My heart was steady but my stomach was in knots. I stood on a platform near the ceiling of the fire-gym, listening to the sound of my breathing as it echoed off the walls of my starting box. I wondered if I had ever felt as alone as I did in this moment. A surge of longing for my parents rose in my breast and I put a hand over my heart. What was it about being nervous that made one revert to a state of child-like ache for the safety of home? I'd been in many nerve-wracking situations in my short life, but this challenge felt more serious than the rest, and I hadn't even seen the gym yet.

Feeling like I had to move or I'd go crazy, I knelt to retie my fireproof boots. My hands moved systematically. I straightened, plucking at my vest and fireproof pants.

A shaft of light appeared by my feet. The door at the end of the platform rose, revealing the artificial world the game-makers had created. Stepping forward as the gym came into view, my gaze was drawn to the small figure of Eira where she stood on a platform just like mine, directly across from me.

Her body was encased in black clothing, her pale face and even paler hair stood out like disembodied parts. We locked eyes, stepping to the edge of the platform, then surveyed the terrain below. Our own private battleground.

The game-makers had manufactured a city skyline, and harbor still under construction. I-beams and the arms of cranes with dangling chains and hooks crisscrossed the air. The climbing walls had been unfastened from one another and placed in a staggered line along the far side of the harbor, making artificial building exteriors too bizarre to be real. I recognized the wrought-iron balconies, the brick wall, and the nylon ropes. One wall looked like a building taken over by nature, choked with tree branches, vines and roots, leaving a tangled green mass. Leaves fluttered gently in the artificial wind. Air was being circulated by the gym's powerful ventilation system. It smelled earthy but artificial at the same time. Like the outdoors, but laced with the smell of neoprene, rubber and nylon.

The most remarkable part of the engineered landscape was the artificial harbor. Half the gym floor had been lowered, sealed and filled with water, though it couldn't be more than five feet deep. A red light flashed in my mind upon seeing the harbor and I was reminded of the conversation in the cafeteria yesterday.

Three docks—of different lengths and various materials—stretched out into the water from a road running along the artificial shoreline. Across the road were a string of false shop-fronts. In the harbor sat three miniature vessels, large enough for a couple of people to stand on but scaled down too far to function as actual boats. One craft resembled a narrow speedboat that looked like it would tip over from a single occupant. Another was a fishing trawler with gear extending into the air from the back. The last vessel was a kind of barge stacked with colorful, miniature metal sea-cans. The sea-cans made me think of Gage, which made my heart ache.

Setting thoughts of Gage to the side, my gaze went to the middle of the water. To the platform, the place where the victor would be decided.

It was flat, black and square, large enough for two people to do an exuberant polka without falling off the edge. It looked solid, but hovered above the water by a foot. The sight of four cuffs set into the surface jarred me and I wondered, *am I going to throw up?*

Crouching, I reached back for a last swig from my water bottle. Swishing the water in my mouth, I swallowed, set my bottle aside and straightened. I felt a little better, but lamented useless questions. Why couldn't the game-makers have planned something less in-your-face for the final challenge? Less primal. I could defend myself and had good instincts, I thought, but this was different. I needed to be offensive, aggressive, dominating. None of these traits came naturally to me. Somehow, I had to manufacture them ... synthesize them from nothing.

My gaze lifted to the observation pods where I made out the silhouettes of Basil, Christy, Gage, Mr. Bunting and Babs. In the other pod sat Guzelköy and Davazlar.

I wondered if they'd speak to us over the intercom with some final words of advice or wisdom. The sound of an amplified chime blasting from the speakers gave me my answer. There would be no final words. The game had begun.

My pulse quickened as my gaze fastened on Eira. She didn't move. Was she expecting me to make the first move?

I took a steadying breath, the blood rushing past my eardrums loud enough to hear. All I had to do was get her into those cuffs. Tomio's voice rang in my memory: *Make chaos for your opponent.*

Make chaos? How? I hated chaos. I didn't even like it when my library shelf was out of alphabetical order. Why hadn't I asked him to elaborate on that instruction?

A flash of fury licked through me. Not at Tomio, but at the game-makers. They had no business setting Eira and me against one another in this barbaric manner. But it wasn't the game-makers fault, either. This was Babs' doing. She was the one who wanted a show. That's why all the effort had gone into making this artificial arena. They could have used the VR, where the stakes were real but no one would get hurt.

I shook myself and thought of Dante, what he'd done to me, what he'd done to Federica. That had been worse than this, surely. He'd almost killed me. If I could deal with that then I could deal with this. What right did I have to dream of working for the Agency if I couldn't handle a little combat?

Eira moved, preparing to jump.

Suddenly, I wanted to move first. I already knew that her plan for me was the same as my plan for her. Neither of us could strategize until we had engaged and seen how each of us fought. I gulped, turned off my brain, cranked up my fire, and leapt.

Detonating in every joint down my right side, I vaulted across space to land on the arm of a crane. I caught a flash of Eira's hair as she went for the closest stable structure, the top of a climbing wall. The one festooned with brightly colored ropes.

Scampering to the end of the crane with my arms out for balance, I dropped over the side. The cold metal chains slid under my hands until I latched, halting my fall. Hand under hand, I fed the chains through my grip in a controlled descent. Slow-burn alternated from one shoulder to another in smooth liquid bursts of heat. I reached the hook to dangle twenty feet above water. Looping a hand over the large iron hook, I locked my grip. A few forceful swings were enough to bring me close enough to the stack of sea-cans.

I let go.

My stomach lurched up through my throat. It was a long drop but the landing came quickly. Too quickly. Mis-timing my detonations, I hit hard and rolled my ankle. Gritting my teeth, I ate the pain and looked for Eira.

She was running along the water. I blinked and stared. Her movements were jerky and strange. It rose gooseflesh on my body to watch her.

She'd soon round the artificial bay and reach the road in front of the shops. I wanted to get there first, but... what was with her body? The way she moved rattled me. Maybe that was the intention. I ignored the desire to shudder, calculating the distance to the road. It was far, but if I detonated just right this time...

Backing up as far along the containers as I could

get, I exploded into a sprint. Reaching the end, I detonated so powerfully I could hear soft popping sounds reverberating in my eardrums. Water sailed by beneath me, my eyes teared up against the wind.

I landed on an exhalation and dropped into a forward roll, going too fast to just stop. A flash of blond hair to my right made my heart leap. She loomed, speeding up. Now she was too close.

She attacked!

Acting on pure instinct, I detonated as I came to my feet, shooting into the air as Eira flew by beneath me, hands grasping empty air. Still airborne, I cocked an arm and released a fireball at her back, intending to give myself time to land and orient.

With a thwap against her fireproof jacket, Eira staggered forward as if shoved from behind. With those jerky movements, she arrested momentum and whirled as I landed.

Gone was the sweet doll-face, the demure expression. Her upper lip curled in a snarl, one eye glowed red while the other was piercing white. I didn't have time to absorb her fierce appearance. She cocked her own arm back and, with a scream, released a shower of projectiles.

I put a hand up and ducked, protecting my face, not knowing what to expect. They weren't fireballs she'd thrown.

I gave a cry as my skin was blasted with tiny sharp objects: ice pellets. When it ended, I looked up. Water dripped from my eyelashes. My face stung like it had scraped along an iceberg. My hair dripped and my clothing was damp. On the floor around me lay a scattering of melting pellets.

That was how water was her weapon.

With a flare of heat, I could steam away most of the moisture but there wasn't time to do that and defend myself and it wasn't like being wet was a problem. It was the ice-pellets that were dangerous.

Panting, I wiped my face and reassessed my opponent. My hand came away with traces of blood.

Eira stood there with her hands up, grim and determined. My lantern gaze clashed with her red and white one.

"You're a fraud," I growled. "Is that what Babs teaches her students? To use deceit?"

"Don't be naive," she hissed. "In the real world, the best deceiver wins." Then she came at me, charging like a mechanical ram.

Fire blossomed in my torso, filling every limb with explosive power. It raced up my neck and crackled across the top of my scalp. I was ready.

Rational thought got checked. Fire blossomed in beautiful sequences, an orchestra of impeding violence. I blocked fists and feet, sent my own punches, kicks and thrusts. Arms collided, shins clashed. Neither of us landed clean blows. She was hardly ever where I expected her to be. Eira's frame and limbs moved fast but not smoothly. She jerked around like a stop-motion puppet. It was unnerving, and impossible to predict where she'd be next.

She went for a hold on my upper arms, I broke it and made to sweep her off her feet. She jumped, jerked away, moved in. I tried to knock her into the water, she used my strike to pony me off my feet. I got an arm through her legs and lifted, detonating in my shoulder and back. She rolled in my grip, using me as a vault. She summersaulted and landed on her feet.

Still, my hopes lifted. As our battle continued, it became apparent that I was faster, more precise.

She sent another shower of ice pellets that took me off-guard and half-blinded me. I brought a hand up to wipe my eyes as she hit me like a train, full in the side.

My quads flexed and I slid along the neoprene. My ankle struck the edge of the road. I was weightless, then I was floundering, fully submerged in water. She'd thrown me into the harbor.

Thrashing to find the floor and get upright, I gasped for air as I surfaced, hair sticking to my cheek. My skin stung with a burning sensation not like that of fire. I was sure I had multiple lacerations across the side of my face; even my ear was burning.

Eira knelt at the water's edge, a smug smile on those petal pink lips. My heart spasmed with fright. I knew what was coming and thrashed away from her as quickly as I could.

She put a hand in the water.

A sharp crackling sound cut through the air. The water's edge turned a brilliant white where she touched it, then spread rapidly, advancing toward me.

Ice closed around me and beyond, stilling all movement and locking around my shoulders. It wrapped me up like a huge snake, a python, squeezing and squeezing. Ice pressed against my skin, filled every space. The compression increased as it expanded, forcing air from my lungs. My arms locked into place. The unforgiving hand of panic gripped my throat.

My vision blurred, the white and red of her eyes fuzzed and grew, like looming, mismatched headlights. I blinked in an effort to see better. The blood in my body compressed upward. My head pounded.

Eira straightened slowly, like a victor. Surveying her handiwork. A smile crept across her face. The details of her features were lost, but my murky vision was enough to see it.

I grit my teeth and snarled. It was a small sound only I could ear, I hadn't enough air to talk. I could produce thousands of degrees of heat. I had this.

Panic backed away like a frightened mutt.

My fire hissed and bellowed. Steam rose through the fabric of my clothes. Heat baked from the top of my head. I closed my eyes and redirected it down, sending out through my legs. The ice compressing my thighs relaxed. The pressure around my ribs lessened.

Wait. The word whispered past my ears from some unknown corner of my brain. *Patience.* She had to come out onto the ice.

Sending invisible heat below the surface of the ice, I opened my eyes. My hips were free now, water sloshing around them. I could burst the ice away from my torso in a moment, but Eira didn't know that. She thought she had me trapped.

Eira took a step on the ice toward me, then another, and another. Cautious, but not cautious enough. She was halfway to me now.

Oozing heat into the water, the ice encasing me grew thinner by the moment, crackling as it surrendered to my fire.

The water around me began to bubble. Then it began to roil. I was free, standing shoulder deep in a hole in the ice.

I turned up the heat. A satisfying crack filled the air

with me as its center. The ice spiderwebbed, breaking into chunks.

Eira stopped, her eyes widened. Her arms shot out for balance as the surface beneath her came apart.

I wasn't locked in ice any more, but I had to get out of the water. With all the heat I'd built—enough to melt copper—if I detonated like this it would be overkill. It didn't matter, I had to jump.

Dull pops of sound echoed through the gym as I vaulted from the water like I'd been shot from a cannon, aiming wildly for the platform. A wash of liquid and chunks of ice trailed me, making a calamitous sound. I landed on the edge of the platform, teetering for balance and cushioning my landing with fire.

I spun to see Eira following, desperately leaping from floe to floe. I half-squatted, waiting. With a final jerky leap, she landed on the opposite side of the platform in a crouch.

Our eyes met.

"What are you?" I asked, hands up but relaxed, unafraid enough to be curious.

All the fuss so far had served to settle a kind of patient confidence within me. I'd observed and tangled with her enough now to know that Eira was fast and strong, but I was better. I was going to win this. I just had to keep an eye out for those freezing pellets.

Mirroring my stance and breathing hard, Eira let a few breaths pass before giving a sarcastic answer. "I'm half-mage and half-mage."

She advanced and we exchanged a flurry of punches and blocks, her movements jarring and electric, mine smooth and liquid.

We broke apart, panting, circling like a couple of wild dogs, teeth bared.

We advanced again, but she was visibly flagging now. Biding my time, deflecting a few glancing blows, I watched for the opportunity I knew would come. When it came, I drove a fist through an unguarded pocket. She took it full on the chin. She wobbled, dazed, and probably seeing stars.

I shot out a foot and swept at her ankles. She jumped valiantly but too late. She stumbled and fell, rolled away then scrambled to her feet. Her bottom lip was bleeding.

She was at the edge of the platform now. Any further back and I could push her into the water, except I didn't want that. I needed to get her down on her back.

"That doesn't make sense," I said, as she panted and recovered her balance. I allowed it. I'd have her down with my next attack, but before that, I wanted an answer. All of my insecurity was gone. In its place was a sense of dominant power. It surfaced in my thoughts that this feeling could be dangerously addictive.

I could see in her eyes that she knew she was about to lose, too. Which meant she was at her most unpredictable right now.

"I'm nobody," she said quietly, wiping a trickle of blood from her chin. It left a smear of pink across her jaw.

I arched a brow. "Self-pity doesn't become you."

"Fine," she grated. "Look at me. I'm what they say, just a doll. What are you?"

My skin prickled at her words. I recalled what

Harriet had said, how sad it was that a woman was known for her looks rather than her abilities.

I'd had enough. I wanted this finished now, before I started thinking too much and made a mistake.

"I'm *pure* fire-mage," I replied, then lunged.

TWENTY-SEVEN
CATASTROPHIC CONSEQUENCES

Someone was crying, a woman. It had to be Babs because I was surrounded by men. I should be crying too but my mental processes were weighed down with shock.

I stood in the academy's lobby. Someone put a blanket around me. Silly thing to do for a fire mage who was never cold. On top of that, I deserved no charity.

It was Gage. He had his arm around me. I was thankful for his solid bulk against my side as I stared at the gurney with Eira's body on it. She was covered head to toe with a white sheet. I was glad for that small mercy. I couldn't bear the look of her gray skin, the blue lips. The dead eyes.

Gage was talking. His words echoed like they were coming from far away.

"Dr. Price did everything she could," he was saying. "The other medics arrived in moments, but it was just too late."

There had been more blood. Not a lot, but its vivid

brightness was the hook from which all my other memories hung.

Eira shouldn't be dead. She *couldn't* be dead. But somehow, she was.

The gurney was almost to the lobby doors now. Eira was going into the back of a van.

My face felt numb, my lips and legs were numb. I couldn't stop staring at the sheet, the shape under it. The head that would never raise itself. She'd never see through those pretty doll-eyes again, thanks to me.

My eyes felt so dry they ached.

Basil was there, and Dr. Price too. Davazlar looked grim and ashen pale. Guzelköy looked like he'd already been sick.

I wished I could be sick, could cry, could anything. I felt like I was made of wood.

"Come, sit down," someone said. I was led to a couch and given a glass of water. I wanted to ask where they would take Eira's body, I wanted to ask what would happen to her next. I wanted to ask about her family.

"This is all your fault," Babs said to Basil with a choked whisper. "If you'd just accepted the will as it was, she wouldn't have died."

"That's not helpful." Christy's voice, sounding very calm. Maybe she was better able to handle death than the rest of us, being a doctor and all.

I lifted my eyes to look for Basil. He was seated at the other end of the sofa, looking like he'd aged a decade. Another death. The death of an aged father was one thing, horrible enough on its own. The death of a young woman, barely out of her teens...

And it was my fault. I'd killed her.

"I don't understand." Basil put his hands on his face and rubbed up and down, bringing a flush to his skin. "She's been trained to deliver non-lethal blows, even at speed. It's automatic for her by now—"

"Clearly, your training has been inadequate," Babs snapped. Her wailing had ceased and had been replaced by hostility and anger. "And you, young lady, will answer to a tribunal for your actions."

I supposed she was talking to me, trying to instill fear. But I wasn't afraid of a tribunal, they could do what they wanted with me. I was still back in the fire-gym, reliving the events of the past hour.

I'd never gotten any of Eira's limbs into the hafnium cuffs. We'd exchanged blows at the edge of the platform. Hers were delivered in desperation. Mine, with confidence. In spite of that she had caught me with a fist in the mouth, a glancing blow but it stung. I fired one back.

There was a moment when all I saw was the bright blood pouring from her nose. Then Eira coughed and gathered spittle and blood in her mouth. She spat. It landed in my eye, a heavy gob of bloody saliva. Half-blinded and momentarily lit with rage, a monster surged to the forefront, something dark and uncontrollable. I detonated into a single shot.

There was the solid sound of my fist connecting with flesh and bone, somewhere below Eira's collarbone. Yes, I'd detonated, but even half-blind I knew how to make non-lethal contact.

That sound filled my mind. Helplessly, I watched her eyes roll up in her head.

She collapsed, folded in on herself and crumpled. She slipped into the water with hardly a splash. She'd gone boneless, totally limp, with an unconsciousness impossible to fake.

Still, I'd been surprised that my strike had knocked her out. It wasn't like I'd hit her in the head, or the throat. I expected her to come to at any moment. She'd leap from the water with renewed strength and I'd take her down again and put her into the cuffs.

But she lay still and face down, a swirl of red drifting from her head, staining the water with a little pink cloud. Spread-eagled and motionless, she drifted between half-melted ice floes.

Then I was in the water, splashing and floundering to get to her.

"Eira!" I screamed, repeating her name over and over.

Voices yelled. A red emergency light flashed.

I rolled Eira's body over. Her eyes were open. Dead. Her pink lips already turning gray. Her hair stuck to her jaw in clumps and lay across one open eye. My heart convulsed, my brain froze.

Numbly, I floated her to the closest dock and hauled her body onto the platform. My whole body was trembling. Footsteps coming. The water draining away... swirls and funnels, floes jostling.

I began CPR, but then Dr. Price took over, her movements confident, well-timed.

My eyes dried out as I stared, straining, begging and hoping to see life. All I could see was how Eira's body moved as Dr. Price worked on her. I sat on the dock with my knees pulled to my chest, my arms around my shins, my body shaking with desire to see Eira's chest rise with an inhale. I'd have given anything to bring her back.

Christy lowered her ear to Eira's chest. She checked for a pulse under the jaw, that small place at the wrist. It felt like Dr. Price worked on her forever. More medics arrived, in their dark clothing encrusted with equipment, they lifted Eira to a gurney. A complicated looking box, wires hooked to Eira. Her body bucked under the paddles.

I couldn't remember getting from the fire-gym to the lobby. There was a lot of shouting as the medics continued their fruitless efforts.

Babs couldn't seem to do anything but emote at the top of her lungs. A glass of water was shoved into my hands. Someone asked me something but I didn't answer. I thought it was Gage, maybe. My backpack appeared at some point. Someone had set it on a coffee table. I'd retrieved my phone and put it into my pocket, wondering who I should call first when I could piece together rational thought.

The front door of the villa slammed closed behind the medics.

"We need to analyze the recording. She shouldn't have—it shouldn't have... killed her," Basil mumbled.

I gathered the presence of mind to move closer to him and take his hand. It was trembling but he squeezed back and we shared a look of torment and shock.

"I'm so sorry," I whispered.

He put the fingers of his other hand on his lips, as if to keep them from quivering and shook his head. I wasn't sure what that meant but I felt too weary to converse further.

I thought of Eira. Where was she from? Did she have family? I knew nothing about her, and now she was dead. She'd signed the release just like all of us had. There would be no legal repercussions for Babs or Basil or the game-makers. But for Eira's family, there would be nothing *but* repercussions. Shock waves. For years. Shock waves from a death weakened over time, but never truly went away. I knew that from personal experience.

"Babs?" I croaked, looking around for Basil's twin.

She was conversing with Guzelköy. She paused and looked my way.

Getting off the sofa I crossed the lobby. As I approached she seemed to draw herself up to her full height and lift her nose, like I was something disgusting that had emerged from under the carpet.

"I cannot begin to say—" I paused. Sorry didn't even begin to cover it, there weren't words for what I wanted to express. "Have you called Eira's family yet?"

"Of course I have," she snapped. "What do you take me for? Do you know they have no other children? Eira was their only baby. I don't know how you're going to live with that."

Steeling myself against her barbs, I kept on track only with great effort. "So you have their contact information in your phone?"

I fished my cell out of my pocket, turning it over and over in my hands.

Her gaze flashed down to my phone and back up to my face. Her expression seemed to open fully for a moment. It was like driving by a large house at night when all the light were on. The interior made stark and radiant. Fear came into Babs eyes, then it was gone, shuttered up so quickly I wondered if I had really seen it.

Her upper lip curled and her superior disdain was back. "You're insane if you think they'll want to hear from you."

"They will." My voice calm in spite of the grief in my heart. "Maybe not today, maybe not tomorrow, but soon. They'll need an apology from me. It will help them heal."

She stared at me, her expression horrified. She lifted her hands up, turning her torso away from me in a defensive posture, like she thought I was going to snap and attack her, or maybe like she thought my vileness was contagious.

"They'll need one from you, too," I added softly.

Her expression darkened. "How dare you speak to me in this way. Basil, get her under control." What started as a bark soon became a shriek. "It's not enough that she's murdered one of my best students, she has to turn the blame back on me?"

I caught Basil out of the corner of my eye, getting to his feet but moving like he needed a cane.

"That's not what I meant."

It was a struggle not to raise my voice, but if I did I would lose it. I was already teetering on the edge. The wooden numbness was being replaced with emotion as reality took hold. A breakdown was inevitable but I needed to have it in private, not here in front of Babs. I might be numb and in shock for the moment, but the real pain was lurking at the edges of my consciousness, waiting to sweep me up in its arms and cradle me in a nest of razors I might never fully extricate myself from. I'd taken Eira's life. What that meant was yet to fully manifest itself.

Babs shoved her face into mine, her breath hot and sour. "You leave those poor people alone."

"She is right, Barbara," said Basil, who was now at my elbow. "The Nygaard family will need apologies from all of us. It will help give them closure. You and I are indirectly responsible for Eira's death."

"I do not agree, and I won't be giving you any access to her family whatsoever." Babs words came out on an acid hiss.

"You don't have to," Basil replied wearily, and I felt his hand against my back, a silent and invisible support in the face of his sister's mania.

I appreciated that small touch more than anything in that moment, and clung to it the way kittens cling to trees.

Guzelköy raised his hand cautiously, like he was sneaking up on a nest of snakes. "I have all the contact details for next of kin. I can give you Mr. and Mrs. Nygaard's information."

Babs rounded on him. "You *what?* I am the sole contact for all of my students."

Guzelköy stepped back, alarmed at her venomous demeanor.

Davazlar materialized out of nowhere, his height and breadth imposing. I'd never stood this close to him before. Authority radiated from him.

"It's a matter of course, Headmaster," he said, smoothly and with a low, powerful voice I could feel vibrating in my knees and ribcage. "The day you were late in arriving we collected all the pertinent details. It's a basic before all tournaments."

Babs eyes widened then shrank to slashes. Two red spots of color rose high in her cheeks. "I forbid it." Her gaze slid around the group. "You will not disturb the grieving family."

Dr. Price released the medic she'd been speaking to and caught the tail end of this. She approached, a mildly interested look painted on her face. "Who wants to disturb the grieving family?"

Babs pointed a finger at Basil, then me, and the game-makers, as if we'd been colluding behind her back. "They do. The body is barely cold and the first thing they want to do is impose themselves upon the girl's family. Their privacy needs to be respected. I'll not allow it."

Dr. Price crossed her arms in a casual gesture. "Certainly the family will need privacy and time to grieve, but my good friend and psychologist Dr. Bud—you may know him from the agency—has waxed long about the grieving process. At some point, they will be ready and needful of an apology."

I felt like I'd slipped into a twilight zone of weirdness. Why had this become such a big deal? Why was Babs fighting so hard to keep us from reaching out to Eira's family? The idea of talking with them made my palms sweaty, but I couldn't walk away without giving the bereaved a chance to vent at me, look into my eyes and see real remorse.

Babs seemed to become aware that her behavior was drawing attention. She puckered her lips and crossed her arms, but made no more screaming attempts to bully us. I could see the gears turning under that glamorous auburn hair.

After a moment of tense silence, she said, "Then, let's leave it up to Dr. Bud. Shall we? If he gives his consent for Saxony to reach out to Eira's parents, I won't intervene. But let's give them at least a week before we consider it." Her voice softened and she sounded almost reasonable now. "Let's do that. Yes?" She raised her brows at me, pointedly.

I nodded, but my hackles rose with dislike and suspicion.

"Excellent." She eyed the game-makers and Basil. "I presume Mr. Pendleton has been notified of the outcome and is on his way with the paperwork? I need to get it out of the way quickly. School begins in eight weeks and I need all the time I can muster to prepare."

Basil made some tired sounding reply to this, but I was barely listening.

I was still stuck on Babs' reaction. Was asking for a week just a tactic to stall for time? But time for what? A lot could happen in a week and I trusted Babs about as much as I trusted Enzo. Dr. Bud could be coaxed to a certain point of view, for instance. If not coaxed, then coerced.

I watched Babs through narrowed eyes as she followed the medical team out the front door. Something was wrong, and it was more than the death of Eira. Yes, Babs could get up to a lot in one week, but so could I.

TWENTY-EIGHT

STUPID CUPID

"Stamppot?" Mr. Hoedemaker asked, eyes bright.

I peered into the pot. It contained a lumpy, green-tinged mash. Since I wasn't likely to taste my food anyway I nodded and let him scoop his concoction into my bowl, besides I'd had it before and survived.

The cafeteria was quiet but not empty. Gage was seated beside Dr. Price and across from Cecily. Basil had excused himself claiming a headache. He'd retired to his suite, a suite that wouldn't be his for much longer.

The thought of Babs moving into Basil's suite and taking over his office was utterly depressing.

Carrying my food over to the table sent a whiff of the food's scent into my nostrils. The smell was more pleasant than its look. Potato, butter, vegetables, and a smoky, sausage-gravy. My stomach growled and I felt a wash of guilt. I shouldn't have an appetite but my body was starving. Fire burned calories, and I'd used it a lot today.

Setting my tray down beside Gage, I took a seat. From my back pocket, my cell phone vibrated. Shifting onto one hip, I retrieved my phone, intending to ignore the call. I didn't want to talk to anyone. Then I saw the caller ID.

Excusing myself with a quiet murmur, I headed for the exit. I waited until I was out of hearing range before bringing the phone to my ear.

"Hi," I said as I passed into the hall.

"Hi," replied Tomio.

My pulse quickened at the sound of his voice, more from anger than anything else. "You left. You just vanished."

"I know."

"Right before the biggest, most important, challenge in the games, my combat coach and sparring partner just *disappeared*." Heat was rising in my cheeks as the horrible, nightmarish day came rushing out through an emotional opening Tomio had unwittingly made by calling me right now.

"I know. I'm sorry." He sounded genuinely contrite. "But what happened between us—"

"I get that that was unexpected, but couldn't you have put the personal aside until the games were over? I mean, come on, Tomio. I thought you had a backbone, some kind of honor."

He gave a hiss and paused before responding. "Honor is why I left."

"Oh, really?"

"Yes, if you would just—"

"You think it's honorable to ditch one of your best friends in an hour when she needs—"

"Saxony, will you shut up for a minute!" He barked this loud enough that I pulled my phone away from my ear.

I grit my teeth and barked back, "So, talk then!"

"I'm sorry I left, but I was ashamed. I'm still ashamed. I didn't know what to do and I thought the best thing was to extricate myself from the situation so you could focus on what you needed to do to win."

I gave an exasperated laugh. "You couldn't have told me that before you left?"

"I'm not finished."

I clenched my jaw and exhaled through my nose.

"I did a bad thing," he continued. "I've been dying to kiss you since we first became sparring buddies. I tried to ignore it. Gage is my best friend. I knew it was foolishness to fall for you but my heart—" he paused suddenly, like he'd veered off into terrain he hadn't been aiming for.

"Your heart what?" Some of my anger had receded.

"It doesn't matter. I dealt with it in a less than ideal manner."

"You sound like Basil," I muttered. "Less than ideal."

"I dug myself into a hole and I'm doing my best to get out of it. I'm sorry for what happened, I'm sorry I left, okay? I'm ashamed, and, I mean," he huffed, "well, aren't you?"

"Of course I am," I whispered. "And as soon as I figure out a way to tell Gage, I'm going to."

Tomio was quiet for so long I thought he'd covertly hung up on me.

"Tomio?"

"I'm here."

"I didn't know if you were going to be making a habit out of disappearing."

He was quiet again.

"Tomio?"

He sighed. "Somehow, you've managed to make me feel even worse. Why are you so bloody honest? Couldn't we just put it behind us? Pretend it never happened?"

"Is that what you would want If you were Gage?"

He sighed again. "No."

I closed my eyes. A flashback came unbidden, invading my mind, the feeling of Tomio's mouth on mine, the way I felt everything. The way my fire sat back with approval, like *this* was a match it could get behind.

I rubbed at my temples. "I'm not entirely sure it was a mistake."

"What do you mean?" Tomio sounded like he was holding his breath.

"It's complicated. Too complicated to untangle right now. I'm confused, about more than just this. Today, I—"

I gulped and my nose began to tingle.

"Today, what?" Tomio sounded on high alert now. He didn't know the last challenge had already happened.

"Today, I fought Eira—"

"Really? Because, that's the other reason I was calling," Tomio interjected. "I guess it's too little, too late."

"What? I'm not following."

"I figured out what she is. She's a cryohäxa, an ice mage from Scandinavia. Fairly rare."

A tear slipped down my cheek as he put a name to the species of being I had ended today. I didn't trust my voice so I just said, "Mhm?"

"Yeah. I wish I'd found out sooner, I wanted to

warn you. I'm sorry about that too. I seem to be failing all over the place lately. So, how did it go?"

I sniffed and ran a sleeve across my nose.

"Saxony, are you... are you *crying*?" He sounded mortified.

"Nope," I sniffed again. "Yep. A little."

He cursed softly and I could picture him raking his hair into spikes.

"She's dead, Tomio. I killed her," I blurted, facing the paneling in the hallway and putting my forehead against the wood. I curbed the desire to thump against it repeatedly.

"No." He choked out the word, pregnant with disbelief.

"I can't—" My lower lip was trembling now. I felt like I was made of glass.

"Saxony?"

I whirled at the sound of Gage's voice, the cell stuck to my ear.

"Your food is getting co—" he stopped when he saw my face. Then he was there, taking me into his arms, folding me against his body.

"That sounded like Gage," Tomio said in my ear.

I gave a sniffly affirmative grunt.

"I'll let you go," he said quietly. "I'm so sorry. I'm in shock. You're in shock. I'll call again soon. I promise. Okay?"

"Mhmm." I pressed my face against Gage's denim shirt.

It felt surreal. Like a kind of torture invented by a deranged and maniacal cupid. Wrapped up in Gage's arms, his smell filling my nose. His lips on my hair. His fingers drawing tracers of fire on the skin of my neck as he stroked my curls back. And Tomio's voice in my ear, the man whose kiss I could really feel.

With a last whispered apology, Tomio disconnected the call.

My phone slipped from my grip and Gage caught it, hugging me more tightly as the dam holding back my tears finally broke.

I LAY AWAKE WATCHING the beam of moonlight as it crept across the floor. Gage lay beside me, his breathing slow and steady. I was still, but only because I didn't want to wake him. My mind was a thrashing animal caught in a trap.

Lifting my head for a glimpse at the clock on my nightstand, I saw it was almost five. The sun would make its presence known soon. My eyes felt hot and full of sand. I hadn't slept at all.

Gage murmured something unintelligible and I felt him touch my shoulder.

"Did I wake you?" I whispered, turning to look at him.

He lay on his side with his face mashed into the pillow. The blond-tipped lashes of one eye lifted. His iris looked black in the gloom of early morning.

"Mope," he croaked.

It was the first time we'd ever shared a bed overnight and it was the exact opposite of what you'd expect. He wore a t-shirt and pajama pants. I wore a long-sleeved night-shirt and shorts. We went to bed without talking. Cuddling only meant we'd slowly build so much heat we'd soak the bed with sweat, so that was out. But I didn't want to be alone and he didn't want to leave me so we lay side-by-side without touching.

He cleared his throat and adjusted his pillow, cracking both eyes open. He had pillow marks on his face and his eyes were puffy. He studied me for a moment, blinking away sleep.

"You look tired. Did you sleep?"

"A little," I lied.

I had passed the night replaying what had happened with Eira and the scene with Babs in the front lobby.

I still couldn't wrap my mind around how my blow could have caused Eira's death. Yes, I'd had a moment of anger when she'd spit in my face, but even then... Non-lethal strikes had been drilled into me for months now. They were automatic. I could only hope that the autopsy might shine light on an explanation. Maybe she had some unknown heart condition, like Targa's father had had.

Gage's arm snaked around my waist and pulled me to him. He nuzzled into my neck and pressed my chest to his.

Immediately my fire sprang to life, sizzling at my collarbone and under my ear, sending loops of heat cascading from Gage's lips down my torso. My upper lip felt damp almost instantly. I so loved to be close to him, so wanted to feel him next to me. Why couldn't my fire just butt out of my relationship?

Gage's lips found mine and he kissed me, softly at first, then with more passion. My lips and face sparkled with heat, well along the way to where I knew it would lead: numbness.

I broke the kiss. Even in the dim, early morning

light I could see the moisture gathering on Gage's forehead. I shuffled back a little on the mattress, making space and air between us.

"Too hot?" Gage asked, rubbing a hand across his upper lip.

I nodded, taking a deep breath. "You?"

He pressed his lips together briefly, like someone spreading lipstick. "A little numb."

I groaned and flopped onto my back.

"It's okay, we'll figure it out." Gage reached for me but pulled back, not wanting to build more heat.

"How will it be okay? Our fires don't want us to be together."

He shifted his torso up to lie on his elbow, propping his head on his hand. "Is that really what you think?"

"What else *can* I think? Every time we get physical, I get so hot and sweaty that my nerves shut down. I like you so much—"

He blinked a couple of times at that and I saw a flash of hurt. I knew he wanted to hear me say that I loved him. I did love him, but neither of us had said it out loud before and saying it right now would only make this situation more difficult.

"But it doesn't seem to matter how we feel about each other. If it's going to be like this..." I gestured at us and my sentence trailed off.

"I keep hoping it's just a bump we have to get over," he said. "Maybe if we ignore it, just keep going, it will realize—"

"How much I want that not to be wishful thinking," I replied, shifting to mirror his stance so I could see his face better. I took a breath and forged ahead before I thought about it too much. "Tomio and I—we kissed."

He froze, his eyes fastened on mine. They widened a fraction as what I'd just admitted fully registered.

My heart began to pound but there was no going back now. The words tumbled out of me. "I am sorry, it wasn't planned, we were sparring and then it just... happened. It's been eating at me, and Tomio feels horrible."

"So *that's* why he left?" Gage sounded so calm, so reasonable, and that scared me.

I nodded, stomach turning inside out.

"And that was him on the phone, in the hall?"

I nodded again.

The room was silent for a long time. An owl hooted somewhere outside the window.

Gage held out a palm in supplication. "So what does that mean, Saxony? Where does that put us?"

I opened my mouth but had no answers, only a useless stutter.

Gage let his hand fall on the duvet. "Do you want to be with him?"

"I—no. I don't know." This is a nightmare, I thought. A living nightmare. The hurt in Gage's eyes, the calm in his voice, it was slicing my heart to ribbons and I just wanted to take away his pain, but if I lied to take away this pain it would only mean more pain later.

"It's not a complicated question." Gage sat up, the covers falling to his waist. He shifted on the bed to lean against the wall.

"It is, though." I sat up myself now because I couldn't have this conversation lying down if he wasn't lying down. Already I felt a horrible chasm growing between us and I was desperate to close it again. But at what cost? How could we go back to the way things were five minutes ago?

"Was it good?" Gage's voice broke, his features were stricken now. I hated myself for putting that look there, for messing up his beautiful face like that.

"It was..." It had been amazing but I could not, would not, say that out loud. "There was no fire, no heat getting in the way. So it was different."

Gage dropped his head forward and plunged the fingers of one hand into his bedhead, tugging at it. Then he left his hair alone to rub at his eyes. "This is a nightmare," he murmured.

I was nodding but he couldn't see it because he was grinding his eyeballs into his head with his knuckles.

"Yes," I croaked, hoping he could hear how much I agreed with him. "I'm sorry."

He left off the grinding to look up, his eyes bleary. "Why is it a nightmare for you? It sounds like you're perfect for each other."

"We're not perfect for—" I swallowed without finishing my denial. Truthfully, I had no idea whether Tomio and I were good for each other or not. We were friends, friends who had shared a kiss that felt the way a kiss was supposed to feel.

My heart had been set on Gage since that day in my bedroom just before Christmas, when we'd made up. My heart still wanted Gage, but my fire was doing everything it could to show me how much it disagreed.

We were quiet, the tension in the room was so thick we could have hung a garland on it.

"Are you okay?" I asked.

The corners of Gage's lips turned up just briefly, but there was no pleasure in the look, only pain. "I'm not the one who killed someone, so of the two of us, I'd say I'm pretty okay. Yeah."

Stung, I blinked at him. My hands felt sweaty.

Gage pushed the covers off his legs and shoved himself toward the end of the bed, avoiding me to get off. The gesture made me feel like a fish-bone was stuck in my throat.

He stood, looking around briefly for the socks he'd discarded the night before.

"Where are you going?" I hated the weak sound of my voice.

He picked up one sock, then the other, then stood there, his body facing me but his gaze on the floor. "To go back to sleep. Maybe when I wake up, I'll discover this whole thing was all just a bad dream."

He opened the door and was gone, leaving me to wonder what he meant by "this whole thing"; the conversation we'd just had or our entire relationship?

TWENTY-NINE
KENTISH TOWN

If Gage was able to sleep after that, more power to him. For me, it was impossible. After another couple of hours of agonized tossing and turning, I dressed and left my room for the library.

Morning light poured through the diamond-panes in soft shafts. I headed for the section on supernaturals. My footsteps made the floor boards creak and groan. Skimming a finger over the titles, I selected an encyclopedia of supernatural species.

I set the big book on a table, slid into a chair and opened it. I found the C section and ran my finger down the page until I found cryohäxa.

It described Eira almost to a tee, leaving out the extra abilities that she had due to her hybrid nature. The section was only a page and a half long and revealed a few things of interest that led me to take other titles from the shelves. I became so lost in my reading that when the library's clock chimed that it was nine. I straightened with a start at the sound. I'd been worlds away.

Gage sprang to mind immediately, the way he'd looked when he reminded me that I'd killed someone. As if I needed reminding.

My heart spasmed painfully and I winced. Taking a few deep breaths, I put away the titles I'd gathered over the last hour and left the library. My mind kept wanting to review the conversation with Gage, like a tongue going to the tender place of a missing tooth. But I'd come across some interesting facts about cryohäxa, facts that led to more questions, questions that led to strange answers, so I tried with only moderate success to ignore the pain in my chest.

My first stop would be the game-makers. If they wouldn't help me, then I'd hit a brick wall.

I headed for the mudroom exit. The day was shaping up to be a beauty, with birds heralding summer and only a wisp of cloud hanging out over the Channel. Passing under the arch, I opened the door to the fire-gym's lobby, then the fire-gym itself. There was no reason to keep it locked up any more.

Unlike the yard and garden, which were still peaceful, the fire-gym was full of activity. People in construction belts carrying power tools, mostly screw-guns, swarmed all over the gym, dismantling the last of the course. Already the gym looked more like its old self. The floor had been returned to its normal height and all traces of the harbor were gone. The boats had vanished. Only the climbing walls remained to be put away.

I spotted Guzelköy in a rear corner holding a black box with cables looped over one forearm. He was talking with Davazlar, both of them looking grim and serious.

Hopping over a pile of two-by-eights and rows of

chains, I ducked under an I-beam being carried by four men. Someone reproached me for being there but I ignored them, intent on my targets.

The game-makers saw me coming and stopped talking.

"Morning." I stopped in front of them, looking from one face to the other.

"Hello, Ms. Cagney," Guzelköy said, probing my features. "How are you?"

Davazlar shot him a look that said, *why did you ask her that? She's traumatized, obviously.*

I cleared my throat and opted for polite and direct. "I'm okay. I was hoping I could get Eira's parents contact information from you. This morning if possible."

The game-makers exchanged a look.

"I thought we agreed to give it some time," Guzelköy replied, shifting the box from one hand to the other. He rubbed at his forehead. "Wait for the psychologist to give the okay? I'm sorry, I've forgotten his name. I'm a little absent minded this morning."

I nodded, feeling sorry for him. I wondered if the game-makers had ever had a death during their games before. I wasn't about to ask them.

"I wasn't planning on contacting them right away," I said, "it's just, I've been away from my family for a long time and I'm feeling pretty homesick. I want to go home as soon as I'm allowed and I'd rather go knowing I have their information. I'll wait for permission from Dr. Bud before I call."

Guzelköy looked hesitant but Davazlar said, "Give it to her, Zafer. She's not going to make the situation any worse than it already is."

I sent Davazlar a grateful look and the corners of his mouth turned up in a sad smile. He looked at the floor.

"Alright." Guzelköy sighed. "Babs won't like it, but I'm past caring what that woman likes or doesn't like."

The way he said 'that woman' made me wonder how many pushy conversations the game-makers had found themselves in with the headmaster of Firethorne.

Guzelköy took my email and said he'd text the information to me as soon as he had the file open. I thanked them and left them to their cleanup.

Phone in hand, I went by Gage's room. His door was closed. I listened at the keyhole and heard nothing. My knuckles hovered over the wood, but I pulled away without knocking. I wasn't sure he'd be ready to talk to me so soon. I wasn't sure I was ready, either.

I made myself a coffee in the third-floor students' lounge, checking my phone every minute. When an email from Guzelköy dropped into my inbox, I opened it and consumed the information like a brushfire consumes dead grass.

Eira's family had a home in Kentish Town. It would be a two hour journey from the academy but I counted myself lucky that I wouldn't have to cross any borders. A big plus on an observation project like the one I'd assigned myself.

The name of this task would be: See, but do not be seen.

I went to my room and exchanged my sneakers for boots and my sweater for a light jacket. I grabbed a hat and sunglasses and checked the bus schedule for the next one to Dover's train station.

I should be back at the academy in time for dinner. If that wasn't possible then I'd eat on the train and be back by sundown. These days that was after nine pm. Maybe by the time I returned, Gage would have warmed to the idea of reopening our conversation, though what was left to say, I wasn't sure.

I took a shuddery breath as the thought passed through my mind that we'd broken up this morning. It didn't feel for the best right now. Right now, it made me feel shaky and ill. But maybe it was for the best. I was too close to it to think rationally.

Setting my private issues aside, I left the academy hopeful that this little expedition would bear fruit.

THE TRAIN from Dover pulled up at St. Pancras Station just after eleven. From there it was a five minute walk to the tube and a twenty minute train ride to the Kentish Town stop.

I stepped onto the Kentish Town platform with my nose in my phone, watching the little blinking blue dot (me) and following the trail the navigation app gave me. It would be an eight minute walk to the Nygaard's house.

Tucking my phone into my pocket, I twisted my hair back into a low bun, tucked it under my hat and turned my collar up. I'd chosen a thin, tan-colored double-breasted coat. It was a little too warm for an English summer, but the light wind meant I could get away with it. I slid on a pair of oversized sunglasses and my non-disguise/disguise was complete. Not that the Nygaard's would know who I was even if they did spot me.

Kentish Town was a middle-class borough filled

with cute antique pubs, flower shops, newsagents, cafés and corner grocery stores. Turning down the Nygaard's street revealed a long, gently sloping hill lined with three-story town-houses without a millimeter of space between them. The sidewalks were cracked and uneven, the gardens were unkempt but pretty with untamed profusion, and the houses—while some were freshly painted—were a little rundown. Most of the front walkways and steps were crumbling, some of the windows were taped up. The Nygaard's neighborhood was old but expressed the efforts of its residents to maintain their homes, a battle some of them were losing.

The Nygaard's lived at number 72. It was a building that fit perfectly in with all the others. Run down, but cared for. Old and a little decayed. Loved and lived in.

I parked myself on a bench across the road from their house and sipped the coffee I'd purchased from the Costa outside the tube station.

In contrast to Canadians (whose habits resemble that of squirrels), the habits of most Brits involved visiting the shops daily for food. Fridges were small and kitchens were cramped, plus fresh fruits and vegetables were best on the day they were purchased.

My assumption was rewarded just before twelve-thirty—around the time my butt was growing numb from the wooden bench.

The door of number 72 swung open and a woman with a silvery-blond pixie-cut stepped down onto the stoop. I guessed she was in her early sixties, and with those cheek-bones, she definitely looked the part of Eira's mom. She carried a handbag and wore a pale cardigan and a wispy scarf with feathers dangling from one end. She leaned into the open door and called, "Popping off to the shops, luvey. Get you anything?"

A man replied from within the house, too far away to make out his words, but his words weren't important. That had to be Mr. Nygaard, since Babs had helpfully informed me Eira had no siblings to comfort her grieving parents.

But that was just the point. Mrs. Nygaard did not look the grieving parent. Neither did her husband sound anything short of sprightly. So Babs had to have lied about calling them.

Mr. and Mrs. Nygaard exchanged a few more pleasant words. As she closed the door and rearranged her scarf, she began to hum.

Mrs. Nygaard was halfway down the front walk, gracefully stepping over a lifted bit of pavement (she had none of her daughter's jerky way of moving) when the front door of 72 opened again. A head emerged. A young head, with bright blond hair and a doll-face with a bruised and scabbed lip.

"Don't forget cream for the coffee, Mummy," said Eira.

My heart turned a summersault and bounced off my ribcage. I liberated my cell phone from my pocket, opened my camera app with a trembling finger, zoomed in on Eira and took several photographs of my very non-dead opponent.

Mrs. Nygaard paused with her hand on the front gate. "We have milk, darling."

Eira spoke patiently, her demeanor as sweet as her features. "I don't like milk anymore. I take it with cream, now. Remember?"

The Nygaard women spoke simultaneously. "Fat is your friend."

I surged to my feet, hardly aware that I'd made the spontaneous decision to throw out my earlier aim not to be seen and heard now that I'd seen Eira in the flesh. I was scared that the door would close and I'd lose my chance.

Pulling off my beret and sunglasses, I let my twisted hair spill out into the sunshine, knowing it would attract Eira's attention.

"Hello, Eira," I called, pleasantly but with enough confidence to let The Doll know she'd been caught and I wasn't just going to go away. I stowed all of my amazement and wonder and fury at the impressive trick she'd played behind the expression of someone pleased to have accidentally run into a friend.

Mrs. Nygaard turned to look at me, missing the look of shock and guilt that washed over her daughter's face.

"Hello there, Miss," she said with a sweet smile. "You're a friend of Eira's?"

I nodded, tossed my coffee cup into the nearby bin and crossed the street, holding my beret and sunglasses in one hand, my phone in the other. "We know each other from school. Don't we, Eira?"

Mrs. Nygaard looked at her daughter.

Eira's wide blue eyes were on my face. Her gaze dropped down to the phone in my hand, and bounced back up to my face. The pale pink had drained from her cheeks, though she reclaimed enough presence of mind to plaster a look of happy surprise as her mother looked at her.

The exchange spoke volumes.

If Eira's parents even knew about the games, they

didn't know about Eira's deception. The reason for Babs' desperation to keep me from contacting Eira's parents was shockingly apparent. They were clueless. She could hardly allow me to call or visit them, apologizing about their daughter's death.

"Invite your friend in for coffee, darling. I'll be back in two shakes." With that Mrs. Nygaard stepped out of the walkway and onto the sidewalk, holding their front gate open for me.

"I'm Saxony." I held out a hand to Eira's mother. "Lovely to meet you."

She shook my hand with warmth, smiling into my face. "It's lovely to meet a friend of Eira's. She never brings anyone to the house. How lucky you happened by."

"Thank you." I stepped through the front gate and Eira and I watched her mother disappear down the street.

I turned to my opponent, emotions boiling inside me. Fury, amazement, disbelief, but the dominant emotion was relief. Eira was not dead. Babs and Eira were in breach of contract in a huge way. The school had to be returned to Basil. I intended to make sure they admitted what they'd done in front of the games committee.

"Aren't you going to invite me in?" I asked. "Or did you want to keep up with the corpse impersonation? See how far you can take it?"

Eira shushed me and stepped onto the stoop, pulling the door closed behind her. She spoke under her breath. "For my parents' benefit, you're a good friend from school. We've been away at camp together."

I might have laughed if the circumstance hadn't been so serious.

"What kind of camp?" I asked, falsely bright.

She gave an exasperated sigh then turned and entered the house, holding the door open for me. Her look was an odd combination of pleading and warning.

I started to kick off my sneakers when she said, "Don't bother."

She led me down a narrow hall then through a cluttered kitchen. There was no sign of Mr. Nygaard. She put her hand on the handle of a glass door leading into their back yard.

"In the garden, Daddy," Eira yelled, making me jump. "Got a friend from school whose popped by for a bit."

"Have you really?" answered her father from an upper floor. He sounded worn and dry, even elderly. "A friend? Blimey. Shall I come down?"

"No, it's fine," she called back hastily.

"Alright, Plumpy."

"Plumpy?" I mouthed.

She opened the back door and went out into the garden in her bare feet. I followed her to a set of wicker patio furniture near the back fence. The back yard was cluttered. Garden gnomes, stained-glass images of birds hanging from trees, brightly painted ceramic mushrooms, and a profusion of flowers and ivy.

I didn't remind her that if she really wanted to convince her parents we were friends, she would offer me coffee.

"How did you figure it out?" She asked as she settled into a wicker seat and pulled her feet up, a petulant look marring her features.

"Tomio tipped me off. He told me that you're half cryohäxa, which led me to do some research. There wasn't anything I read about cryohäxa that rang alarm bells, it was all consistent with your abilities. Until I stumbled over a short passage suggesting that cryohäxa descended from a commonly-known but long extinct species with unusual gifts. The Valkyrie. Which led to a whole new line of research."

Eira didn't deny it. She chewed her bottom lip, her gaze on the grass.

"Which of your parents is which?" I folded my hands in my lap.

She coughed and gave a sigh of defeat. "My dad *was* a fire mage. His fire went out suddenly in the spring."

I stared at her. That was news. "Wow, I— Really?"

She nodded. "We know it wasn't isolated now. It happened to a few mages, and on the same night. Sent the mage community into an uproar."

"I know," I murmured, thinking of April, and Jade's old babysitter, Maggie.

"Initially, he was devastated. He used to work for a department of the UK government. His placement there and his security clearance hinged on his supernatural status, even if it was mostly a desk job. A few others in his department lost theirs as well. While it was a shock for all of them, they supported one another, and the government arranged for retirement packages and therapy for all of them."

I felt a little dazed. This wasn't the direction I'd expected this conversation to go it. I half wondered if it was a lie to distract me, but something in her face said she was telling the truth. "Is he okay?"

"I've never seen him happier." Eira shook her head and blew out a shaky breath. "He's in his eighties. Twenty-two years older than my mum. He refused to retire even when we begged him. His work was stressful but he was addicted. I think he was afraid he wouldn't have a purpose once he retired. But after the initial shock wore off, he started painting and writing. He's a whole different person now."

I'd never heard Eira string so many words together at one time. Seeing her like this, in her own back yard, talking about her dad with such affection, it raised mixed feelings.

"So your mom is the cryohäxa?"

Eira nodded. "Quite a force in her day, but unlike my dad, she always wanted to retire early. She lived hard and fast through the late-seventies in to the early-nineties. Burned herself out, no pun intended, and decided she wanted to have a family. She switched jobs. They met at work, then had me in ninety-eight."

"Did they also call her The Doll?"

Eira met my eyes for the first time since sitting down. She shook her head. "She can't do what I can do."

"And shame on you for it," I breathed, "but you have a chance to set things right, and that's what you're going to do."

Eira dropped her gaze, picking at the cuticle of her right thumb. I could see moisture gathering in her eyes. "She's going to kill me."

"Who? Babs?"

She nodded.

I thought about this. When two people committed a crime, the police often used a strategy that set one against the other to elicit confessions. What Eira had done was reprehensible, but Babs had put her up to it. It was Babs who should take the brunt of the consequences.

"I have an idea that will exonerate you, at least partially, without putting you under any risk from Babs. Can you trust me enough to follow my lead?"

She hesitated.

"I asked to be polite," I said, my gaze never leaving hers. "You don't actually have a choice."

She looked away and began chewing at her thumbnail again.

I opened the audio recording app on my phone and lay it on the table.

"Eira?"

She looked at me, still chewing her cuticle.

"Start talking." I pressed the record button.

THIRTY

THE FINAL SIGNING

I crouched in the AV booth at the back of Lecture Hall C, trying not to sneeze. Evidently, the cleaning crew had neglected the tiny cubicle at the back of the hall. A layer of dust covered the cables, the floor, the single chair, the small desk and the control board's switches and dials.

If a sleuth had been wondering what I was doing here, their first clue would be that one of the knobs on the control panel had no dust. I had used it to lower a big screen down from the ceiling. It now hung in front of the blackboard. Less obvious was the fact that I'd connected my phone to the projector via Bluetooth.

I sat among the dust-bunnies, breathing quietly with a finger under my nose. When the lecture room door opened and the footsteps of the games committee proclaimed that it was almost showtime, my heart began to pound so loud I worried someone would hear it.

I could picture them easily.

Mr. Pendleton wearing some kind of fitted tweed vest. Basil with his beautifully coiffed hair and creaseless sports jacket, even in the face of the loss of his inheritance and everything he'd worked for, he'd look calm and in control, if a little worn at the edges.

Babs, probably in a painted-on dress, her usual forties hairstyle and patent leather pumps. Mr. Bunting with his rolling gait and twitchy mustache. Guzelköy would be fidgety but dashing, while Davazlar would dominate the room with his silent, menacing good looks. I wasn't sure if Dr. Price would be here for this or not. I hoped so.

"Let's get through this quickly, shall we?" Babs' Monroe-voice pierced the silence of the room. "I have a hard stop at eleven. I'm swamped with meetings. Everyone wants time with the new headmaster."

"This should only take fifteen minutes." A chair squeaked against the hardwood as the lawyer spoke.

"The screen is down," Dr. Price said, confirming her presence. "That's odd. Shall I tuck it away? They get so dusty."

"I'll do it afterward," replied Basil. "Must be a glitch."

I smiled. This was going to be the most fun I'd had all year. Clutching my phone in my hand, I woke it up and scrolled through my contacts. I knew the committee could see what I was doing on the big screen.

There was a moment of shocked silence, then Babs' voice rose. "Where is *that* coming from?"

She sounded mildly alarmed but she'd not yet clued in to the fact this was no accident.

I dialed the Nygaard's number.

The sound of my cell phone's call echoed through the speakers.

"What is happening?" Mr. Bunting asked. "Who is making a call? And why can we hear it?"

"Must be a bug," replied Basil, sounding bemused but faintly smug.

"How strange," said Guzelköy in a melodramatic tone of wonderment. He was uber intelligent and an excellent game-designer, but sucked as an actor.

"Hello?" Mrs. Nygaard's warm voice filled the lecture hall, pouring through the speaker in crystal clear quality. Good ol' Basil and his love of technology.

"Hello, Mrs. Nygaard," I said into the phone. "It's Eira's friend, Saxony. Is Eira there?"

My voice, delayed by microseconds, thundered through the speakers with only a little crackle of static.

"What the hell is going on here?" Babs screamed. "This is a very sick joke. This is not funny. Basil—"

"One moment, Saxony," said Mrs. Nygaard. "She's in the back yard. Are you alright? I thought I heard someone screaming. Was that on your end, or is it someone outside here? I'm afraid I can't tell."

"Sorry about that," I said through my grin. "It's from my side. Just a hysterical woman on the street."

Babs' shrill voice made me wince. "I demand to be told what—"

I got to my feet, cell phone against my ear. As I pulled my phone away and switched over to video call, I waved down at Basil. He waved back. The rest of the committee saw the wave and looked up toward the AV booth.

All eyes on me, and Babs' as big as saucers, I took the narrow steps down to the lecture room floor. Now the screen displayed my face on half and a circle with an N on the other half.

"Saxony?" Eira's voice came through the speakers.

"Yes," I said, now close enough to the committee to see the vein pulsing in Babs' forehead.

"Hang on, I'll turn on my video," Eira said.

Babs' mouth dropped open and her hands flew to her face. All the blood drained out of her complexion. She wheezed a few times, probably trying to scream.

Eira's doll-face appeared beside mine on the huge screen hanging at the front of the room. "Hey."

"I'm here with Mr. Pendleton, the game-makers, the headmasters and a few others," I said to her. "Care to say hi?"

"Sure." Eira sounded cheerful. I guess she'd warmed to my idea after I'd called to fill her in on the final plan.

Turning the phone to capture the group at the main table, they could now see themselves on half the screen. Necks craned back and forth between my phone and the big screen. Clearly this was no recording, but was happening right now. Live.

Mr. Pendleton lifted a hand. "Hello, Ms. Nygaard. Lovely to see you looking so well."

Eira waved. "Hi Mr. Pendleton, nice to virtually meet you. Hi, Headmaster Chaplin."

Basil fluttered a hello with his fingers, smiling enigmatically.

"Eira?!" Babs screeched, coming to her feet. Her scream started outraged, then changed halfway through, into a question. As if pretending she didn't know Eira was alive could save her now.

Davazlar shifted to stand beside her, his big body a wall of threat.

"We'll need silence for this, please," the lawyer said, with a glance of disdain at Babs. "Sit down, Barbara."

Babs was frozen, except for a twitch in her cheek. Her face was waxy, her eyes so round I thought they might pop out of her head. For a second I was worried she might faint and miss the show. That would be no good. All this effort was for her sake.

Davazlar guided her helpfully back into her seat.

Mr. Bunting looked like he was trying to catch as many flies as possible in his mouth. I couldn't tell yet if he'd been part of the plot, but the truth would make itself clear.

Eira waved at everyone. The game-makers waved back.

After I'd emailed Eira's audio confession to Basil while I was on the train home the previous evening, he had wasted no time bringing everyone but Babs and Mr. Bunting into the loop. Once I'd arrived back at the academy, we'd closed ourselves in Basil's office and got Mr. Pendleton on the phone to work out how to approach the situation. The live video call had been my idea. While Eira had taken some convincing from Basil, she'd agreed to go along with it on the understanding that she'd be admitted into Arcturus Academy for the upcoming school year. She would never have to be face-to-face with Babs again. She understood there would be consequences for her part in the deception, but Basil also promised that Babs would be issued a restraining order, which would be enforced by the agency. She wouldn't be permitted to come within five-hundred meters of Eira.

"Please state your name for the record," Mr. Pendleton said, taking on a professional air.

"Eira Nygaard. People also call me The Doll." She brushed a lock of wheat-blond hair away from her face.

"And, why do they call you that?"

She cleared her throat. "I'm half cryohäxa, a supernatural group with control over sub-zero temperatures, winter conditions, snow, ice, that sort of thing. It's how I got past the tilting game-board. I froze the casters in place and just walked across it. Same with the pool of water. Basically, I'm the opposite of a fire mage, my other half. Cryohäxa evolved from the Valkyrie, a species now believed to be extinct. But a tiny portion of our population have a rare gene, a kind of atavism."

"Can you define atavism for us?" Mr. Pendleton had his specs perched on the end of his nose, his pen hovered over his notebook.

"Sure. It's when an ancestral genetic trait reappears after having been thought to be permanently lost. Evolutionary changes seem to eliminate the gene, or at least its expression, but centuries later, the trait occurs in an individual member of the species. That's me."

"And what is this ancestral trait?"

"The ability to become inanimate for a period of time."

Babs put her face in her hands as Mr. Bunting turned his head slowly to look at her, an expression of vile disgust on his face. Either he was an exceptionally good actor, or he really hadn't known.

"Interesting," said Mr. Pendleton. "How is such a trait useful?"

Eira gave a kind of ironic chuckle. "It's mostly not useful, that's why it evolved out of our species. But it *was* useful to the Valkyrie. According to legend, one of their jobs was to visit battlegrounds and escort the souls of the dead to Valhalla. Many times, the battles were not over, and they had to wait for the dying to pass away. Often it was dangerous, especially since enemy armies would attempt to keep the dead from making it to Valhalla. To combat this, the Valkyrie could shapeshift. They could appear as a soldier, and shift into an apparent death-state. No pulse. No breath. No circulation. Nothing. I haven't got the shapeshifting gene, but when I become "The Doll" no technology we have today will tell you I'm alive." She put up a hand. "To be honest, I've never really valued the trick. Babs never valued it either until these games came up."

"So it was Babs idea to use your ability?"

Eira nodded. "I don't think she thought we'd have to use it, to be honest. She's got some very strong students, much stronger than me. But when I kept making it to the next round, we realized it might end up being me and Saxony in the final, and the likelihood of me winning was low."

"Even with your hybrid abilities?"

"Even with them. Saxony is Burned. We had two students who were also Burned. Liu and Serenamen, but when they were eliminated, it was down to me."

"You are not Burned?"

"I *can't* Burn. My hybrid nature means my fire can't get hot enough to do the job. It also hampers me from moving smoothly. You'll have seen the difference between Saxony and me if you've watched the footage. I'm a hybrid, but that doesn't mean my abilities always work synergistically. Fire and ice are kind of opposites, after all, which can make for a struggle as I try to control both at the same time."

"I see. So what is clear to all of us now, is that the

rules were broken and that you and Babs colluded to win the games by using your ability to appear dead."

"We didn't collude, exactly. She... bribed me."

Babs took her hands away from her face and sent Eira an ugly glare.

Eira seemed to gulp, but braved on. "I've never been a favorite of hers. When she began to favor me, I liked it. I went along with it. And when I saw the amazing facilities at Arcturus, I wanted us to win. She promised me a bonus and no fees next year if we won. My family isn't particularly well off because my dad never properly prepared for retirement. It was appealing." Eira swallowed and looked to the side for a moment, chewing her cheek. She looked at the screen again. "I am sorry. I know you'll just say that I'm sorry that we got caught, but in actuality I am relieved. My parents didn't raise me to lie. I'll accept whatever punishment the committee decides."

"Thank you, Ms. Nygaard. Do you have anything else you want to add?"

She shook her head then stopped. "Maybe one thing."

"Go ahead."

"Babs," she began, her fine brows pinching together.

Babs looked at the ceiling and crossed her arms.

"I know it doesn't look like it, but I didn't break your confidence. Saxony found me at home and when I knew we were caught I thought the best thing would be to own up to it."

I shook my head, fighting the urge to snarl. Eira didn't owe Babs anything, but relationships were complicated, and if Eira had spent the last year looking up to Babs and wanting her approval, it wouldn't be a habit that would break overnight.

Mr. Pendleton gave Babs a deadpan look, allowing her to respond if she wanted to. Babs looked away.

"Thank you for coming forward, Ms. Nygaard. We'll be in touch after the committee reviews your contribution to the crime."

Eira nodded, lifted a hand, and her side of the screen went dark. I hung up my cell and the visual of the committee disappeared as well.

There was a moment of quiet where everyone in the room looked at Babs except for Mr. Bunting, who had his infuriated and embarrassed gaze on the table.

Mr. Pendleton broke the silence. "The foul play involved here means a full reinstatement to Basil Chaplin as estate owner and headmaster of Arcturus Academy. Further, the consolation prize we had set aside will be stripped and returned to the estate's coffers, leaving Barbara Chaplin no worse off than before Chaplin Senior passed away. A castigation far too light, in my opinion." He tipped his pen toward Basil. "Do you wish to pursue this matter with the agency's tribunal?"

Babs eyes widened with fear but Basil shook his head.

"I'm just relieved that it's over."

Mr. Pendleton retrieved a stack of papers from his briefcase. "Yes, thanks to Ms. Cagney here." He nodded to me but addressed Basil. "You could do worse than to consider her for an investigative position at the agency, Mr. Chaplin."

"I know." Basil took the pen Mr. Pendleton held out.

My cheeks heated with embarrassment. All I'd done was a bit of reading, then sat on a bench in Kentish Town for long enough that I got lucky.

"The arrows will direct you where to sign," Mr. Pendleton told Basil.

Guzelköy and Davazlar had moved to the side and murmured between themselves while the rest of us watched as the legal ties binding Basil and his property together were tightened and finalized.

Babs got up and headed for the door without a word to anyone. Mr. Bunting did not rise to follow her.

"Barbara," Davazlar called in his rumble of a voice.

She paused but didn't look back.

"You are barred from working with SG for life. Firethorne's students and graduates will be barred from entering any of our games, including the ISG, as long as you are headmaster at Firethorne Collegiate. This penalty will be grandfathered to any educational institution, agency or organization you form or are a member of. It takes effect today and it will never expire."

Davazlar finished and the room felt blanketed by a heavy silence. Babs lifted her nose and walked out.

The paperwork was witnessed by Dr. Price and Mr. Bunting, who'd shaken off enough of his wrath to sign. Mr. Pendleton took the documents and excused himself, saying he'd be in touch with Basil.

The spindly lawyer came over to me with his hand outstretched. We shook firmly.

"Well done, Ms. Cagney. When you graduate, I happen to know a well respected law firm who may still be looking for a PI. Good ones are hard to come by, and often very hard to keep."

My face heated again. "I didn't do anything but a little digging."

His bushy brows rose. "Yes, and isn't that all that lies between deception and the truth? A little earnest digging?"

He plonked his tweed fedora on the top of his silver-gray head and left the room at a brisk walk.

Basil, Dr. Price, and the game-makers passed looks between them. Mr. Bunting nodded at Basil and left, cheeks flushing furiously.

I suddenly remembered that I had never found out. "What's SG?"

"That's our company," Guzelköy replied. "Supernatural Game-makers."

"Oh. And what's ISG?"

The game-makers sent Basil a reproachful look at this question.

"Really, Mr. Chaplin," said Guzelköy, a little sulkily.

Basil cleared his throat. "International Supernatural Games. Their version of the Olympics. Games in our society don't get any bigger."

"Oh." I blushed for the third time is as many minutes, wishing I'd known that.

"She didn't grow up as one of us," Basil told Guzelköy by way of explanation.

Guzelköy and Davazlar looked at me with renewed curiosity. Guzelköy said, "Really? Plenary endowment?"

I nodded.

"I should like to hear that story," the game-maker said with a little bob of his head, "but, at some future date. Davazlar and I have work to do."

With that, the game-makers headed for the door.

I watched them go, thinking. Their blacklisting of Babs from the games might not seem a harsh sentence, but if the game-makers didn't allow any supernatural athlete from any organization Babs was even on the board of, she would be very hard pressed to be accepted anywhere. I wondered what explanation she would give to the contacts she had to date. I didn't doubt for a moment she'd come up with some clever spin to make herself appear as the victim.

But it wasn't my problem. Basil had the school back, and that's what mattered most.

THIRTY-ONE
RUNAWAY

"Gage?" I poked my head into Gage's room to find it empty.

His bed was neatly made, his chair tucked into his desk. Gage was always neat, but my stomach gave a twist. There was no luggage in the closet and no toiletries visible in the bathroom. I left his room and made my way to the students' lounge where I discovered the Prices.

Cecily looked up from the sofa and began to applaud. "Well done, Saxony. A very satisfying ending, I must say."

"Thanks." I smiled, wringing my hands. "Have you seen Gage?"

Dr. Price glanced at the watch on her wrist, her brow creased. "Didn't he say goodbye to you? He took a cab to the airport just before the committee met this morning. Maybe he couldn't find you. How long were you hiding in the AV booth?"

The bottom dropped out of my stomach, I felt like screaming. What was with the men in my life running away from their problems? I made an effort to keep my features neutral. "A while."

"What a shame. I can't believe he would leave without telling y—"

My chin wobbled and the astute doctor didn't miss it.

"Oh, dear. What's happened? Did you have a falling out?" She got up and made as though to come to me.

I put up a hand. "I'm okay. I'll just call him."

I left the lounge before their sympathy undid me, misjudging and banging my shoulder against the doorjamb on the way out. My vision was a blur as I made my way to my room where I could fall apart in privacy. My heart literally felt like it was ripping into two, shredded, bleeding chunks of muscle.

When I got to my room, I found his note. It lay on my pillow, neatly folded. Pressing the sleeve of my cardigan into my eyes to soak up the moisture, I began to read Gage's handwritten scrawl.

Saxony,

I know you're wondering how I am. I can't answer that question honestly because I don't know myself. One minute I think I'm okay, the next I'm not. One thing is clear, I need time. I'm sure you do, too. I tried to find you to say goodbye, but not that hard. I think it might have made things worse. Anyway, I might be on a plane by the time you read this. I'm not saying we can't talk. If I see you in Saltford, I'm not going to ignore you. But I am saying that maybe breaking up is for the best. We won't know until we live with it for a while, and you obviously need to think about what you want.

Gage

More tears welling up to replace the old, I fumbled for my phone. Scrubbing at my eyes, I scrolled for Gage's number and tapped the call button. I sat on the edge of my bed, fighting for control. Holding the phone to my ear, I listened to the dashes. I realized I had my other hand over my heart, as if to protect it.

"Hello?" Gage's voice sounded flat. He knew it was me.

"Gage." My throat closed up and his name came out as a cough.

"Hi." He let out a long, slow sigh.

"I'm sorry." I sniffed, then hiccupped. "I'm really, really sorry."

"I know you are. Tomio is, too."

"He called you?"

"On my way to the airport. Listen"—he took a slow shaky inhale—"I know, this sucks."

I nodded and wiped my nose, thankful we weren't using video chat. I probably looked like a muppet with swollen eyes and a red, puffy nose. How could Gage sound so calm? There was physical pain in my heart with every contraction.

"I should have tried harder to find you, but I figured since the games were over you'd be coming back to Saltford soon. We won't have a school to go back to in the fall."

"Actually, we will," I choked out, feeling my chin tremble. "Eira's death was a ruse."

Gage was quiet for a long time, then incredulous. "She's alive?"

"Yes. She's absolutely fine."

He let out a breath and the relief in it was palpable. "Well, that's crazy and amazing. So... how?"

"It's a long story. One I'll tell you in detail if you meet me at Flagg's in a few days?"

My heart bobbed like an inflatable toy in water at the thought of seeing Gage so soon, but my mind was backpedaling, taking me back to that moment with Tomio. The moment I'd felt what one was supposed to feel. Should I be trying so hard to salvage this?

"Maybe. Yeah," Gage replied.

I closed my eyes, weak with relief and confusion.

"Let's not put pressure on ourselves to be anything more than friends. Okay?"

"Okay."

"It was just a kiss. My parent's relationship has survived much worse, and I think they're stronger for it. So, I have hope."

"Me too," I croaked, but even as I said it, I wondered. Was I being truthful or was I just wanting the pain to stop? I still believed our fire didn't want us to be together. Why would it randomly change its mind?

I sniffed and reeled in the desire to break down bawling. Gage didn't sound angry anymore. He was willing to be friends. That was enough to live on until I got home.

"Text me when you're back and we'll make a date," he said, then added hastily, "just coffee between friends. Yeah?"

"Yeah." I smiled through my tears. "You're wonderful, you know that?"

"Well, one of us had to be," he murmured.

I cringed as his words pierced me. He was still angry, and he had every right to be. I began to agree with him when he spoke again.

"I meant between Ryan and me."

"Oh." I looked up, blinking. "Have you spoken to him?"

"A little. He's up to something. But I can't talk about it right now. They're calling for final boarding. You tell me about the games and I'll catch you up about Ryan when we see each other."

"Okay."

"Bye, Saxony."

"Bye, Gage." I wanted to tell him I loved him but pressed my lips together. This was confusing enough without deepening the emotional waters we were wading in.

I waited until the phone went dead then tossed it aside. Sprawling on my back, I pulled my pillow over my face to muffle the sound of my tears.

EPILOGUE

Fifteen minutes later and hoping I was all cried out, I went to my desk for a tissue, sniffling. I was dabbing at my eyes and blowing my nose when a knock came on the door.

"Yes?" I honked into another tissue.

Cecily poked her head in. "There's—Hey, are you okay?"

I nodded. "I'm okay. Just looking forward to having an actual summer break."

She opened the door wider. "I bet. Me too. We're driving to Inverness this afternoon. I can't wait to see my dad."

I nodded. "What's up?"

"Basil sent me. He said to tell you, you have a visitor waiting in the headmaster's office."

"Who is it?"

She shrugged. "Didn't say. I'll walk with you?"

I nodded and picked up my phone. Tucking it into my pocket, I didn't bother to close my door. All I wanted to do was get on a plane, think about my own problems, over-sleep for hours, and have pancakes with my family.

Walking with Cecily, I made a mental note to text Brooke and Harriet about how Eira got through the obstacle course so quickly, as I had promised I would. Dr. Price had notified all the competitors about Basil getting the rights to his school and property back due to broken rules, but I looked forward to sharing the juicier details with Brooke and Harriet.

As we approached Basil's office, Dr. Price appeared at the end of the hall wearing a light trenchcoat.

"Ready, darling?"

Cecily nodded.

Dr. Price pulled me into a hug on the landing outside Basil's office. "Well done, dearie," she said, rocking me a little. "You made us all proud. Well, done."

When she pulled back she touched my chin. "Cheer up, love. Supernatural education has been saved from a tyrannical dictator. We have a school to come back to in the fall."

I found some nice words for the Prices and waved them off as they descended the stairs, but my mind was full of Gage.

I pictured walking into Flagg's Café, making the familiar wind chimes hanging in the doorway tinkle. He'd be seated at the couches at the back, where we'd sat on our first date, a date which had been cut short by Ryan. This time we wouldn't be cut short. Gage would look up. He'd smile. I'd hold the thought of that smile in my mind all the way home.

With a soft knock on Basil's door, I listened for his invitation.

"Come."

Basil was seated behind his desk, looking like the headmaster I'd come to know and love. All had been made right in his world, well, almost all. At least he could grieve his father in peace without having to worry about the fate of his school.

An older man wearing a fedora faced him. One hand rested on a cane. He shifted in his seat to watch me come in, his bushy eyebrows raising over big brown eyes I hadn't seen in almost a year.

My palms instantly felt clammy.

"Buongiorno, Ms. Cagney," said Enzo Barberini. "It's been a long time."

I halted, frozen on what felt like a pair of hollow legs. "No, Senor Barberini. It has not been nearly long enough."

END BOOK 3

I KNOW, I know! GAH! How could I end it this way! Don't worry, I'm already hard at work on the next instalment...

Legends of Fire, Arcturus Academy Book 4

Bound by an oath she cannot retract, Saxony must save an old enemy from a new one.

Preorder *Legends of Fire* Today!

AFTERWORD & ACKNOWLEDGMENTS

Did you think I wouldn't include the answers to the riddles Saxony was unable to get? Naw. I wouldn't do that. Although you probably already guessed the right answer, I'll put them here, just for affirmation.

Different lights do make me strange, thus into different sizes will I change. What am I?

ANSWER: PUPILS OF THE EYES

It cannot be seen, it cannot be felt, it can't be heard, nor can it be smelt. It lies behind stars, it lies beneath hills, it ends life, and laughter kills.

ANSWER: DARKNESS

Writing *Fire Games* was an angsty blast. That's the best way to describe it. Incredibly difficult, but so much fun. Thank you to Ryan Schow for your help with the combat scene between Saxony and Eira, thank you to Nicola Aquino for the fantastic suggestions and editing, and thank you to my VIPs for being my amazing support network. Authoring is hard. Wonderful readers make it all worth while.

What's next for Saxony? Things don't get any easier for our favorite redhead, I'm afraid. You won't want to miss the next instalment, *Legends of Fire*.

If you loved *Fire Games*, please consider leaving a review for it. Reviews help new readers find books they'll love, plus they give encouragement and support to the authors you love.

See you soon, in the halls of the academy.

Abby

XOXO

COME A LITTLE CLOSER, MY DEAR...

Want to be kept updated on new releases, be the first to know about sneak peeks and 'read by yours truly' audio snippets? I'm no Judi Dench but I do try not to make too many swallowing sounds. I host the occasional sale and sometimes join themed multi-author promotions that are good fun. Join my newsletter at www.alknorrbooks.com or request access to my private VIP Reader Lounge on Facebook (don't forget to answer the three questions to get in). I also have Instagram for those who are curious about the life of a traveling fantasy novelist. I tend to visit a lot of ancient places, there's inspiration to be found there, doncha know. See you in them virtual hills!

    Love, Abby

ALSO BY A.L. KNORR

Elemental Origins Series, Season 1

Born of Water, Book 1

Born of Fire, Book 2

Born of Earth, Book 3

Born of Æther, Book 4

Born of Air, Book 5

The Elementals, Book 6

Elemental Origins Series, Season 2

Salt & Stone (The Siren's Curse 1)

Salt & the Sovereign (The Siren's Curse 2)

Salt & the Sisters (The Siren's Curse 3)

Elemental Origins Series, Season 3

Bones of the Witch (Earth Magic Rises 1)

Ashes of the Wise (Earth Magic Rises 2)

Heart of the Fae (Earth Magic Rises 3)

Elemental Origins Series, Season 4

Firecracker, (Arcturus Academy 1)

Fire Trap, (Arcturus Academy 2)

Fire Games (Arcturus Academy 3)

Legends of Fire (Arcturus Academy 4)

Source Fire (Arcturus Academy 5)

Elemental Origins Spin Off Series: Rings of the Inconquo

Born of Metal, (Rings of the Inconquo 1)

Metal Guardian, (Rings of the Inconquo 2)

Metal Angel, (Rings of the Inconquo 3)

Elemental Origins Spin Off: The Returning Series (Mira's Story, Completed Series)

Returning, Book 1

Falling, Book 2

Surfacing, Book 3

Elemental Novellas

Pyro, A Fire Novella

Heat, A Fire Novella

The Kacy Chronicles (Completed Series)

Descendant, Book 1

Ascendant, Book 2

Combatant, Book 3

Transcendent, Book 4